TWILIGHT
AT THE
EQUATOR

BOOKS BY JAIME MANRIQUE

FICTION
El cadáver de papá
Colombian Gold
Latin Moon in Manhattan

POETRY
Los adoradores de la luna
Scarecrow (chapbook)
My Night with Federico García Lorca

CRITICISM
Notas de cine: Confesiones de un crítico amateur

TWILIGHT AT THE EQUATOR

A NOVEL

Jaime Manrique

Faber and Faber, Inc.
Boston · London

Library of Congress Cataloging-in-Publication Data

Manrique Ardila, Jaime, 1949–
    Twilight at the Equator : a novel / Jaime Manrique.
      p.   cm.
    ISBN 0-571-19901-1 (cloth)
    I. Title.
    PS3563.A573T85   1997
    813'.54—dc   96-43422
                                                    CIP

Jacket design by Hania Khuri
Printed in the United States of America

For my grandmother,
Serafina Ardila,
to whom I owe
Twilight at the Equator

CONTENTS

ACKNOWLEDGMENTS

Most of the chapters were originally published in somewhat different form in the following publications: *Men's Style:* first half of "To Love in Madrid"; *Callaloo:* second half of "To Love in Madrid," under the title "Barcelona Hunger." *Mānoa:* "The Documentary Artist." *Christopher Street, Exceso* (Caracas, Venezuela), and *Men on Men 5* (Plume): "The Day Carmen Maura Kissed Me." Portions of "Twilight at the Equator" appeared in *Open City; Shade: An Anthology of Fiction by Gay Men of African Descent* (Avon Books); *The Chattahoochee Review,* and *The Writer's Journal* (Dell). "Papa's Corpse," under the title of "El cadáver de papá," first appeared in a collection of short stories and poetry translations published in 1978 in Colombia by the Institute of Colombian Culture. Later, in 1983, in a vastly altered and reduced form, and under the title of "Carnival," it became Part I of *Colombian Gold* (Clarkson N. Potter).

In appreciation of their support I would like to thank the Corporation of Yaddo, The MacDowell Colony, The Virginia Center for the Creative Arts, The Ludwig Vogelstein Foundation, The Writer's Voice of New York City, Mount Holyoke College, Eugene Lang College, and the New School for Social Research Writer-in-Residence Program.

And deepest thanks of all to my friends.

TWILIGHT
AT THE
EQUATOR

1

To Love in Madrid

∿℮℈∿

I arrived in Madrid to become a poet. The year was 1976, and I was twenty-five years old. I had one friend in the city, Lulu Mercurio, a historian who was working on her doctoral dissertation. Lulu was a big, platinum-bleached curly-haired Andalusian who chain-smoked Camels using an elongated silver cigarette holder. I also went to Madrid to self-destruct. I wanted to die young like Sylvia Plath, Jimi Hendrix, Janis Joplin. I wanted to immolate myself while writing dazzlingly scorching poems; like Janis Joplin, I wanted to split from this world with a shattering cry.

Lulu lived in a studio apartment, so she arranged for me to sub-let a penthouse in Moratalaz, a working-class district. The penthouse belonged to a friend of Lulu's who was in Morocco for the year; it was on the twentieth floor, and it had a terrace the size of a tennis court, with a magnificent view of the city.

Madrid was a place lost in time. Because of the media censor-ship of Franco's forty-year rule *Madrileños* were still living with the attitudes of the 1950s. Franco, who had not tolerated misfits, had created a society that outwardly seemed free of everything unpleas-ant one associates with metropolises: there were no beggars in the streets, the city was spotless and perfectly preserved for the tourists. Best of all, it was safe: one could walk Madrid's streets, av-enues, and boulevards at 3 A.M. without fear of any kind of danger.

After a few weeks of sightseeing, I realized I would have to get a job. I spoke English well enough to teach it as a second language, so Lulu directed me to a language institute, the Instituto Inglés. The director hired me with the condition that I impersonate a native speaker, a Chicano. Monday through Friday, from 10 to 2, I posed as a Chicano from Texas to my highly suspicious students (Madrid matrons and middle-aged businessmen) who bombarded me with questions about Texas: What did armadillo meat taste like? What were my favorite Tex-Mex recipes? What kind of hat did I use to protect myself from the scorching Texas sun? Did I know anyone who owned oil wells? I learned to improvise quickly, fearlessly, since all I knew about Texas I had learned from the movie *Giant*.

Usually after I finished teaching my lessons at the Instituto Inglés, I'd grab a ham and cheese *bocadillo*, and take the subway to Madrid's *Filmoteca*, where I arrived in time for the 3 o'clock show. Later, on my way home, I'd stop at the gay bars for drinks. To my surprise, my type was popular. In those years, because of my unruly Afro, people often mistook me for a Moor. I tricked indiscriminately.

The *Filmoteca* had organized a retrospective of the Italian director Pier Paolo Pasolini, who had been murdered in the fall of 1975. Up until that point Pasolini's movies had been banned in Spain. Religiously, I attended the afternoon showings where I noticed a couple of boys who also showed up every day. They sat a couple of rows in front of me, and often flirted with me. I flirted back, but thought nothing of it. Then one day they barged in as the movie was about to start and sat next to me. As the credits of *Mama Roma* were rolling, the one closest to me offered his hand and introduced himself as Jose. Minutes later, I felt Jose's arm resting against mine. The sensation was pleasant, and I resolved to go along with it. When Jose pressed his leg against mine, I turned to face him and our noses touched. He was grinning so innocently that, feeling audacious, I grabbed his hand. The rest of *Mama Roma* is a blur to me.

When the film ended, Jose introduced me to his friend Carlos. Now I saw that they were both skinny, tall, somewhat gawky yet good-looking prep school boys. Both of them carried their school bags. I announced that I was leaving because I had already seen *Accattone!*, the following feature. I suggested, however, that we have coffee during the intermission. Carlos declined, saying that he was afraid to lose his seat, but Jose was quick to accept my invi-

4

tation. Drinking coffee in the cafeteria, I was enthralled by his effusiveness. He had eyes that glowed like summer fireflies, long eyelashes, charcoal black hair parted in the middle and cropped above his ears, the long nose and fingers of a Velázquez hidalgo, and a voluptuous mother-of-pearl lower lip. Jose chattered vehemently about literature and movies, and, clapping his hands, he laughed raucously without self-consciousness. The fifteen minutes flew by. I remarked he should go join his friend or he'd miss the movie.

"I don't care if I miss the movie," he said, suddenly serious. "Santiago, can I go home with you?"

On the bus to Moratalaz, Jose fired a volley of questions at me: who were my favorite film directors, poets, novelists, actors? What did I think of Madrid? What was Colombia like? And New York? Did I have a boyfriend? Had I ever had one? How long had I been out of the closet? He reminded me of a toddler going around a room, pointing at objects and asking, "What is it?" I learned that Carlos was his best friend, that they were in the same school, that Jose's father was a fascist colonel in the army, that he despised the school he attended and Franco's legacy.

Once inside the apartment we started kissing as we undressed. Jose stood naked in front of me, fully erect. For the first time, he seemed unsure of himself. "What do I have to do?" he asked.

I stared at him incredulously. Somehow I had assumed that he routinely picked up older guys at the *Filmoteca*.

"It's my first time," he mumbled.

"How old are you?" I asked, nervously.

"Fifteen."

I froze.

"I'll be sixteen in October," he said eagerly, as if that made it much better.

I noticed now that he only had incipient pubic hair. Losing my erection, I sat on the bed, confused. Jose sat next to me, took my face in his hands and gave me an awkward kiss that was almost a bite. I nudged him back on the bed and, with my finger tips, began to massage his face, his tight nipples, his stomach, his long, uncut penis.

5

"Please, Santiago, teach me," he pleaded, trembling.

Grabbing his cock, I pulled back his foreskin. With my tongue I licked the head of his penis tenderly. Jose shook and moaned in ecstasy. Coating the head of his penis with saliva, I grabbed his cock in my hand and placed it in my mouth. He came immediately. I pulled back.

"I'm sorry," Jose apologized. "I pissed."

"No, you didn't," I said laughing, almost choking with his sweet-tasting come. "You came."

"Oh," he exclaimed with embarrassment.

Since I had just come out of the closet, I was no expert in love-making myself. It turned out Jose had never given anyone a full kiss. Up until that point, shame and guilt were the two feelings I had associated with sex. We became each other's teachers.

As Madrid's benign winter thawed, Jose and I met at the *Filmoteca* every afternoon, and then we'd nest in the penthouse where we'd drink wine, make love, and later read poetry to each other. While Jose read aloud the poems of García Lorca and Manuel Machado that he loved, I listened, sipping wine, my head on his chest. He had a dulcet voice, enunciated beautifully, and declaimed his favorite poems. As crazy as we both were about the movies, poetry was our greatest love. Jose taught me about Spanish verse, and I shared with him (translating as I read) my passion for Plath and the other extremist poets. Around eight o'clock every night, I'd walk him to the bus stop, where we shook hands till the following afternoon.

Lulu called one day, alarmed because she hadn't heard from me in a while. I suggested we meet for a drink. I told her I was having an affair.

"Many young *majos* make their living that way," she said, assuming that I was having an affair with an older man. When I corrected her impression, Lulu lost her composure. She started banging her bejewelled hands on the table and flapping her arms laden with silver bracelets that clanged as she gesticulated. "Your behavior is completely hallucinatory. Are you insane? This is Spain. Do

6

you know what Franco did to homosexuals? And the boy's father is in the military. . . . Do you realize what will happen to you if they catch you? I can't even begin to imagine it," she finished, her lips quivering with anger. "*Me tienes alucinada.*"

My friendship with Lulu cooled considerably. Yet I didn't mind losing her as long as I could continue seeing Jose. I was learning that love wasn't synonymous with agony and rejection. Jose and I drank out of each other insatiably, as if we were hungry humming-birds attacking honeycombs bursting with ambrosia. I realized that my body was an entity that had lain dormant until Jose awakened it with his ardent hands, voracious lips, impassioned caresses. At first there was no anal sex. But one day, as we were taking a shower together, he said, "*Fóllame.*" Standing under the warm spray, he rested his chest and head against the tile wall and I entered him, feeling completely aroused by his wet ass. "Fuck me, fuck me, Santiago," he repeated in a paroxysm. As I came, Jose started screaming, "I'm coming, I'm coming." Feeling faint, I pulled out, dropped on my knees, and took his cock: Jose shot a blast of semen that I swallowed hungrily, as the water from the shower entered the corner of my lips. With his back against the wall, Jose lowered his body to the floor, legs spread out. I rested my head on his shoulder and blacked out.

In love for the first time, I was happy. Spring arrived, and gypsy ladies singing *cuplés* stood on Madrid's street corners selling bouquets of violets. Beautifully landscaped beds of black and scarlet tulips decorated the parks and boulevards of the city; weeping willows shot slithering emerald ribbons, and gaggles of chirruping swallows imbricated the diaphanous turquoise skies.

I decided to start writing my first novel. One morning an image came to my mind: my old and sickly father was in a hospital, and I was in the room with him, applying a pillow to his face—asphyxiating him. I hated my father; I couldn't forgive him for abandoning my mother when I was a child. Influenced by Sylvia Plath's poem "Daddy," I decided to write a novel that would kill my father when he read it.

That morning, on the way to teach, the idea of facing my students—three middle-aged Exxon oil executives—was repulsive to me. I just wanted to stay home until I completed my novel of revenge.

We had just finished drilling the sentence, "I've moved to Texas to work for Exxon, and I like barbecue very much," when one of my students requested that I teach them to pronounce the sentence with a Texan accent.

To this day, I do not have the vaguest notion of what Texans sound like, and I've never been gifted at mimicking accents.

"Professor Martínez," a student said, "we'd really appreciate it if you could teach us Texan English, since our goal is eventually to relocate to Texas."

"I'm Colombian, not Chicano," I snapped, not believing the words that came out of my mouth. Now there was no going back. "I've never been to Texas; it sounds like a hideous place and I hope I'll never have to visit it," I finished, glowering at them.

The executives exchanged puzzled looks of disapproval. The atmosphere became tense, and the remaining minutes seemed to drag on forever, yet I managed to finish the lesson. As the students exited the tiny somber classroom, I kidded them in a mock Texan drawl, "See yawl tom-merrow."

That evening, in the apartment, I babbled excitedly to Jose about the novel. After he left, I banged away at my typewriter, writing in a frenzy, until I had drafted the first chapter. It was dawn when I got up from my desk. I opened the door to the terrace and stepped out into the frosty air. The stars, like minuscule throbbing diamonds, were extinguishing their shine; the city lights were beginning to dim. In the distance the buildings reminded me of El Greco's views of Toledo from his studio. Bathed in a luminous sapphire gauze caused by the incandescent ivory-pink lip at the horizon, Madrid glowed like a vision that expressed a great past and a thrilling present—all my own.

I was so wired from the writing that I knew I wouldn't fall asleep if I went to bed. I wanted Jose by my side to make love to him; I wanted to hear the drumming sound of his heart after he came; I longed to caress his chest, his skin as smooth as the flesh of a grape, and to lick its sweetness and its warmth, like a grape that had ripened in the sun, with the tip of my tongue. Feeling a tremendous potency, I walked to the end of the terrace, took my cock out and began to beat off. Crying out Jose's name, my come shot over the wall framing the terrace and fell to the city below, into the expanding brightness.

I arrived at the Instituto Inglés still reeling from my nocturnal orgy of writing. On the classroom door, I found a note asking me to stop by the director's office before my first class began. The director received me with a chilly greeting. Since Señorita Mendeiveítia always dressed in black, when she wasn't friendly she could be forbidding. She had a beaked nose, razor-thin lips, and she reminded me of an ostrich with a wig on. I knew I was in trouble. She informed me that my students had demanded my replacement with a native speaker. She reminded me it would be extremely difficult for her to replace me right away. Therefore, Miss Meindeiveítia demanded, in her sharp admiral-manner, that I apologize to my students, explaining that I had been joking.

"My Chicano sense of humor, I suppose?" I bitched, emboldened by the surge of *cojones* that my newly begun novel gave me.

I walked out of the Instituto Inglés as an unemployed full-time budding novelist. I went home, re-read the chapter I had written overnight, and decided that for the next two weeks I would write a chapter a day, until I had 150 pages. To celebrate my freedom and the start of my career as a novelist, I drank a bottle of Marqués de Riscal. Afterwards, drunk, I went to sleep, peacefully, like a shipwreck that has finally reached a benevolent shore.

I didn't have a penny saved. But a dam had broken in me, and I didn't stop to think about the consequences. I was afire, the story of my life bursting out of me uncontrollably. I wrote for long stretches at a time, until I collapsed. I would stop only to meet Jose at the movies or to make love. Very soon I was broke. I found that the kitchen was stocked with containers full of chickpeas, lentils, and rice. I subsisted on these and wrote a chapter a day, according to my plan. My energy never flagged; I was in a trance.

I was no longer able to go to the movies, so Jose would come to visit me late in the afternoons. Usually he'd steal a bottle of wine from his parents' cellar; when he realized the monotony of my diet, he started bringing me ham and cheese sandwiches.

It would have been easy to call or write my mother asking for money, but I was quite determined to be the Colombian Sylvia Plath. In my novel, after the hero murders his father, the corpse is stolen from the funeral parlor. From Carnival Sunday to Ash Wednesday (when the action of the novel takes places) a terrifying amount of sex and sexual debauchery goes on. Dressed in drag, the main character watches a gang of boys rape his father-in-law at the country club, is fucked in the ass by a man he runs into at the beach, and finally, when the father's corpse is still missing on the morning of the burial, the hero stuffs the coffin with cement bags and buries it. I worked hard to make the book as sacrilegious as possible: I not only wanted to kill my father, but also to shit on the Catholic Church, Colombian society, and my bourgeois family. The book had the mad insolence of the would-be suicide who has nothing to lose. It was meant to be my farewell letter to the world. As long as I could write it, I didn't mind burning all my bridges behind me. I thought that to die in Madrid a writer, in love, young, was the stuff of myth.

The seething anger that consumed me kept me going. But when I typed the words "THE END," I crashed. I was spent, lost. It was as if my entire life had been leading to the moment when I could finally assume my homosexuality and strike back at everything that had hurt me as a young man. Now that I had accomplished my revenge, life seemed to be ebbing out of me.

April was coming to an end, the full glory of the Castilian spring was peaking, summer felt just around the corner. For days I lay in bed, recovering from the brainfever that had seized me during the writing of *Papa's Corpse*. Melodramatically, I listened to Maria Callas recordings, read the extremist poets, and, in outbursts of energy, I revised my manuscript—which I was beginning to memorize. I knew I was having a nervous breakdown and I didn't want to do anything to stop it. Although Jose tried to hide his concern for my well-being, he grew more and more alarmed. However, faith-

fully, he showed up every afternoon with food, wine, and sometimes a little money. He was quite determined to keep me alive.
There was such sweetness and desperation in our sexual encoun-
ters, in the way we gave ourselves to one another, that afterwards,
when we lay in bed, I felt sad, thinking that this was the purest, the
most unselfish love I would ever experience.

One evening in May we were in bed, caressing each other. The
room was suffused with a toasty African breeze that had traveled
over the Mediterranean, across Andalusia, past the parched hills of
Castile. Through the window, Madrid's sky pulsated with filigreed
stars. Breaking the silence, Jose said, "Santiago, do you love me?"

Even though we had been lovers for a few months, these words
had remained unspoken. "Yes," I said without hesitation, kissing
him on the lips. "I love you more than anyone in the world."

"If you really love me," he said, "you have to promise me you'll
live. If you die, I'll die, too."

I burst out crying. We held each other tightly and sobbed and
petted each other until I fell asleep.

I made up my mind to live. After all, Plath had died at age
thirty-three, and Berryman and Sexton much later. I still had half
of my twenties to get through. The following morning, I dropped
off *Papa's Corpse* at a well-known Madrid publisher. Next, I went
around the city looking for work. Since I couldn't produce my
working papers, no one was willing to hire me even for the most
menial jobs. I was directed to the fruit market where I was told I
could make some *pesetas* unloading trucks. Working all night, I
made enough money to pay for an ample breakfast. I ate ravenously and went home where I slept until late in the afternoon.
When I awoke, I could barely move—I had thrown out my back.

Days went by and my luck didn't improve. I survived on the
sandwiches and fruit that Jose snuck out of his parents' kitchen. In
my desperation, I decided to sell a pint of my blood. After I was
paid in cash, I went directly to the Moratalaz market where I spent
half of the money on food and a large bottle of cheap red wine. On
the way home, I fainted. When I came to, a couple of neighborhood
housewives surrounded me. The bottle of wine had broken in the
fall. The women were alarmed, but I insisted that I was all right,

just weak. Nonetheless, they insisted on walking me to my building and carrying the shopping bags. I thanked them profusely when they put me in the elevator. I felt awful: I was convinced the women knew I was trying to survive by selling my blood. I went upstairs where I rested for a while, then I cooked a feast. Jose arrived late in the afternoon with his sandwich and bananas, and I surprised him with a *cocido* of pork, lima beans, carrots, and potatoes. He didn't ask where the money had come from, and I was too ashamed to tell him the truth.

That night we celebrated by going to the movies and to a café. For the first time, our plans for the future were mentioned. At the end of the school year in May, Jose, his mother, and sister closed the apartment in Madrid and went to the family farm in the mountains of Jaén, in Andalusia, where they stayed until early September. I couldn't conceive of staying in Madrid without him.

"I won't go, if you don't want me to," he said, his eyes blazing.

"You'd move in with me?"

"No. You don't want to be here in the summer. Madrid is unlivable, unbearably hot and dead." He paused. "We can run away," he finished and there was a mischievous twinkle in his eyes.

The idea was romantic and cinematographic. I thought of Bonnie and Clyde and God knows what else! Then I remembered Jose was a minor and his father a colonel in Spain's fascist army. I could hear Lulu shouting, "Are you insane? This is Spain. Do you know what Franco did to homosexuals?"

Obviously, Jose had given the idea some thought. "We'll go to Cataluña. We can find work in the Costa Brava, in the hotels. They're desperate for workers this time of the year. We'll go to Cadaquéz, where Dalí has a house. They'll never find us there. It's beautiful, and very close to France. And when we've saved enough money, we'll go to Paris or to America. I'm sick of Spain. I can't stand my parents. Santiago, I love you. I want to be with you always."

The madness of our love became so clear to me. Although Jose was brilliant, I realized he reasoned like a child.

After that conversation, I knew my days in Madrid were numbered. I couldn't conceive going with Jose to Paris or to Colombia or to New York. I didn't know myself what to do with my life. But I was young, a bard, and the world's vastness beguiled me.

I returned to the blood bank to sell more blood. They refused, arguing that I was too thin and in danger of becoming anemic. I consoled myself by thinking that for the first time in my life I was really thin.

My fate was sealed the following morning when a curt letter arrived from the prestigious Madrid publisher rejecting my novel.

I hadn't bottomed out enough, so I held to my stubbornness. I made up my mind that no matter what I wouldn't contact my family for money. Now I was determined to live, to become like George Orwell in his *Down and Out in Paris and London* period. I was convinced that if nothing else all this would be good for my autobiography, and I determined to go to Barcelona alone, looking for work.

I decided I would hitchhike, but I wanted to have enough money to take a room in a *pensión* when I arrived. Feeling feverish, I wrote a letter to Lulu, explaining that I would return in the fall for the rest of my belongings, and that as soon as I made some money, I would pay the back rent. Next I wrote a missive much harder to compose—a letter to Jose, asking him to forgive me for departing without saying good-bye in person; reassuring him that I adored him, that it broke my heart to part from him, but that I would return.

Late that afternoon, I walked all the way downtown to the *Oficina de Correos* and, using the last of my money, I mailed off these letters. Then I headed to a gay bar in the neighborhood that catered to tourists looking for hustlers. Around six o'clock the bar began to fill in, and soon a foreign-looking man entered the premises. The combustion was instantaneous: we exchanged glances, he came over and offered to buy me a drink. Rasmus was a Belgian, a count (which didn't mean anything, he informed me), and he was in Madrid on business. He was married, and he showed me snapshots of his wife and his two blonde daughters. Rasmus was in his mid-forties, with salt-and-pepper hair, hairy chest and arms, extremely handsome and likable. In other circumstances, I would have gladly paid him to go to bed with me! He was practical, too. He wasted no time informing me he would pay me to fuck him, and that he loved to be whipped on his buttocks with a belt. Was I interested? S&M sex was a mystery to me, but a little spanking sounded harmless enough.

"How much?" I asked, remembering my reasons for doing this.

"Fifty dollars?" he offered, astonishing me.

"Seventy-five," I countered. After all, I was supposed to be the sadist!

Off we went to the penthouse. Rasmus was a consummate lover: he licked my body, nursed my nipples, sucked my balls, fellated me, and finally sat on my cock, riding it until I came. Subsequently he lay face down on the bed and asked me to whip him with his belt and to call him a bad boy. At first, I was very tentative, but Rasmus kept asking for harsher punishment and verbal abuse. "You horrible, bad boy," I screamed, relishing my suddenly awakened dominatrix nature. "Bad, bad, bad. *Muy malo.*"

The harder I whipped him, the more he wriggled on the bed moaning with pleasure and begging for more. A while later, his ass extremely bruised, he asked me to stop and to fuck him again. "*Quiero leche en mi culo,*" he begged. "Give me *leche*. Pump me full of it."

I was incredibly turned on. I felt close to this man, united in a bewilderingly intimate bond. Later, we lay kissing, our sweating and bruised bodies entwined. "My little Moor," Rasmus called me, tenderly. "My beautiful Moorish boy. I have a secret apartment in Brussels," he said. "Why don't you come there? We could be lovers. You like your bad boy, don't you, Papa?"

The idea was appealing. I told him of my summer plans, and that perhaps later I might join him. Rasmus left around midnight. He gave me two crisp $50 bills, told me that I had made him very happy, and that he looked forward to seeing me in Brussels. He gave me his card. We kissed passionately, as if we were lovers. He made me promise I'd write to him.

I was too excited to go to sleep. I packed a shoulder bag with some clothes, Plath's *Ariel*, and the manuscript of my novel. Around 4 A.M., lugging my typewriter and traveling bag, I walked out of the building where I had written my first novel and had been in love for the first time. I headed south, away from Morata-laz. The deserted city had never looked more inviting than it did at that hour when it was all mine. It was dawn when I found myself in the outskirts of Madrid, walking along the highway that leads out of Castile. Automobiles, buses, and trucks whizzed by in ever-increasing numbers. I was terrified of what lay ahead, but I was in a hurry to go meet it. When I got tired of carrying my stuff, I put my arm out, thumb up. Almost right away, a VW slowed down and pulled up on the side of the road, some hundred feet away from me. I picked up my possessions and, before sprinting toward the waiting vehicle, I turned around, kissed the tips of my fingers and thrust my hand in the direction of Madrid. Jose was probably in bed, dreaming. I sent my kiss out to him, hoping it would sail down the highway, past the tall buildings, the monuments, the parks, and into his bedroom, as a final caress, to thank him for his love, for being my first love.

It was during my stay in Barcelona that I became interested in Christopher Columbus. I had rented a room with a sink in the Hostal Alfonso X, a malodorous dive in the Barrio Gótico. In the late afternoons, before I started cruising Las Ramblas, and later the bars, I'd sit on a bench on the quay in front of a replica of one of Columbus's caravels, the *Santa María*, and marvel at the Admiral's boldness to wander off into the unknown in such a flimsy vessel.

Sitting on the hot bench for hours, with no money and no place to go, scanning the promenade for cigarette butts, dreaming of taking a long shower and having a good meal accompanied by a bottle of red wine, I'd think of Jose and get sad, thinking that perhaps I would never see him again. I didn't even have an address for him in Andalusia, and he had no way of contacting me in Barcelona. Mesmerized by the stagnant waters of the bay, I'd daydream about him: Jose in the mountains of Jaén, reading poetry in an olive grove; Jose working in the family orchard, sweating, wearing shorts and a hat.

June had come to an end and I had plantar warts on the soles of my feet from making fruitless rounds to restaurants, *fondas,* and hotels looking for work as a waiter or dishwasher. But without a work permit no one would hire me. I was behind in the rent. It was weeks since I had taken a shower, and although I cleaned myself at the sink every day before I went out and after I came back late at night, and washed my hair often with soap, I was convinced I smelled like rotten fish. I was tired of sneaking out of the *pensión* in the morning, and coming in late at night, when the ancient clerk behind the desk was so drowsy he'd mechanically hand me the key to my room in his sleep.

Although I had sworn never to do it again, I went to sell my blood. Somehow—I can attribute it only to the sea air, and the many hours of inactivity on the bench, and all the water I drank from the stone fountains all over the city—I had gained weight, so I wasn't turned away. After I caught up with the back rent, paid for a shower, and devoured a deluxe paella in a cheap restaurant, I was broke once more.

To aggravate the situation, it was impossible to write anything in my room. Because the hostel was on the Calle del Barro, in the heart of the Gothic section, throughout the day and night the ancient churches clanged their bells, keeping me awake at night and incapacitating me so that I could not compose a single line during the day. Besides, I was so hungry all the time I could think only about the succulent dishes of seafood I saw the tourists wolfing down in the outdoor restaurants. In that state of slow starvation, fetid, the unthinkable occurred to me: I'd pawn my typewriter. It was an electric typewriter my mother had given me as a birthday present. I figured I'd get a few thousand pesetas for it. I wasn't ready to go back to hustling again. What had happened with Rasmus, I reasoned, was a freak occurrence, and I was determined to make money in a more conventional manner.

I hauled my typewriter to the nearest *Monte de Piedad* and got in a long line of indigents who were pawning their china, their silverware, and their finest linen. I consoled myself by thinking that pawning my typewriter would be just a temporary measure. Sooner or later, I figured, I'd get a job off the books. When I handed my typewriter to the window person, she plugged it to an outlet to make sure it worked. Satisfied, she said, "I need to see some proof of ownership."

I couldn't believe my ears. All strength seemed to ebb from my body.

"The bill of sale will do," the woman said.

"For Heaven's sake, it was a present from my mother," I protested.

The woman shrugged. To indicate she couldn't help me, she started looking over my shoulder to the next person in line.

"Wait," I said. "There must be some other way. I need to eat."

This caught her attention. "Where are you from?" she asked— my South American accent gave me away.

"Mexico," I lied, since all South Americans—not without reason—had a reputation as crooks and swindlers in Spain.

"Go to your consulate," she said, "and ask the consul to give you a letter attesting that the typewriter belongs to you; we'll accept that." She paused, then, raising her voice, she called, "Next in line."

I wasn't keen on going to the Colombian authorities and announcing my poverty. But the truth was that in the last two days all I had eaten was a sandwich I had swiped from one of the cafés on Las Ramblas. The Colombian consul at that time was a well-known intellectual, a patron of writers, and an intimate friend of Gabriel García Márquez. I had already published a few poems and short stories and reviews in Colombia, so I thought the consul would be sympathetic to my plight. Surely, I thought, he'd be familiar with the story of authors who had had to starve in order to write their first great work. García Márquez himself had gone hungry in Paris in order to write *No One Writes to the Colonel*.

The following morning, I arrived at the Colombian Consulate as soon as it opened its doors. While I waited all morning for the consul to see me, I was offered coffee half a dozen times, which I drank with lots of sugar to get some energy. My empty stomach began to make alarming rumbling noises, which the people sitting in the waiting room could hear; the coffee and sugar made me feel light-headed, supernaturally lucid, and jittery. Finally, around one o'clock, the consul's secretary, a friendly young man from Bogotá, told me that the consul was not receiving anyone else and asked me to come back in the afternoon. I hadn't eaten in twenty-four hours, but there was nothing I could do except go to a park and wait until the consulate reopened in the afternoon. If everything went according to my plans, I'd be able to eat in one of the cheap eateries in the Barrio Gótico that evening.

I had reached the first floor, feeling weak and dejected, and as I was crossing the building's entrance, I bumped into a young man who was entering the building in a hurry. I was about to curse him, then realized he looked familiar.

"Martínez," he called first, in a Barranquillero accent that I immediately recognized. "Rivadeneira," he said, tapping his chest with his fingers. "Carlos Alberto Rivadeneira, from Barranquilla."

I was astonished that he recognized me. I hadn't seen Carlos Alberto since the days when, as adolescents in Barranquilla, we had participated in declamation contests. Back then we were friendly rivals, though I kept my distance from him because he already had a reputation as a homosexual—something that was truly shocking and unacceptable in the Barranquilla of those days. As much as I had wanted to be his friend, I was afraid of the buzz our friendship might create. After I had moved to the States with my family, I had never seen him again.

"Where are you going?" he asked.

I explained that the consulate was closed for lunch and that I'd return when it reopened in the afternoon.

"Damn it," Carlos Alberto snapped. "I get my mail here; I was coming to get it. Damn these bureaucrats. Leeches of the people, that's what they are. Every week they close earlier and earlier. It's a wonder they get any business done. So Macondiano." When he had finished railing against the Colombian functionaries, he asked, "What are you doing now anyway? Want to have lunch with me?"

The mention of the word lunch reminded me of my hunger. I was about to excuse myself, when Carlos Alberto said, "It's on me. Come on, it will be so great to catch up with each other after all this time."

Hardly believing my luck, I accepted his invitation. We headed for Las Ramblas, and entered one of those restaurants I had passed many times, and which I thought I'd never be able to afford. Over a huge paella, which we bolted down with plenty of wine, we talked excitedly as if we were intimate friends who had not seen each other in ages. Carlos Alberto told me he had arrived in Spain the prior year, to study Romance and Arabic languages at the university in Barcelona. Soon after his arrival, however, he realized that what he really wanted to do was to become a playwright. For a Latin American writer there was no more attractive place than Barcelona in those years. García Márquez and Vargas Llosa had lived there for many years just prior to our arrival. It was there they had their scandalous falling out (it was reported in the press that the Peruvian had given the Colombian a black eye). The Chilean José Donoso, as well as other famous writers of the Latin American boom, resided in the city. The most important literary agents and publishing houses in the Spanish language were located in the capital of Catalonia.

Carlos Alberto, whose ancestors were Catalonian, was lanky, sandy haired, fine featured, and conventionally good looking. He was also boisterous, vehement, and intellectually passionate. Eating with him was not altogether a pleasant experience because he spat pieces of food as he got carried away expressing his opinions. As a student, he had been able to get a work permit and made his living as a translator. He informed me that in the summer business was dead, however, and that he'd have plenty of work again in September. Since I knew English, he promised to get me work translating in the fall. Because he was owed money for some jobs he had done in the spring, he thought he would be able to squeeze through the summer without having to get a job. His plan was to spend July and August working on his play, a kind of *Long Day's Journey into Night* set in the garden of his parents' house in Barranquilla.

Carlos Alberto was a renaissance man, knew several languages, and had an encyclopedic knowledge of European history and literature and of Barcelona's architecture. He regaled me with many stories about his conquests in Barranquilla and in Spain. I had never had an intimate homosexual friend, and meeting him this way I felt as if I had encountered a long lost cousin. After lunch, Carlos Alberto suggested we go for a cognac to a bar in the neighborhood. By then, because of the wine, because of the warmth of the couple of hours we had spent together, I felt relaxed enough to be frank with him. "Look," I said, "I'd love to go with you, but I have to get back to the consulate. I need to pawn my typewriter." I explained about the letter I needed from the consul.

"Santiago, don't hawk your typewriter," Carlos Alberto exploded. "You're a writer. Sell your mother first."

"But you don't understand," I insisted. "I don't have a penny to my name. If I don't pawn it, I won't eat tomorrow."

"Don't worry so much about money, man. The world is full of money. How much money do you think I have left after I paid the bill?"

"I don't know. How much?"

"Enough to buy a pack of Spanish cigarettes. Santiago, money is not as precious a commodity as you think it is. As long as I'm here in Barcelona, you'll eat. So don't worry about it. The drinks are on me. I have a tab at this place where I'm going to take you."

We went to a bar, El Peruano, in the Barrio Gótico. Carlos Alberto knew the owner, who greeted him effusively. The bar was a smoky, cavernous room in a medieval building—a catacomb with a liquor license. The walls looked as if they had last been painted before Columbus sailed for the Americas. Although it was early in the afternoon, the seedy joint was packed with over-the-hill hookers, sailors, and scruffy, dangerous-looking South Americans. Nineteen-fifties romantic boleros by Roberto Ledesma, Olga Guillot, and Lucho Gatica played in the juke box.

We drank cognac after cognac, eyeing the sailors we fancied, talking about writers, literature, movies, politics, sex. I had never met anyone who engaged me intellectually the way I felt engaged by Carlos Alberto. Just the thought that soon enough the day would come to an end, and we would part, seemed unbearable.

It was already evening when Carlos Alberto said, "Look, Santiago, when was the last time you took a good shower? It's one thing to be a bohemian, and another one to stink like a dead vulture. Why don't you move in with me? It'll be a lot cheaper. I have a large room with two beds and a shower and we can write in the mornings and then hang out together and have fun. What do you say to that?"

It sounded like a great idea, but I owed a few days rent at the Alfonso X, so I couldn't move until I paid.

"What floor are you on?" Carlos Alberto asked.

"The second," I told him.

"No problem, man. I'll show you what to do. Manolo," he called the bartender, "put our drinks on my tab. We'll be back tomorrow."

Manolo didn't seem the least bit worried about this; he produced a bill and Carlos Alberto signed it. I was so entranced by Carlos Alberto's energy, the freedom and ease with which he moved in the world, that I followed him without questioning anything.

We walked to my hostel. On the way, Carlos Alberto outlined the plan of action for me: I'd go to my room, drop my suitcase to the street hanging from a sheet, and then climb down in the same manner. Emboldened by all the cognac we had consumed, I did not hesitate. The maneuver was achieved with a smoothness that surprised me. Carrying my suitcase and typewriter, we wended our way through the sombrous streets that led to the Hostal de la Alondra, deep in the heart of the Barrio Gótico. My career as a petty criminal had begun.

Back then, Barcelona was not the amusement-park city it is today. A spattering of tourists visited it in the summer to admire Gaudí's architecture, but most Europeans bypassed it on their way to Ibiza and other trendy islands, and to the beaches of the Costa Brava. Barcelona summers are hot and humid, and many of the natives abandon the city early in July for the coolness of the countryside, the mountains, and the seashore.

The old part of the city, in particular, had a decaying aspect that was appealing to me. Barcelona was like a ruined Venice, without the canals and without the gondolas, but it was more surrealist because of Gaudí's colorful, deracinated structures. Even the buildings constructed earlier in the twentieth century had a grayish patina to them, as if they were entirely covered by pigeon drop-pings. The grand structures made me feel I was living in a set designed by De Chirico. And the Gothic barrio, with its narrow, sun-less streets, was an endless labyrinthine maze that I imagined Borges would have loved. It was a lumpen neighborhood of old, decrepit people, starving artists, and South American thieves. Because it contained museums, impressive ancient churches, cheap eateries, and the sleaziest bars imaginable, once I settled in the Hostal de la Alondra, Carlos Alberto and I ventured out of the Barrio Gótico only to get our mail at the Colombian Consulate, to visit the quay in the late afternoon, where we'd sit, exchanging stories about Christopher Columbus, and to cruise Las Ramblas, which was always—day and night—like a bazaar out of the *Thousand and One Nights*. The other place we frequently visited was Gaudí's un-finished Cathedral of the Sacred Heart, which we never tired of ad-miring. For hours we'd argue about how we'd finish Gaudí's mas-terpiece if we had the chance. At night, we'd sit in the plaza in front of it, smoking cigarettes, and talking until it was time to go to a gay bar for a night cap.

Carlos Alberto's little checks from his translation jobs kept drib-bling in, giving us extra pocket money. He insisted in sharing everything with me. "If you had money, you'd do the same for me, right?" "Right," I agreed. He had credit in the crucial places. Manolo, the owner of El Peruano, was always happy to see us come in, and would let us drink as much as we wanted, even though days and days passed, and our dire monetary situation re-mained unchanged. More important to our predicament, Carlos Alberto had credit at the *fonda* Reina Isabel, a restaurant in the Barrio Gótico that opened only for lunch. The Reina Isabel was one dark hole in a crumbling medieval building. It was the cheapest imaginable place, and all kinds of derelicts with a few pesetas fre-quented it. The restaurant was strictly a family operation: mother and father cooked, and the daughter, Concha, was the waitress. Concha was a matronly girl in her twenties. She had beautiful black hair, which she wore in a long ponytail, and kind, luminous, chestnut eyes. One of her legs was shorter than the other, giving her a bad hobble. Concha had a crush on Carlos Alberto. In July, when her parents went on vacation to their family home in the country, she ran the place all by herself. In August, she'd join her parents, and the restaurant would close for the month. During the month of July, Concha had a young boy who helped her in the kitchen washing the dishes and serving the food. She was so taken with Carlos Alberto that an expression of ecstasy came over her face when she saw us come in. Concha was an amazing cook: her rabbit *al ajillo*, her chicken stewed in olive sauce, and her ham and chick peas with laurel leaves were marvels of Catalonian cuisine. The carafes of fruity, rich red wine were from the family's vineyards. Since the Reina Isabel served only lunch, we would usually show up around three o'clock, when most of her customers had left, and eat until we were full. Then she'd sit at the table with us, and ask us how our writing was going. Every other day or so, Carlos Alberto would scribble a poem to her that he would read aloud to an enraptured Concha.

Our lunch at the Reina Isabel was our only meal of the day. I was delighted to be eating again, especially such delicious food, but I felt guilty; I felt that we were exploiting Concha. It was obvious that she was in love with Carlos Alberto and would do anything to make him happy. One day I confronted him about it. Carlos Alberto blew up. "We are not doing anything unethical," he shouted as we loped down the narrow sunless streets reeking of urine. "I bring that girl the only happiness in her life. You should see what monsters her parents are, and how they mistreat her. Besides, the place will close in August, and her parents will be back in September. When they return, our credit won't be honored anymore. So let's enjoy our good luck while we have it. Remember this Santiago, good things have a way of not lasting."

"But she's in love with you," I protested. "She doesn't know you're a homosexual."

"I've never hidden it from her. I just don't discuss with her the men I go to bed with." He became thoughtful for a moment, lowered his voice, stopped walking, and placed a hand on my shoulder. "Santiago, this is a piece of wisdom I'm gonna pass on to you: women don't care about whether the man who loves them is homosexual or not. What women want is a man who's attentive to them, who appreciates them. Women need constant praise, the way a plant needs water. I'm probably the first man who's ever treated Concha nicely. And why not? I like the girl. I'm not faking anything. I think she's the sweetest thing on earth, and a great cook. If I weren't gay, I'd marry her. Besides," he continued, "don't I write beautiful love poems to her? Has any man ever written love poetry to you?"

I thought of Jose, of whom I was beginning to think less and less all the time because I had begun to fall in love with Carlos Alberto. At night, when he lay on his bed in his underwear, it was hard for me not to make a pass at him. One day I told him how I felt about him. "We're sisters," he snorted. "Forget about that stuff. You're not my type, anyway."

To my surprise, Carlos Alberto was a disciplined writer. By 9 A.M., he sat on his bed and wrote with a pencil on his notebook all morning. His work habits were irritating and distracting to me: he enacted the different characters to test his dialogue. The main character in the play was based on his mother, whom he referred to as Eleanor, after Eleanor of Aquitaine. When he was impersonating her, he'd drape a sheet over himself, and traipse around the room, mouthing somber lines. At first, it was hard for me to get any work done with such goings on in the small space; but after a while we established a good working relationship, and I'd read to him the beginning stanzas of what I envisioned to be an epic poem about Christopher Columbus.

After lunch at the Reina Isabel, and a brief stop at El Peruano, we visited our bench in front of Colombus's caravel. If we had any money, we'd go to the movies. When one of his little checks arrived, we'd go to the gay bars, buy a drink, and nurse it for a long time.

The dreaded month of August came, and Concha placed a *Tancat per vacances* sign on the door of Reina Isabel. The last of Carlos Alberto's checks for his translations had arrived a couple of weeks before, and we were broke and with no prospects of money coming in. I called my mother collect; and Carlos Alberto wrote to his estranged parents. My mother sent a check for $50 and informed me that it would be the last money she'd send to me in Spain. If I couldn't get a work permit, she wrote, it would be better for me to return to the States and go back to graduate school.

Every day, we made the trip to the Colombian Consulate, waiting for a check that never arrived. It was clear that we'd have to do something about money. Since I had sold my blood twice over the summer, Carlos Alberto offered to do it too. He was too slim, however, and the clinic turned him down. Things were becoming really grim, and we hadn't eaten for two days, when a packet arrived at the Colombian Consulate from Carlos Alberto's eccentric aunt Lucila, a millionaire. When he realized who the packet was from, Carlos Alberto tore it open on the spot, hoping she had sent cash. Inside, he found six envelopes of instant Knorr chicken soup, and a note from Lucila recommending the soup as very nutritious. We both broke up laughing.

We were hungry, and bloated from drinking so much water from the fountains in the streets. Carlos Alberto knew a Colombian writer a few years older than us, who had made a big splash recently with—what else?—a magical realism novel. We had called him a few times, hoping he'd recommend us to his publisher and introduce us to other Latin American authors, but he had refused to see us, perhaps sensing how desperate we were. Carlos Alberto swallowed his pride and called him again, explaining that all we wanted from him was to borrow his kitchen to boil some instant soup. The writer replied he was on his way to the Costa Brava right that minute and would be away for two weeks. He regretted he couldn't help us, he said, and hung up. "The bastard," Carlos Alberto screamed, blanching; he slammed the public phone. Enraged, he started shaking the cabin and kicking it. As he did this, hundreds of coins started pouring out of the telephone—a squall of *pesetas*. We filled our pockets with coins, even as astonished passersby watched us. We headed for the bench on the quay and, in front of the replica of the Santa María, we counted our booty. We had enough for a good meal and celebratory drinks afterwards.

We went by El Peruano and paid Manolo some of our tab. We were having a wonderful time, laughing, celebrating our unexpected good luck, when an older gentleman approached us.

"Are you South Americans?" he asked us, sitting at the bar on the chair next to me. "Tomás Castillogrande," he added, introducing himself. He was a gentleman in his sixties, plump, balding. Something about his manner betrayed the fact that he was well off, although he was dressed in frayed clothes so that he could blend in with the riff raff at El Peruano.

In our expansive mood, we decided to include him in our conversation. As the afternoon turned into evening, Don Tomás revealed more and more about himself. He lived in the town of Sabadel, an hour away from Barcelona by train. He was married and was a grandfather. He owned a wool-dyeing factory. Don Tomás laughed constantly at our *boutades* against the literary establishment, the Church, Colombian diplomats in Barcelona. Finally, around eight o'clock, when we were beginning to feel the effect of the alcohol, he asked us if he could take us out to dinner. He said he knew a wonderful restaurant on the water, and that he would be honored if we accepted his invitation. We did. And we had the best meal we had had in Barcelona. As dinner was coming to an end, Don Tomás said in a very matter of fact way that he had to go back to Sabadel that night, but that he would be happy if one of us came to visit him next week. He had, he said, "*una casa para mis devaneos.*" We understood this was a place that his family did not know about, and to which he took his tricks. He said he would give us the equivalent of $100 if one of us came to visit him for the evening. Although he never specified which one of us, it was clear that he preferred me. Carlos Alberto was the good-looking one of us, but clearly not his type. I had suspected this was what Don Tomás (or Monsieur Sabadel, as we came to call him), had in mind all along. Despite his worldliness, Carlos Alberto had no experience with hustling. He was genuinely surprised when Monsieur made his proposal. When we parted that night in front of our hostel, Monsieur handed us an advance, gave us his address, and said that he expected us—all the time looking at me—next Friday night in his "house of peccadilloes."

The thought of going to visit Monsieur didn't thrill me, but for the past month Carlos Alberto had been supporting me. And, as he pointed out, I was "the experienced hustler."

Friday evening I took the train to Sabadel. It was a ride that made stops in towns that looked sleepy, clean, and melancholy. When the train arrived in Sabadel, I began to get anxious. I found Monsieur very pleasant as a drinking and dining companion, but I wasn't sure I'd be able to have sex with him. Rasmus, after all, had been an extremely handsome man. As I followed the elaborate instructions that Monsieur had drawn for me, I started to get nauseous. At that moment I would have returned to Barcelona, except that I didn't have the money for the return trip. In a little plaza along the way, I sat on a dusty bench to collect myself. Not to go to bed with Monsieur Sabadel, considering that Carlos Alberto was in Barcelona—hungry—waiting for me to return with money, was a cowardly action. "I'll do it once," I muttered to myself. "Just once."

Monsieur's house of peccadilloes was in the kind of lower-middle-class neighborhood where I imagined the people who worked in his factory lived. I knocked on the door, my knees weak. The door opened and Monsieur appeared wearing a loose house dress and slippers. I hesitated. Perhaps I should go back to Barcelona, even if I had to walk all the way back. Monsieur smiled sweetly and said, "Come in *majo*, what took you so long to get here?"

I remembered why I was there; that this was a job; and that I couldn't disappoint Carlos Alberto. I followed Monsieur into a homey living room. He pointed to a reclining chair, which I took.

"Would you like a drink while I finish preparing dinner, *corazón*?"

It dawned on me that I was supposed to play the husband coming back home to his wife after a hard day's work.

"Yes, a glass of wine will be nice," I mumbled, ill at ease.

"And the paper too, *corazón*?"

"The paper too."

Monsieur left the room, and I didn't know whether to laugh, to cry, or to run away from his house. I tried to reassure myself that so far his fantasy seemed harmless. Monsieur returned with wine, cheese, olives, and fried squid, which he set on a little table next to my chair. He took a cushion from the sofa and placed it under my head. Then he picked up a pair of worn slippers from under the sofa, knelt in front of me, untied my shoes, removed them and put the slippers on my feet.

I decided I'd go along with it, as long as he didn't force me to do anything that was unacceptable to me. The smells coming from the kitchen were enticing. At least, I thought, I'd get a great meal out of it. Monsieur was obviously a gourmet cook. I began to relax as I read the paper. After a while, Monsieur came into the room to announce that dinner was ready. He carried a bathrobe in his arms.

"Take off your clothes and put this on," he prompted me, handing me the bathrobe.

I balked. "I'm fine like this; I don't need to change."

"Your clothes are filthy, *corazón*," Monsieur said lovingly. "I'll put them in the washing machine while we dine, and when you leave you'll have clean clothes for tomorrow. I want you to look your best."

He did have a point. All my clothes needed a trip to the laundry. I obliged him, removing everything. Discreetly, he looked the other way when I took off my underwear. I put on the luxurious velour bathrobe.

Lighted candles, flowers, pretty china, and fine stemmed glasses decorated the table. Monsieur had prepared a sumptuous meal: rabbit stew with mushrooms, potatoes au gratin, garlicky sautéed vegetables, a salad of greens, olives, fruits, and tart flowers, freshly-baked bread, a rich velvety red wine, and for dessert a flan, dried fruits, poached pears and plums, cognac and coffee. Over dinner, just like any couple comfortable with each other, we talked about the news. The Olympics were on that summer. Nadia Comaneci had hit a perfect 10 in one of her routines and Monsieur was fascinated by the tiny athlete. That summer were the celebrations for the American bicentennial, so we talked about American democracy and how different it was from the Franco regime of the past thirty years. Not once did he ask any personal questions, as if he already knew everything there was to know about me. At one point during dinner, Monsieur got up to put my clothes in the dryer.

The fine food, the wines, the lively repartee had had a positive effect on my mood. I was having a wonderful time. After we finished eating, we went back to the living room for cordials. Around nine, Monsieur said that he was tired and wanted to retire for the night. The moment of truth had arrived.

I had decided that I liked him very much as a person, but the idea of making love to him was still revolting to me. He took me by the hand and led me to the bedroom. There was a lamp by the bed draped with a red shawl, so that the room was amber colored. Monsieur helped me to remove the bathrobe and asked me to lie down on the bed. Then he handed me a bunch of German porno magazines.

"Look and see if there is any *majo* who arouses you," he instructed me. "I'll be back in a minute." He stepped out of the room.

Alone, naked in his bed, I got nervous for the first time. What was he up to, I wondered? Without my clothes, though, I couldn't go anywhere. What had I gotten myself into? As these thoughts raced my mind, Monsieur entered the room carrying an ironing board, an iron, and my clothes.

"Found anybody you like?" he asked, referring to the magazines of naked men on my lap.

"Oh, uh," I mumbled and started flipping through the pages of men performing sex in more ways than I'd thought possible.

Monsieur plugged in the iron, put my shirt on the ironing board, sprinkled it with water from a bottle, and sat next to the board, waiting for the iron to heat up.

I stared at him.

"Look at the magazines," he directed me. "Is there anyone who makes your balls hard?"

I decided to play along. Now that he had a hot iron in his hands, I was at a disadvantage. I knew he wouldn't kill me, because Carlos Alberto knew where I was. Nonetheless, I was anxious. Since he sat there, waiting for me to look through the magazines, I obliged him. Eventually, after looking at hundreds of photographs of hunky men fucking, I began to get a hard-on. Then I saw Monsieur beam, get up, put on his glasses and start ironing.

I thought I understood what he wanted from me. He wanted me to get a hard-on, while he ironed. When he saw that my cock was erect, Monsieur started saying, "Oh, your balls are hard now, aren't they? Oh, oh," all the time meticulously ironing my shirt. I started playing with myself, looking at a picture of two men engaging in sex. It wasn't easy to concentrate and keep an erection with Monsieur looking at me, with a hot iron in his hands. He put the shirt in a hanger behind the door and started ironing my pants. As he ironed, he kept talking smutty to me. If all he wanted from me was to watch me jerk off, I had gotten off easy, I thought. I closed my eyes and thought of myself in bed: making love to Jose and Carlos Alberto at the same time. As I was climaxing, I heard Monsieur cheerleading me, "Shoot, shoot, *corazón*, let me see that come all over your chest. Make your wife happy, *corazón mío*."

When I opened my eyes, Monsieur was furiously ironing my jeans and leering at me. After I while, when my breathing began to stabilize, I decided to get up to clean myself.

"Don't," Monsieur ordered me. "Don't. Let me do it, please. Let your wife clean you." He hung my pants and my shirt and left the room. He returned with two steaming washcloths and cleaned me. When he finished, he buried his face in the washcloths, kissing them.

Monsieur walked me back to the train station, where he handed me the equivalent of a hundred dollars, a large sum of money in those days. He said he would be happy to see me again, the following week. That he'd be waiting for me.

Carlos Alberto was in our room at the hostel when I arrived. Since he hadn't eaten, I took him out for a big midnight meal at a restaurant in Las Ramblas. While he ate, I regaled him with all the details of my visit to Sabadel. He howled with laughter as I described myself on the bed with the magazines and Monsieur ironing my clothes. After I paid for dinner, I gave Carlos Alberto half of the money I had made. He declined it, but I insisted. After all, he had been bringing in more money than I had, and he had shared everything with me. That night, we celebrated in grand style. After dinner, we went to El Peruano for drinks, and later we went to a club where we danced nonstop until dawn. With the threat of starvation lifted from our heads for a while, the euphoria of the disco music worked on us like an aphrodisiac. On the dance floor, it was easy to believe that that night was all there was to life: that if we kept dancing, the music would keep us forever young, that we would never be hungry or alone ever again.

When we returned to our room, I waited until we turned the light off to muster the courage to say what all night long I had suppressed. "Carlos Alberto, are you awake?" I asked.

"Yes."

"I think I've fallen in love with you," I said without any hesitation.

"Cut it out, will you?"

I pressed him. "I want to know what you feel for me."

"Santiago, *carajo*, I've told you many times. We're sisters."

"The hell we are," I said. "I'm in love with you."

"You're not my type, Santiago. Why can't you understand that?"

It was hard to believe that he loved people because of a type. As far as I was concerned, we were a match made in heaven: we were both Colombians, coevals, writers, gay, we loved many of the same things. He was European looking, I was dark. I said so.

"Santiago," he mumbled angrily. "I want to go to sleep, okay? Just don't spoil this beautiful night."

Hurt by his rejection, I didn't say another word, but I stayed awake, tossing in bed. It was becoming painful sleeping in such proximity to each other, my desire unrequited. I wanted to get up from my bed and wrap him in my arms. It hurt wanting him and not being able to fuse with him. I began to think about going back to the States to finish graduate school. The life we led was beginning to lose its attraction. It was true that September was just a few weeks away, and that then, according to Carlos Alberto, we'd be able to get regular work as translators. But what if we didn't? The idea of another visit to Sabadel wasn't appealing. Once was enough for me. It was morning when I fell asleep.

When I woke up, Carlos Alberto was writing. "Well, good afternoon, Sleeping Beauty," he teased me. "I've been working for hours. It's almost time for lunch."

"Let me take a quick shower and we'll go," I said getting up.

We were walking up Las Ramblas, in silence, looking for a new cheap restaurant we hadn't tried before, when I heard someone scream my name. I looked up and, running toward me, I saw Jose.

I didn't have time to react before he had his arms around me. We embraced and kissed.

"What are you doing here?" I asked, astonished to see him in Barcelona.

"I ran away, Santiago," he said excitedly. "I knew I would find you. I've been in Barcelona two days, roaming the streets looking for you." He stopped talking, becoming aware of Carlos Alberto's presence.

I introduced them. Carlos Alberto had heard all about Jose, but Jose had no idea who this person was standing next to me. "Carlos Alberto is a friend from Barranquilla. We're roommates. We were going to have lunch. Have you eaten yet?" I asked awkwardly. Though I was happy to see him, I was nervous too.

"No, no. Oh, Santiago, I can't believe it. This is incredible. I knew I'd find you," Jose exulted, holding my hand.

"You two love birds go have lunch," Carlos Alberto said. "I'll meet you later at the hostel. Perhaps we can have dinner together." Then to Jose, "Very nice meeting you." He turned around and disappeared in the crowd before I had time to say anything.

"What's the matter with him?" Jose asked suspiciously. "Is he your new lover?"

"No," I said firmly.

"Well, he seemed jealous to me."

"It's nothing. He was just being thoughtful. He's a very well-mannered guy. He just wanted us to be alone with each other. Let's go have lunch," I said to change the subject.

We took a table under an umbrella. In the months I hadn't seen him, Jose seemed to have grown taller, more handsome. He was very tanned and his hair touched his shoulders. After the waiter took our orders, I said, "Jose, what are you doing here?"

"I thought you'd be happy to see me, Santiago. Are you angry with me?"

"No, no. I'm just surprised. I'm still in shock."

"Oh good. Because I love you as much as ever. I should be the one angry with you for leaving Madrid without saying good-bye."

Guiltily I said, "I sent a letter. Did you get it?"

"Yes, I did. And I'm not angry with you."

The waiter arrived with a pitcher of *horchata de chufa*. I poured the drinks. I was afraid to ask Jose any questions. I liked him as much as ever, but my changeable heart was now infatuated with Carlos Alberto. Yet I realized I couldn't tell that to Jose.

"Well," Jose said, "I ran away to be with you. We can go to France: I have 200,000 *pesetas*."

I gasped. "Where did you get so much money?"

"For a while I've known the combination to my parents' safe in Jaén. My father showed up last week to be with us for the month. Right away he started berating me for not doing manly things, for my long hair, for reading poetry all the time. He threatened to send me to a military school in the fall. So, a few days ago they left to visit some relatives in Cádiz. I feigned having a virus. I said I would join them later. After they left, I opened the safe and took all the money out. I knew you were in Barcelona, and I was ready to comb all the towns of the Costa Brava looking for you." A feverish light shone in his eyes, as if he found it romantic being a thief on the run.

"I did it so we could go to Paris, Santiago. We can live together and be happy."

I smiled, not knowing what to say. Finally, after lunch had been served and we had been eating for a while, I said, "Jose, you've got to return that money before your parents get back. If you go back now, they'll never know you did this."

"Is it because you don't love me anymore?" he asked, crestfallen.

"No, no, it's not that, Jose. It's just that . . . when they find out, they'll send the police after you." As I said these words, I remembered Lulu Mercurio's words: "Are you crazy? The guy's father is in the military? Do you know what Franco did to homosexuals?"

"France is just a couple hours away by train. They'll never find us in Paris. Or we can go to Germany. Or to Sweden. Or to New York," he insisted.

I realized that I would not be able to get him to change his mind right away, but that it was in my interest to convince him to go back and return the money. If they caught us together, I could go to jail for a long time.

After lunch, we went to Jose's hostel. We made love as passionately as ever, and then took a nap. It was late afternoon when we woke up.

We were in bed, caressing each other, when Jose said, "Let's go to Cadaqués. I want to show it to you before we leave Spain. We'll take the train to Figueras tonight and tomorrow we'll be in Cadaqués."

I became pensive. Perhaps I should go to Cadaqués with him. After a couple of days together, he might calm down enough to become reasonable.

"All right, let's go."

Jose kissed me, enraptured.

"I have to go to the hostel to say good-bye to Carlos Alberto and to get my things. You get ready, and I'll be back in an hour."

Carlos Alberto was reading in bed. I told him about the money, and how Jose wanted us to go to Paris, but wanted to stop first in Cadaqués. I would return in a few days, I reassured him, after I sent Jose back to his parents.

"Are you sure you don't want to go to Paris with him? I hope you're not feeling guilty about leaving me behind. Jose is really cute. I'd follow him all the way to the tundra if he asked me," Carlos Alberto said.

"He's adorable, I know. But I don't want to spend the next twenty years of my life in jail. If his fascist father doesn't kill me first. No, I'll return because I want to return"—to be with you, I wanted to add, but didn't dare.

Carlos Alberto walked me to the hostel where Jose waited for me. Then he accompanied us to the train station, and stayed with us until our train pulled away in the dark, in the direction of France.

It was late when we arrived in Figueras. After we found a room for the night, we went looking for a place to have dinner. Jose and I spent our first night together. In Madrid, we had always met in the afternoons, and then Jose had to go back to his parents. This was the most time we had spent together. It was our honeymoon. When I woke up in the morning, with Jose in my arms, it was hard to accept that I would have to give up the great pleasure he represented. Yet, deep down I knew that no matter how happy he made me, how much he fulfilled my desire, I had to let him go.

We visited Dalí's museum in the morning, and by noon we were on a bus to Cadaqués. As we traveled over the mountains on unpaved roads, Jose babbled about Lorca and Dalí together in Cadaqués in the 1920s. For him, this trip together was half literary fantasy, half pilgrimage. I got excited as we began to glimpse the Mediterranean from the top of the hills, but I also dreaded our destination, because I'd resolved that after Cadaqués we had to part.

We arrived in the tiny quaint village, which seemed underpopulated, except for a score of German tourists. In a little hotel in the hills, we took a room with a view of the beach. That afternoon we went sailing, and later we swam until it got dark. The following morning, after breakfast, we set out to walk over the hills that led to Dalí's house in Port Llygat. We arrived at the mansion, enclosed by white walls. It had its own private bay, and next to it, on a small hill, there was a dilapidated, unoccupied structure. We swam and waited for a sign of life from Dalí's house. When the hours passed and nobody came out, we walked around the walls to see if we could get a glimpse of Dalí. We returned to the front gates and began calling out, "Dalí, Dalí, we're here. We've come to see you. Come out." We did this for a long time, and not once was there a sign of life in the silent mansion. Finally, as it was getting late, and we were hungry and needed shelter from the sun, we returned to Cadaqués, disappointed we hadn't seen the artist but happy to have visited his house.

Cadaqués's sleepiness had begun to work its magic on us. We felt relaxed, tired from the swimming and hiking, in a state of heightened sensuality from the constant contact with each other. That night, after dinner, we sat on the dark beach, and I looked for an opening to carefully broach the issue of our future plans. Jose kept talking about how in a few days we'd be in Paris, the city of lovers just waiting for us. We were sitting next to each other on the sand, and I had my arm around his shoulders, when I said, "Jose, you know I love you very much. But we can't go on like this."

A pained look came over his face. "What do you mean? Aren't we going to Paris?"

"No, Jose. I don't think it's wise to go on like this. We really shouldn't risk the consequences." I paused and kissed him on his forehead, caressing his hair; his grimace wouldn't go away. "I have a better plan," I said. "Go back to your parents. Put the rest of the money in the safe. We've spent so little they probably won't notice it for a long time. If they do, just deny it or admit that you took some to go visit a friend or something like that. Anyway, I'll go back to the States very soon," I went on. "I'll get an apartment in New York, and then you can come to live with me." As I said these words, I started believing this scenario.

"But we can do that right now," he said. "I have my passport. We could be in New York tomorrow. We have enough money for that."

"It's not the same, Jose. I don't want to live with you feeling like a fugitive. If your parents find us, I'll go to jail. You have to understand that."

Jose pulled away from me and began to sob loudly. Then he got up and bolted into the darkness. I didn't run after him—my job was to be firm.

The next afternoon, when the train arrived in Barcelona, I got off at the station and Jose continued on, to Andalusia. I waited until the train pulled away. It broke my heart to see him in the window, crying. This wasn't the last image I wanted to have of him.

I went directly to the hostel. When I asked for the key, I was told that Carlos Alberto was in the room. I knocked on the door.

"Who is it?" Carlos Alberto asked.

"It's me, Santiago," I said. "I'm back."

There was a pause. Then Carlos Alberto opened the door. He was sweating, and had a towel wrapped around his waist. I understood he was in bed with a man.

"I'm sorry I came in like this," I said apologetically. "I'll come back later."

"Wait," Carlos Alberto said. "Here, let me take your bag. I'll meet you in half an hour on the bench in front of the caravel."

"OK," I said, trying not to appear perturbed, although I felt deeply wounded by his betrayal. "Take your time."

"I'll be there in half an hour," he said, taking my bag and closing the door.

As I sat on the bench, dejected, muddled, I said good-bye to the *Santa María*. Like Columbus's voyages, my trip to Spain had caused me pain and suffering, and had left me with a broken heart. I couldn't foresee then that many years would go by before that experience yielded its real treasures. Or that I'd complete my poem to the Great Admiral years later, in the countryside near Medellín, where I was with the man with whom I lived many years of my life.

When Carlos Alberto joined me, we walked up Las Ramblas and all the way to the little plaza in front of Guadí's unfinished cathedral. As we sat there, smoking cigarettes, I mustered the courage to tell him that I was leaving as soon as I could book my flight. He said that he was hurt, that he thought we'd be business partners for a long time, that he had dreams of the two of us opening a translations agency and settling in Barcelona, to write our great books. I couldn't tell him that I was going back home because it had become unbearable to live with the man I loved knowing all the time that he didn't desire me. We stayed there for hours, chatting about everything we hadn't had time to discuss in the two months we had spent together.

We returned to our room well past midnight. After we undressed and lay down to sleep, when the lights were off, Carlos Alberto came to my bed and got in with me. He turned on his stomach, and said, "Fuck me, isn't that what you want?" I turned to face the wall. That wasn't what I wanted; I wanted his love; I wanted to be his beloved. When I started sobbing softly, he put his arm around me and we remained in that position until we fell asleep. When I woke up the next morning, I was still in his arms.

We never spoke about that night again. A few years later, we met again in Gotham. The friendship was rekindled, though we had changed by then, and would never be with each other the way we had been that summer in Barcelona. Finally, we were able to be sisters, which we remain to this day.

Jose I saw four years later, after my first novel had been published in Colombia and I traveled to Spain to attend a writers' congress. By then I was in love with another man. I hardly recognized the sophisticated dandy who met me in a Madrid café one refulgent autumn afternoon. Jose was the wunderkind of Spanish poetry. He had published his first volume of poems and lived with a wealthy marquis who was a novelist. But his metamorphosis did not surprise me. After all, even stodgy Madrid was a different city—it had entered the twentieth century: gay people ambled down its boulevards, holding hands and kissing. And why not, I thought. Why not? By then I had come to accept that life is a succession of miraculous changes and transformations. And, I reminded myself, we were still young, the future as yet unwritten.

2

Papa's Corpse

❧

"Victims engender torturers."
OCTAVIO PAZ

I've been dreaming all night, I don't remember exactly what. In any case, it was a long, uninterrupted dream, composed of several dreams, almost all of them related to my childhood, to open fields, blossoming trees, fiestas, rooms full of people; and I, in the midst of it all, gabbing away, saying witty things, happy at last; at last triumphant. It must be 6 A.M. when the phone rings. At first I think about disconnecting it to continue sleeping. Then I think, It must be important, and I pick up. The room is still in penumbra, but outside it must already be dawn. The sun caresses the red curtains on the window, wrapping the room in a dense reddish color, like the color of the entrails of a very young animal that has been bleeding a long time. I answer the phone because I know that Beatrice will not wake up. Noises never awaken her. The house could crumble, her room be set on fire, a band could start playing next to her pillow, but she'd never wake up. I sit up on the bed and take the phone in both hands. I'm not wide awake yet. I'm not conscious of anything, except that I'm in my father's house in Barranquilla, that today is Carnival Tuesday, that Beatrice and I have been in the city for two days, that my father is dying, that it's sunrise.

"Please," says a voice with a tone of urgency, "may I speak with señor Villalba?" I have no idea who it could be at this hour, or what he might want. For a moment I think about saying, "No, señor

39

Villalba isn't here," but I decide against it. I'm still half drunk from the night before, and it's possible that I know the person at the other end. "This is he," I say, not without some impatience, letting a tone of irritation escape from my throat.

"This is Doctor Martínez calling you from the hospital," the voice says. "Excuse me for waking you up so early. But your father is in critical condition," there is a silence, a hesitation, "and he has asked me to call you. It seems he wants to speak with you. He's been repeating your name for quite some time."

That's it: my father's dying in the hospital. That's the reason I'm in the city, the reason I'm in his house, since I cannot call it my house. "Thank you," I say. "I'll be at the hospital right away. Goodbye, doctor." I hang up.

Beatrice continues sleeping, her face covered with a pillow. I don't understand how she doesn't asphyxiate herself. She always sleeps with her face covered. All I can see is her long blonde hair, fanning her shoulders, even more beautiful now in the reddish glow of the room at dawn. I decide to let her sleep. We went to bed very late, at 3 A.M., and we've been traveling for days, without sleeping well, moving from hotel to hotel, city to city, fiesta to fiesta, house to house.

I rise from bed and light a cigarette. I walk to the window and draw the curtain. I've never been in this room before. Only once before I visited my father's house, and on that occasion I didn't go beyond the living room. Now I'm on the second floor, in the room that was his bedroom, and from the window I can see the house's interior garden, planted with yellow and orange *angelitos*, *capachos* and hibiscus, and purple bougainvillea flowering in February, here in the tropics. I open the window. My eyes travel over the garden, over the roof of the house, beyond the roof, all the way to the acacias in the street, also in bloom. For many years I had imagined this house: its interior, the second floor, the bedroom of my father and his late wife. Now I've been here for two days, but I've been so busy I haven't had time to stop to inspect the house, the way I always thought I would do it once I was fully admitted inside it. I haven't been in the city for many years, except briefly, during school breaks. When I hear a bird sing, I remember the troupial we had when I was a boy. Its cage hung by my window, facing the patio, and every morning I'd wake up to its song, although the bird singing now is surely a smaller bird, its song not as acute, its notes lacking in confidence, its voice rather shy and melancholy.

I can't see the sun, but it's almost daylight. A delicate and refreshing breeze blows through the trees and plants in the garden, and the morning tropical air brings a smell of salt, before the sun has come out completely, and things begin to simmer and rot in the heat.

I close the window, go to the bathroom and shower, leaving my head under the cold water for a while. I want to clear my head as soon as possible. I soap my body and then wash it again. When I'm toweling myself, before leaving the bathroom, I notice I'm humming a festive tune, as if I were happy and celebrating something.

I towel myself dry and get dressed without making any noise. I dress informally: jeans, tennis shoes, and a blue T-shirt. I dry my hair with a towel, splash some lotion on, and sit at the desk to write a note to Beatrice: Papa is dying. I've gone to the hospital. I'll call you at noon.

I tape the note to the mirror of the dressing cabinet. I leave the room, walk down the hall, and go down the stairs that lead to the first floor, to the garden. There's more light now, but it's still not daytime. The bird has stopped singing, and an exotic perfume, intoxicating, emanates from the flowers. I walk through the rooms of the house. All the curtains are drawn, but I can distinguish the objects clearly. The rooms are full of flowering plants; there are canvases on the walls depicting seascapes, twilights, dawns, fishermen, great fishing nets, sharks, algae, seashells. I study the furniture of the different rooms, from the modern sofas to the pink and yellow velvet chairs, to the wicker furniture and enormous mahogany chairs. I cross the music room, the library, in which the day before I found a number of books by Teilhard de Chardin, annotated in the margins by my father. The writing was blurry, shaky. I imagine he must have read those books in his old age, when he found himself alone and was trying to give a new dimension to his life. I see the pictures of the ancestors: of my grandfather, the general, whom I never met; and my grandmother, serene, distant, fragile, but with an austere look that hides a repressed tenderness; I see the photo of my aunt Elisa, the nun, who died in her youth; other photos of relatives I don't know. A portrait of my half sister, Lucía, who died some years ago, whom I met once, an afternoon when she came to my boarding school in Connecticut and took me out for an afternoon in Manhattan. It's a picture of her youth, before cancer had begun to undermine her. I don't know whether it is the time of the day, or the fact that for the first time I'm alone in this house, but everything has a chilling effect on me.

Near the garage door I find Pedro. He's sitting on a leather stool, leaning against the wall, half-asleep. Pedro has been my father's driver for over thirty years. He's approximately sixty years old, but he looks older. I try not to make any noise, but when I put my hand to the lock, immediately he jumps up, startled.

"Can I drive you anywhere?" he says, ashamed, as if it were a sin to be found asleep.

I decide I'd rather go alone. At rush hour it would be fine to let him drive; but at this hour, despite the fact that it is Carnival Tuesday, the city must be half-deserted. I love to cruise the streets of cities late at night or at dawn, when there are few people out; I feel then as if the streets belonged to me.

"Pedro, you should go to sleep," I say. "I'm going to the hospital to see my father. I'd rather drive myself."

"Give him my best regards," he murmurs as I walk away.

Pedro opens the garage doors. I begin to back up slowly; outside it's still a bit dark, I can't see the sun anywhere, but a breeze coming from the sea makes the tops of the *matarratón* trees sway. High in the sky, a flock of prehistoric-looking marine birds (they aren't gulls, or ducks, or pelicans, or any kind of bird whose name I know), fly forming a very wide V in the sky, moving a little from side to side, but surely heading toward the ocean.

The streets are deserted. Once in a while I see a drunk weaving a purposeless path. Sometimes, out of nowhere, a car full of people appears, its passengers screaming, recently awakened, or still continuing the party from the night before. I drive toward the hospital, which is more like an exclusive private clinic, and park in a tranquil spot, surrounded by old mansions.

I don't get out of the car right away. I light a cigarette and turn on the radio. Even at this hour Carnival music is playing—a song I've never heard before—and I make myself comfortable, trying to remember some of the songs from my childhood, before I left the city. It's all in vain. I turn off the radio. I light another cigarette and walk to the entrance of the hospital. I've always hated impersonal hospitals, even this one, with its discreet facade, with its familiar atmosphere. I push the glass door and immediately breathe in that odor that is particular to hospitals.

Even though it's almost daylight, all the lights are on. There is very little movement, as if for Carnival sick people had taken a break, as if they had stopped dying. The nurse at the reception desk recognizes me and rises when I approach. "Good morning, Doctor Martínez is waiting for you." I thank her and she sits down to continue reading a book. I'd like to know what she's reading, but I can't read the book's title or the name of its author. I continue on my way. I climb the stairway slowly. This hospital must have been a private residence until a few years ago. Now it has been adapted and remodeled. The marble stairway is wide, not steep, and covered with a dark blue carpet. My feet, the sole of my shoes, make no noise as I go up. There's no sound whatsoever coming from anywhere in the hospital. I arrive at the second floor. The hall is well lit. I approach my father's room, 301, and knock on the door before entering. The door opens immediately, the nurse appearing. "Good morning," I say. She murmurs something and closes the door behind me. Doctor Martínez is seated next to the bed, looking at my father. When he sees me, he rises and walks toward me.

"He's been asking for you all night; that's why I called you," he says, extending his hand and smiling. He looks tired but impeccable. I ask myself why so much ceremony, why so much mystery, as if the death of an old man weren't the most natural act.

"How critical is he?" I ask.

"He woke up a few minutes ago. His condition is critical, but it could prolong for a few days or he could pass away today. It's hard to tell; his heart is giving out. He's getting weaker and weaker."

I sit on the other side of the bed and tell the doctor and nurse that they can leave. I'll be here for a while. If anything happens, I'll call the nurse. At first she protests; the doctor says he doesn't mind the vigil, because more than a patient my father is his friend. But I insist, until both of them leave, Doctor Martínez exiting last.

At last I'm alone with my father. Few times in our life we've been alone together, except for brief instants. I look at the dying man in front of me. He's lying face up. They've removed the respirator under which he had been caged. In his left arm he has an IV. He hasn't been shaved for days, and a whitish growth covers his jowls and double chin. My father must be over eighty years old. I don't know exactly. But whenever he gets ill, he travels to Miami where he checks into a hospital for months, until he's fine again, rejuvenated. It's weird to be next to a dying person, my father, and not to feel anything. For a long time, I thought I hated him. In the last years I had stopped thinking about him altogether, and after the death of Lucía I thought only about inheriting his fortune. By that time I no longer hated him, if I ever did. When my mother died, I was twelve years old. More than pain over her early death, I felt hatred for my father, whom I blamed for it. After that, he took control of my life. He sent me to study in the capital, and I left the school only to visit my maternal grandparents during school vacation. Even then, I hardly ever saw him. I had to write him a monthly letter—the school made me do it—a letter that my father never acknowledged. For Christmas, I'd always get a note with a generous check; and sometimes, when my grandparents took me to his office, I could see him for a few minutes. He'd inquire about the progress of my studies, write me a check, and finally would ask me to kiss him on the cheek.

My grandparents died within months of each other, and I was away in school. I was fourteen years old, and suddenly alone in the world. I never felt again what I had felt at that moment: that feeling of total loss when we've lost the only person who loves us. For months, I had dreams in which I saw my mother come back from death to take me with her; and other dreams, less morbid and more normal, in which I saw my father arrive at school on Sundays during visiting hour, ask me forgiveness for his indifferent treatment, and take me to live with him, giving me all the love I thought parents owed their children. My father did arrive on a

44

pluvial Sunday morning in October, but he stayed only a short time. Vacations were approaching and I had no place to go. Mother had had a younger brother, and I hardly knew my distant relatives. That day father was kinder than usual. He brought me a book: *Uncle Tom's Cabin* (a book I had already read many years before), and a box of chocolates. He said that he was very pleased with my academic progress, that though I probably thought he didn't care about me, he really did; that often he asked my teachers about my progress; that my grandparents' death seemed to have affected me, and that since he didn't have enough free time to devote to me, he had decided to send me abroad, to the United States. There, he said, I'd receive a good education, so that in the future I'd be able to take care of myself and I would not blame him for not giving me the best opportunities available. I heard all this in a quasi-torpid state, without understanding very well what he was saying, except that I understood he was sending me far away, to a place where I could not cause him problems. I saw this trip as a kind of exile, as if my father were banning me from his life—giving me a one-way ticket, and giving me orders to never return.

I've been thinking about all this vertiginously, memories arriving as though in a whirlwind, fast, engulfing me. My father opens his eyes. He remains quiet, his eyes half-open, as if he didn't recognize me. He looks as though he wants to talk. I don't feel anything, and I have no desire to hear him say anything to me. I want only to see him die, the sooner the better. It puzzles me that even at this moment I feel no compassion for this dying man, but I don't, even though he's my father, even though he's responsible for what I've been and what I am. I see his hand move a little, trying to reach mine. Instinctively, I withdraw it, sickened, as if the contact with someone near death would be contagious. At that moment I think of all the times in my childhood when I wished him to come to me and touch me and say kind words, and even that kiss that my grandparents would ask me to give him when they took me to visit him, was, despite the hatred I felt as I gave it to him, something, something instead of the emptiness, the *nada* he had created in me with his lack of warmth. Now he parts his lips and words flow from his mouth. I don't know what he's saying. I don't know whether he

says "Forgive me," or "I wanted to see you," or "I've left my fortune to you." I'm too excited to grasp the meaning of his words.
Suddenly I understand something. Suddenly I realize that he might
not die, that he'll get better in a few days, then go abroad where
they'll prime him up again, and then he'll return perfectly healthy
and will continue to live for many more years. Years in which he'll
expect to see me, will expect my visits, expect me to supervise his
businesses, and what's worse, expect that I give him affection and
love, everything he always denied me. That's when I realize I don't
want my father to continue living. Perhaps he's asking me to kill
him, and then I get up, pull the pillow from under his head and
press it against his face. I press against it for some time (I don't
know how long), time that goes by at a speed that I've never experienced before. I press the pillow with all my strength, expecting him
to wrestle with the object that is robbing him of his life, that life
which he has fought for so long to prolong. But nothing happens. I
feel his hands flutter a bit, his left hand touches my elbow, while I
get excited, and then I feel his body contract, and what I experience
is almost sexual, and then he relaxes brusquely, all his strength
ebbing in the direction of his feet. When I remove the pillow I cry
out and I see that his face is red, but not excessively so, and that his
eyes are open. With my shaking hands, I close his eyes, my fingers
sweaty. I place the pillow under his head. I cover his hands and feet
under the sheet, and he looks like the person who just minutes ago
was asleep, only that now he's dead. I sit on a chair and light a cigarette. It's then I feel something is running down my legs, from my
scrotum: I've ejaculated copiously. I go to the bathroom, turn on the
hot water faucet, lower my pants and underwear, wipe off the
semen with toilet paper, and dry myself with a towel. I return to the
room and light another cigarette and count to a hundred. I look out
the window: it's already daylight, the sun is out. But in the room,
because of the air conditioning, it's chilly. After a while I get up
from my chair and pace around the room. I open the door and step
out in the hall. There's still nobody in the corridors, but the hospital
has begun to awaken and I hear noises coming from far away
rooms. I go back into my room and close the door. I lift the receiver
and dial the receptionist. I say, "This is room 301. I fell asleep for a

few minutes and when I woke up my father . . . " the words won't come out of my mouth and, to my surprise, I burst out crying, first softly, as if I didn't want to, but then convulsively. "Just a moment please," the woman says. "Stay calm. Stay calm." I continue to cry, with growing intensity. I'm still crying when the nurse arrives running. I'm still crying when Doctor Martínez rushes in and takes Papa's pulse and declares him dead and then he offers me a sedative and offers to drive me home. I'm still crying when I step out of the hospital, in broad daylight, under the bright sun, standing in the street that now begins to come to life, crying I don't know why, this morning of Carnival Tuesday.

I drive aimlessly for a while. A strange, hard-to-define happiness takes over me. It's as if at last I have realized my greatest dream. I don't want to go back home right away. I realize, however, that soon I'll be swamped by people, calls, the media, all sorts of inconveniences. I have to think about the funeral, choosing a funeral parlor, and all the things that are going to spoil the last day of Carnival for me; because now I have no doubt in my mind: I want to celebrate.

I drive to the cemetery to visit my mother's grave. I haven't visited it in years. I'm not sure I know how to find it. My mother's buried in the old cemetery of the city, and after her death my grandparents continued to add details to her grave, which the last time I'd seen it looked like a mausoleum. I remember little about mother. I have so few memories, or perhaps I have plenty and they're just confused and chaotic. I remember her as a beautiful woman, living a dangerous life, always moving from house to house, from city to city, from man to man. All these memories, as I said, are very confused. Later, when I was ten years old, I remember her as a sick woman with tuberculosis, dying quickly, perhaps because she was tired of the kind of life she had led.

I don't remember exactly the year my parents separated. I think it was in 1956, because the following year we went to live in the capital, and that year I remember with clarity. My parents weren't married to each other—both of them had other legal spouses. My mother's history I've had to piece together through the years. It hasn't been easy because there are few survivors, and the different versions I have conflict with one another.

My maternal grandfather was a fisherman from a river town. Over a period of many years, he amassed a fortune that made him one of the richest men in the region. Later, during the years of *la violencia*, when the fluvial navigation stopped, my grandfather began to lose his money. By the time my mother died, from the splendors of the past there was nothing left. It's strange that my grandfather, as well as my father, both patriarchs, had a scant male descendancy. My grandfather had been poor in his youth. At age seventeen he had left his mother's side and decided to seek his fortune in Cuba. It was said that in Cuba there were many opportunities for a young man to make a fortune quickly. My grandfather traveled down the river by raft and arrived at the port of Barranquilla, which at that time was a hamlet. There he worked cutting trees in the swamp, until he saved enough money for his ticket to Cuba. The night before his boat sailed my grandfather got drunk, and in the morning, when he came to, the boat had already left port. At that time ships to Cuba left once every three months. My grandfather took this as an omen that he should stay and go back to live with his mother. The Civil War had ended, and my great-grandmother had been hiding all this time in the sierra, near the town. My grandfather began to cut trees again in the swamp for half a year. During this period of hard work, he managed to save five pesos. Using the wood from the trees he cut down, he built a raft, bought mirrors, fans, trinkets, all kinds of artifacts, and he went back up river. The return trip took him several months. Along the route he sold and bought and bartered objects, so that by the time he arrived back in his hometown he had quintupled his capital. When he arrived at the hamlet he found out his mother was dead. It was around that time my grandfather met my grandmother, who was still going to a Catholic school run by nuns in another river village. Because she was of a higher social class, they had to marry behind her family's back. With the money he'd made on his trip up river, my grandfather rented a house in the village, and bought a cow and a plot of land on the banks of the river. He called the cow Sunflower and the plot of land, his first *finca*, Hope.

By the time my mother was born their fortunes had prospered. My mother grew up to be a legendary beauty. When she was fifteen her beauty was famous in the towns of the region. Many wealthy landowners came to ask for her hand, offering my grandfather cows and land in exchange for his daughter. My mother, however, married a man from the town, older than she, also a landowner, and they had a son, who died when he was still an infant. That part of her story is confusing, I don't know when the boy died or exactly how old he was or what illness took his life.

One day my father, an aristocrat from the interior of the country who had moved to the coast to live, and whose passion was fighting roosters, arrived in the village. He and my mother fell in love right away, and when he left the village they had made plans for my mother to follow him. My mother disappeared, leaving behind her husband, her parents, perhaps even her son. She followed my father to one of his banana plantations near the Caribbean. They lived in that plantation, until I was born in the city, which they then moved to permanently.

My father was by then an older man, whereas my mother was still young and beautiful. It must have been hard for her to live in a conservative society full of prejudices, but Mother always did whatever she wanted to do, and her only frustration was not to make her desires a reality. I have vague memories from that time. I was an asthmatic child who spent most of his time in bed. I spent many months of the year by the seaside. I remember Mother had a lover who'd visit us there. The first six or seven years of my childhood went by in this fashion. Of my father at that time I have the vaguest memories. I saw him only on weekends, when he came to our house in Barranquilla. He spent most of his time in his plantations. Saturday mornings, around ten, the nanny would take me to my parents' bedroom, and while they had breakfast and he read the newspaper, I spent a short while chatting with my father. I remember little about him, of the things we did, of what we talked about. I remember clearly only that before leaving the bedroom he'd give me a 100-pesos bill, then he made me repeat a string of seven or eight last names, all his, and at the end he'd made me cry, "OF BLUE BLOOD!" I had no idea what any of it meant, but I was delighted to get the money and to drink my orange juice with him. On Sundays, my father spent all day at the cock-fighting arena, and then he'd go back to his plantations and not return until the following week. The only change in this routine was when I was by the seashore with my mother because he never came to visit us.

I remember their breakup vaguely. I only know that one day my father appeared suddenly while my mother was at a dance with another man. He used this as an excuse to break up. I imagine that because by then he was so much older than she, he must not have pleased her sexually, and so she had to find another man to satisfy her. Perhaps he knew about Mother's lover, the one who came to visit us at the sea resort; what he couldn't bear was for Mother to humiliate him publicly.

When Father left Mother, we became poor. Mother had never saved money, and when her legal husband died she didn't go to claim her share because she was living with my father. Though many years had gone by since her elopement with my father, her parents had not forgiven her. Mother was not educated. It was then that we moved to the capital, where for a while we survived from the sale of the jewelry father had given her. Later, I imagine, she became a prostitute, when she already had consumption and, as I said earlier, she died when I was twelve years old. It was then that I met my maternal grandparents, and that I got to know my father a bit.

The cemetery is deserted, and it has grown a lot since the last time I visited it. Carnival Tuesday must not be a popular day to visit the dead. As a child I was always terrified of cemeteries, and now, walking through these monumental crypts and marble mausoleums and wide avenues of white stones, the same sensation I experienced as a child comes back. After a while I realize I'm lost. I seem to be going around and around and around, always returning to the same spot—the building where the unclaimed corpses are incinerated. I open the door to see if there's anyone inside I can ask about how to find the way to my mother's grave, but as I open the iron door I see a vast blackened room, with floors covered with bones, charred remains and coal and logs burning. I shut the door and run away from the crematorium. I start retching when I reach another part of the cemetery. I stop when I see an old man with a wrinkled face and white hair, dressed in clean but worn-out clothes. As he walks by me, he looks familiar. I turn around and walk in the direction from which I saw him emerge. I find mother's grave, and I realize that the man I had just seen, without recognizing him, is mother's lover, the one who used to come visit her at the seaside resort when I was a child.

There are fresh flowers on her grave. He has been bringing them. The tomb is clean, well taken care of, as if it had been some-one's personal project for a long time. I don't feel well, and I sit on the bench that my grandparents built. The nausea continues. I can't get the crematorium out of my mind. I try to concentrate on mother's grave to forget what I've seen. I don't know why I've come here. My mother belongs more to her old lover—whose name I cannot remember—than to me. I'm not sentimental about the dead, so I don't know why I'm here. Obviously, to think about her unsettles me, and makes me realize that if there's a place for tenderness in my heart, it is for her, who gave me her love and warmth when I was a boy. I remember how at night, when we lived in Bogotá, she'd come by my bed very late at night, after she returned home. She was always resplendent, a vision of beauty. From her parties she'd bring me potato chips, or hors d'oeuvres, or sweets, or a special little gift: a doll, a flower, chocolates. She'd scold me gently for being awake despite the lateness of the hour, and then she'd lie down on the eiderdown, next to me, and tell me stories about witches and mythological creatures, stories from *A Thousand and One Nights*, perhaps the only book she had ever read. That's how I prefer to remember her. And now I know that she was grateful to me for not asking her any questions. I never asked her what she did in her parties, or why she went to so many, or why the mothers of the other children weren't like her. But I also knew that the mothers of my friends weren't as beautiful, or sweet, or mysterious.

The sun is hotter now. The heat is not yet unbearable because there's still a trace of the early morning breeze. I check my watch:

it's 9 A.M. I decide to go back home. Beatrice wakes up around noon; I have to pay more attention to her; in the last few days she's been acting erratically, and when she starts behaving like that, I have to watch her carefully.

As I exit the cemetery, I see mother's old lover seated on a bench under the almond trees, reading a newspaper. A part of me would like to talk to him, to find out what his life has been like; perhaps he could tell me things I'd like to know about; on the other hand, I realize it might be an invasion of his privacy, of what's perhaps his best-guarded secret. The flower sellers and ice-cream vendors have begun to arrive. Young couples, mothers with their children, old people and adolescents, arrive now continuously. I was wrong: on Carnival Tuesday there are people who still remember their dead.

I drive fast. Children, wearing grotesque *marimonda* costumes and silk domino cloaks with hoods and masks, are out in the streets sprinkling people with white starch. In the popular section of the city the cantinas are already open, and the drunks, in profusion, stumble around in great numbers. Carnival music: music from the West Indies, *vallenatos,* all this music plays with almost violence, coming out of the bars, saturating the atmosphere. It's a sad and desperate music, coming out of everywhere, mixing with other tunes from the house I just passed, the street I just drove through, the dance that has just started. As I approach the neighborhood of my father's house, now my house, it looks less and less like Carnival. The rich begin to celebrate much later. Discreetly. Behind closed doors. I drive with my windows rolled up and the air conditioning on. I'm no longer used to this tropical heat. I'm here just passing through, just to settle some accounts. The line "Let the dead bury the dead" comes to my mind, and I can't understand why I'm thinking so much about death when I've never felt so alive, so happy.

When I open the door, I can see on Nury's face that she knows about my father's death.

"I'm truly sorry," she says; there's a sorrowful expression on her face.

"Thanks, Nury," I say, trying to look as sad as she does.

"People have been calling," she informs me. "I disconnected the phone on the second floor so that *Doña* Beatrice would not be awakened. You have no idea how much I loved your father."

I can imagine how much she did. Just like María Eugenia, his secretary, Nury has been my father's faithful servant for many years; like the man who took care of his fighting cocks; like so many others, like Pedro—it's a love I refuse to understand, this servile love. I walk toward the bar. It's a little early to start drinking, but I pour myself a double scotch. The liquor on my tongue produces a mild euphoria, giving me a second wind. I turn on the air conditioning and I sit on a chair next to the window facing the garden. The second sip of the scotch produces another sensation: a soft, nice lethargy, similar to that produced by opium, but more refreshing, less cerebral. It's a state of total lucidity, that one of being awake right here contemplating the immediate future. And yet, memories keep tugging at me, as if only just now I were able to put my life in order. It's like that moment when we have a total awareness that clarifies the present.

Beatrice will wake up soon. I know the face she's going to make at first, a face of pain and guilt, like the face Nury had when she opened the door, even though Beatrice knows that I don't love my father, never have. It's that expression of sorrow that comity demands: the right kind of face for the right moment. Beatrice is also my father's legacy, something that will last longer than money—as long as she and I are both alive.

I met Beatrice in the late 1960s in Washington, D.C. when I was attending Georgetown. I hadn't returned to Colombia since I had left to go to school in the States. Every year, before winter or summer vacations, I'd receive a letter from my father with instructions about what I should do with my free time. At first, he sent me to visit friends in the United States. When I finished high school, he gave me total freedom and I was able to do whatever I wanted. So in 1966 I traveled to Europe for the first time. At that time, Beatrice was living in Switzerland, but we didn't meet each other until a year later, when I was about to graduate from college.

After the death of my half sister, Lucía, my father pinned all his hopes on me. After having paid little attention to me—almost keeping me hidden—he accepted me publicly as his son. At first I was grateful to him. It was only later that I thought I understood why he had changed toward me. It wasn't the pain he felt over the death of his only daughter, nor his advanced age, that had made him change. Nor his reading of de Chardin, which he had been doing for years, and which I suppose he understood only in a formal way. Perhaps he had changed toward me because I was his last hope for continuing his name, at least for another generation. It was then that he recognized me publicly and legally as his son, something that until that moment, even though my grandparents had pleaded with him in my childhood to do it, he had refused to do.

I majored in international affairs at Georgetown, which is not something I wanted to study. I had been a brilliant student, and had I applied for a scholarship I would have received it. I wanted to study literature, my true passion. But I went along with his wishes because I was young and I didn't know what I really wanted, and perhaps because all I wanted was to please my father and to get his approval.

When I entered college I was a total innocent. The only thing I was aware of was of a hatred, a boiling rage, a desire to some day get my revenge for all the pain that my father had caused me. It was the kind of hatred that had no direct target, it was the kind of hatred that comes out of lovelessness. But I was fully engaged in my studies and in politics. As I studied political ideas, I began to question the structured order. The Vietnam War was escalating and my generation vehemently opposed it. The rebellion of those years wasn't anarchic. For many, for me in particular, it was a time to become aware of the nature of imperialism and the condition of colonial people. All these things I understood finally at a theoretical level.

It was through a recommendation of my father that I met Beatrice and her family. Beatrice's grandfather had been named ambassador to Washington, and several members of the family had traveled with him—including grandchildren who came to the States to study. The ambassador was a close friend of my father's. Both shared the same interest in business—cattle ranching and banana growing—even though my father was never interested in politics. The banana business was at that time going through a period of complete decadence, and it was rumored that the new ambassador, who saw his fortune in danger of declining, was in charge of supervising the traffic of marijuana and cocaine into the United States.

During my student years, I had taken sides politically, but the temptation to enter the world of the embassy was too enticing. That's how I met Beatrice, at the embassy, at a birthday party for one of her cousins. I was an excessively timid young man, who had remained sheltered from social life. Parties—which I had started to attend since I entered college—made me uncomfortable. Gloria, Beatrice's cousin, was a student at Georgetown. Little by little, we had become friendly. I became an habitue at the embassy, the ambassador had made it clear that my father had recommended me to him, and he expressed an interest in my future and in my career.

The party where I met Beatrice took place on a spring night at the home of the ambassador. I was sitting by the pool, scanning the sky, when Beatrice appeared. Gloria had mentioned her, but I hadn't paid much attention. I knew she had just arrived from New York, that she had lived primarily in Europe, and that she was an interesting young woman, that is, a good marrying prospect. Beatrice was, is, a few years older than me. I was a bit tipsy, watching couples dance or converse under the trees and around the pool, when I saw Beatrice approach. I'll always remember her first words to me, "You're the gentleman I was hoping to meet." It was a line that sounded like something out of *A Streetcar Named Desire*. I laughed. Beatrice's face was beautiful but not untouched, or youthful. Her beauty was rather plastic, constructed. From that moment, we became good friends, and, weeks later, sweethearts. It was then that I learned her story. And yet I didn't care. Marrying a society girl had not been one of my priorities, but at that moment I realized it was perhaps the only way of getting back at my father.

Despite my fears, her grandfather was pleased with our relationship. For the first time in many years, I received a long letter from my father congratulating me and giving me advice. I was naive. I had no idea who I was, or what was it that I really wanted. I was just dazzled by the grace and beauty that Beatrice represented.

The very rich, I found out later, never completely tell their stories. Honesty with themselves, and with others, is not a valuable commodity for them. Beatrice's story was something that I had to piece together slowly, and that I didn't understand fully until after we were married.

Beatrice's father, Antonio, is a businessman who entered politics. While a student in the United States, he married an American psychiatrist, and from that time on he devoted his life to building an economic empire. Beatrice was an only child. When she was eight, she had been sent to study in Canada. Later, she was sent to finishing school in Switzerland. Beatrice was intelligent and beautiful, but insecure. During these years, she saw her parents only when they went to Europe for their annual tour. She had not returned to Colombia since she had left it as a girl. When she was seventeen, Beatrice went to Paris to study philosophy at the Sorbonne, and later she moved to Rome to study art history. There she met an Italian count with whom she fell in love. They planned to get married. Shortly before the wedding, Beatrice traveled to New York to meet her mother. Two days before returning to Rome, she received a phone call with the news that the count had died in a driving accident. Beatrice returned to Rome and during the funeral ceremonies she suffered a nervous collapse. Her parents placed her in an exclusive sanatorium in Switzerland where Beatrice slashed her wrists with a piece of glass, which she also used to rip her face. After that incident, Beatrice remained in the sanatorium for a long time, only making trips to London for reconstructive plastic surgery.

Beatrice's reaction to the death of the count was hardly exaggerated: he was the only person who had given her something resembling love. She had to be watched constantly, a nurse as her companion around the clock, because Beatrice repeatedly tried to kill herself. When she didn't improve, she was transferred to an institution for the insane in New York; it was there that she slashed her face again. Her process of recovery began all over again. But Beatrice was bent upon dying: she refused to eat, she was fed with an

IV tube, and she began to waste away. Her parents didn't come to visit her. Perhaps they thought that the social disgrace she represented was worse than her own personal tragedy. It was in that institution that a young doctor discovered that Beatrice had a brain tumor. After the tumor was removed, Beatrice began to improve. Her face was reshaped again. That's why around the time I met her she did not go out during daylight hours and wore no make up. Since I didn't know her story, I thought this showed her lack of affectation. Around the time I met her, she had been out of the sanatorium for six months. Behind her back, her relatives made jokes about how her parents offered a fortune to anyone who would take her off their hands. Beatrice was a broken creature, but slowly she began to trust me. I was attracted to her because of her suffering (like Beatrice, I felt I had been victimized by my father), and also because I thought suffering made people nobler human beings. I mistook her weakness for kindness. Beatrice offered me tenderness because she couldn't love. I thought I loved her, and that she loved me back.

I've been thinking about all this time for a while, getting up once in a while to refresh my drink. In the next room, Nury has been answering the phone, taking the condolences and thanking the callers. It's 11 A.M., soon Beatrice will get up. The hum of the air conditioner and the taste of the scotch make me feel disconnected, almost as if I were levitating. Outside, the heat is intensifying. The bushes and plants in the gardens are still. There is no breeze. The morning heat has unleashed. I decide to take another shower. I ask Nury to send me breakfast upstairs. As I'm going up the stairs, Nury calls me. "Señorita María Eugenia is on the phone," she informs me.

María Eugenia has been my father's secretary for over twenty years. She started to work for him in her youth and never left him. For many years, all contact I had with my father was through her: it was María Eugenia who always sent me the checks, who often wrote me letters or notes with instructions. "Thanks, Nury," I say. "I'll take the call upstairs." Climbing the stairs, I feel inebriated.

Beatrice is still asleep, a pillow covering her face. I sit by her side and pick up the receiver. "Yes, María Eugenia. Thanks so much for calling." I wait for her to say something original, something different from what I have been hearing from all the servants.

She says, "You know how much I loved your father."

"Yes, I know," I say, cutting her off, an idea dawning on me. "María Eugenia," I say, trying to imitate my father's tone when he gave orders. "You know, I'm terribly affected by all this. I'd appreciate it very much if you could take care of the arrangements of the funeral."

"Yes, of course. Just tell me what you want done."

I think about it for an instant. I have no idea what needs to be done. I've never been in charge of a funeral. I know nothing about these things. "Perhaps you know better than I do what needs to be done," I say. "As you know," I lie, "my father wanted a simple funeral. I think it'd be better to bury him tomorrow morning. Please make the arrangements for the religious services. Seven A.M. would be a good time, I think. I'm deeply grateful to you. I authorize you to do whatever needs to be done." Before she has time to respond, I hang up.

As I put the phone down, Beatrice wakes up. Generally I don't look forward to this moment. But today I want her to be wide awake for two reasons: First, I want to see how she's doing. Second, I want to see how she reacts to my father's death. In the last few months, her mind has been erratic. Beatrice doesn't like me around when she wakes up in the morning. That's why for the past year we've been sleeping in separate bedrooms. I understand her fear of waking up in the morning and having someone see her before she has had time to tend to her face. As I feared, she wakes up frowning. This, however, is better than to see her wake up with her gaze lost, as if she were coming back from a drug-induced dream and she had trouble getting back to reality.

"What time is it?" she asks, the pillow on her chin.

"It's late. You'd better get up. Father died this morning."

Her eyes open slowly and there is a painful expression on her face. She touches my arm with one of her hands and then sits up on the bed. Despite everything, she looks beautiful.

"I'm sorry," she says. "What do I have to do now?" And then, abruptly changing her tone, she says in a childish voice, "You know I don't like to wear black." And she starts crying.

What is this love/hate I feel for her that I don't understand? I no longer love her, and yet I can't hate her either. Perhaps she's too much like me, and the tenderness I feel for her—which is flooding me at this moment—represents the tenderness that I cannot feel for myself. I drape my arms around her shoulders. I press her softly against my chest and begin to caress her hair.

"Nobody's going to make you do anything you don't want to," I whisper in her ear. "But you should get up. We have to plan the day. You won't have to dress in black, I promise." I keep stroking her hair until she stops sobbing. Then I realize she's gone back to sleep again. I lay her down. I undress, draw the curtains, and stand by the window. As I do this, I think about the sea, and I see myself, fleetingly, on a roseate December afternoon: I'm with my mother, by the sea, we're both laughing, running on the beach, playing in the tide, looking for *chipi chipis* and seashells.

I shower for a long time. The water clears my head and dissipates my bibulous state. I'm more worried about Beatrice than about my father's funeral. Shortly after we were married, when the novelty began to wear off, after her grandfather secured for me a position in the Madrid embassy, reality began to dawn on me unceremoniously, brutal and sudden like a blow to the stomach that leaves one gasping for air. The early days were peaceful and happy. I had just published my first paper on international law and we traveled to Colombia after being absent for many years. We were in a celebratory mood, and we had hopes that in the immediate future there would be political changes. It was a moment of transition. I didn't realize that the brutality of the regime was calculated, so that when the new government took over—with its promises of peace and freedom—people would be fooled into thinking that a real change had begun to take place. I was naive enough to believe the promises of the government. I was reminded of my uncle Andrés, a revolutionary who opposed the system, and who was a firm believer in the tenets of liberalism. My uncle had died as a guerrilla in the mountains, after a futile fight of over a decade.

I didn't understand the enormity of Beatrice's psychological problems until after her first miscarriage. When the honeymoon was over, we settled down in Madrid. At first, life was kind to us. Beatrice was busy decorating the apartment. I threw myself into my job with enthusiasm. The news of her pregnancy made us happy; when my father heard about it, he came to visit us in Madrid. One morning (Beatrice was in her second month of pregnancy), I received a call at the embassy. It was the maid. There was urgency in her voice. Everything had happened quickly. An hour later, Beatrice had miscarried in the hospital. It was a boy. We were all sad and Beatrice became depressed. However, there was no reason to worry about anything. According to the doctors, we just had to be more careful the next time. Perhaps Beatrice should have rested more; perhaps I should not have allowed her to undertake so many activities. Even my father seemed reconciled with what had happened. Little by little, the mishap was forgotten. My father returned to Colombia. I began to study and to write about international affairs with more seriousness than ever before. Once more, Beatrice became pregnant. Life was as pleasant as it can get. My new paper—an apology of the new horizons in Latin American politics—was well received; I was named consul to Tampa, in Florida. We took extraordinary care in the move. Beatrice's mother and Gloria came to help us set up our new home. Beatrice stayed in bed most of the time. Florida's weather, a calm life, all this helped Beatrice to adjust without becoming emotionally upset. My father gave us a beautiful house with extensive gardens right on the beach.

The political situation in Colombia was calm. I started to campaign for the party favored to win the next elections. By that time, I had begun to understand that certain interests had placed me where I was, and I couldn't betray them.

Beatrice miscarried again, this time when she was four months pregnant. After many visits to specialists in New York, we learned that she would never be able to carry a pregnancy to term because she had an atrophied uterus. Beatrice relapsed and she was placed in a hospital in Florida. I was profoundly disillusioned. I would never be able to have a son in my marriage. Any child of mine would have to be an out-of-wedlock child, just like me.

It didn't take me long to realize why Beatrice's grandfather had secured the consulate in Florida for me. A significant portion of the marijuana and cocaine that entered the United States entered through Tampa. The rumors that Beatrice's family was involved in the drug trade turned out to be true. Against my wishes, I found myself involved in this activity. All I was supposed to do was to make the contacts. Generally, the marijuana and the cocaine were transported in plastic bags to a place in the West Indies. The bags were attached to the bottoms of ships. These ships were met near Yucatán, where the merchandise was delivered to American fishing boats. In this manner, the drugs entered the United States in American fishing vessels that had barely left the maritime limits to go fishing.

When I get out of the shower, Beatrice is awake, sitting on the bed, having breakfast. I get dressed as she eats silently on the bed, leafing through a magazine. I pour myself a glass of juice and sit on the bed to chit chat. She hasn't mentioned Father's death yet. I wonder if she has forgotten about it in her sleep. She does look fine, however. It's already twelve thirty. So much has happened to me this morning, but Beatrice is just getting up. I decide to mention Father's death again.

"Beatrice, I've been thinking. I think it'd be better for you to go to your parents' for the day. I'm going to be busy today with the arrangements for the funeral. I want to spare you all that stuff. I've given instructions to María Eugenia to arrange the burial for tomorrow morning. It's better to get this over with as soon as possible."

She nods, to indicate that she understands what I've said. This is her way of communicating when she doesn't want to talk. I don't want to force her to do anything.

It's approximately 1 P.M. when I go downstairs. I start answering the phone. María Eugenia has been very diligent about making the arrangements: Papa's body will be in the funeral home tonight, and early in the morning it will be taken to the church, for a brief religious service. I return the calls of the newspapers and give a brief statement to all of them. The statement is emotional, expressing our grief over the terrible loss. I do all this as I sip scotch. I find the tropical heat unbearable, even inside this house, with its high ceilings, its sombrous corners, its rooms cooled by the profusion of plants and flowers. Even in the rooms that are air conditioned, the heat creeps in. More than anything else, I'm worried about Beatrice.

Last year, when the United States government began to get tougher with the drug trade and the Florida mafia was beginning to get into the business, I resigned from my job as consul, and traveled back to Colombia, which was getting ready for elections. It was then that the future president approached me. With my progressive intellectual image, I could be an asset to the party. That, plus my American education and family connections. I did not wish to continue living abroad, or to be assigned to another consulate or embassy. It was clear that the future president was also interested in me because of the financial backing that Beatrice and I could give him. It was suggested that I run for the senate, and I was reassured that with my name and fortune we could buy all the votes needed. That way, I could live in Bogotá, far away from the sickly tropical weather. I accepted. I had never dreamed of being in a political office, but I was interested in power. Beatrice was the sole blemish on my future political career. It was not going to be easy to navigate high political circles with an insane wife. It was easy to accept that she was barren. But her madness was a heavier burden. Perhaps in the future we could get a legal separation. But at the beginning of my career, that was not an option. I was quite sure that Beatrice would not be able to take the rigors of the political campaigns. What would I do if in the middle of a public act, or an important dinner, or during a speech, Beatrice started falling to pieces?

At two thirty we have a light lunch. We hardly speak as we eat. The servants, who have only known us for a few days, have no idea that most of our meals are eaten in silence. Perhaps they think we are too sad to talk much.

Neither one of us dresses in mourning clothes. Beatrice's only concession is not to wear makeup this morning. I like her face better this way. Her skin looks perfect, unblemished, almost translucent, but tight like canvas on a stretcher. Her face is beautiful, though, and as I watch her pick at her salad, I think how ironic it is that despite her wealth and her beauty, she has known mostly grief in her life. She hasn't even enjoyed the sweetness of revenge.

It's almost three o'clock when we leave the house to go by my in-laws. The sun shines blindingly and the heat is overpowering. The trees are inert, mesmerized. The sky is an intense blue, devoid of clouds. I drive in a northerly direction, toward the newer section of the city and away from my father's house, which is located in the old residential district. As we approach the avenue where the parade will take place, the crowds thicken, the traffic is denser and slower. There's no way to escape it, and all I can do is follow the masses. As we advance, the crowds are more chaotic, less respectful of drivers. Most people, wearing costumes, are heading for the avenue. They wear the usual costumes: *marimondas*, pierrots, tigers, and drag. I drive with the windows rolled down, until someone throws a handful of white starch into the car. Beatrice gets furious and I roll up the windows and turn on the air conditioning. There's nothing we can do now, except wait patiently until we're out of this vortex. I try to appear as calm as possible. I feign to be in good humor, since I'm apprehensive of her reaction. As we enter the heavy crowds, it rains starch everywhere. The people, irritated that we have the windows rolled up, plaster our windshield with wet starch. I turn on the windshield wipers. But the starch, mixing with water, thickens into a gluey substance, adhering to the glass and becoming impossible to clean. Now the sky looks chalky. Beatrice is getting upset. I turn on the radio, which plays frenzied Carnival music, and I start blowing the horn to see if I can get the traffic to move. All the cars start honking and people laughed at us, trapped inside our car. I'd like to laugh, too, but the expression on Beatrice's face stops me. I roll the window down and start screaming, when I see two adolescents jump on the hood of the car and then one of them jumps right above our heads, where he starts bouncing up and down. He howls as he does this. I stop the car and get out to push off the boys, but the car behind me starts to honk hysterically and someone pushes me brutally against the body of the car. "Kill the rich pig," a celebrant screams. As I try to scramble back into the car, a boy throws a handful of starch into my eyes. I get inside the car, lock the door, but I'm momentarily blind. I keep driving, without seeing where I'm going. I drive with my foot on the brake and trying to keep the steering wheel straight. Beatrice starts screaming when she realizes what's happening. I start regaining my vision. The crowd is angry with us. Something lands on our windshield and bursts open. At first I think it's water, then beer, then I realize someone has thrown a plastic bag of urine on our car.

"They're thowing urine at us," Beatrice screams.

"No, it's not," I say, trying to calm her down.

"Yes it is. It's urine," she screams. "I'm going to get out of the car. I'm becoming claustrophobic. They're going to kill us."

"Calm down, Beatrice," I plead, even though I'm shaking.

Another bag lands on our windshield, except this one is full of stones. The window cracks in many places but does not break. When the crowd sees the cracked glass, they start pushing against the car, to jump on the hood and to hit the windows. The window on Beatrice's side breaks. She starts whimpering as she says, "No, no, I won't do it," and she caresses a sliver of glass with her hand, until she cuts herself and begins to bleed. In my mind's eye I see Beatrice breaking the window to cut her face. I start honking desperately, at the same time that I try to pacify Beatrice with my free hand. The crowd continues to press. Beatrice screams and I slap her face. A rock makes a hole on the windshield. People pour starch through the aperture, and the starch enters the car, falling on everything. We've reached the avenue. A policeman on his motorcycle approaches us. The officer turns on his siren and begins to open a way for us through the packed street. I press my foot on the gas pedal.

We cross the street and we leave the crowd behind. There are many people here, but they're not aggressive. I follow the policeman for a few blocks and stop behind him when he stops. He approaches us. He's a rather short man, pale, a little overweight.

"Is she OK?" he asks, when he sees Beatrice sobbing and her hand bleeding. "Is Mrs. Villalba all right?" I realize he recognizes us. "May I escort you to a hospital? They're a bunch of savages," he says, looking south, in the direction of the crowds.

"That won't be necessary. You're very kind," I say. "I don't know how to thank you." I hand him a large bill.

I roll up the window before he can thank me and I drive away. I was thankful to him when he appeared and saved us. But the man's unctuousness makes me sick.

I don't know why I'm taking Beatrice to her parents' home. I don't like putting her in their hands. I have no idea what I want to do. I just don't want her to get involved in the funeral arrangements. I do know her parents won't be happy to see her at their home. But I also know I need to be by myself, far away from everything. Far away from my father's house, from Beatrice, from the city itself.

Beatrice has stopped sobbing, but her hand continues to bleed, though not copiously. I turn the radio off and roll my window down. We're now in the new section of Barranquilla. There are very few people out, here and there some children and adolescents heading south to see the parade. I drive fast. A breeze is blowing, and sometimes, as I reach the top of a knoll, I glimpse the grayish sea in the distance. Beatrice stares straight ahead. Her parents' home is situated in the outskirts of the city, near the highway that leads to the sea. We arrive at a modern mansion, with great lawns and extensive gardens. The house is a construction in the shape of cubes but with many windows. There's a guard in front. He's armed with a gun and stands there like a pillar.

When I park, Beatrice doesn't seem to realize where we are. I ask her gently to get out. Since she doesn't answer, I open her door, give her my hand and smile. There are only two cars stationed outside the garage, which seems to indicate that her parents are home alone. Beatrice studies my hand and smiles, but she doesn't move. I don't want to rush her. The heat is intense, but in this sector of town a pleasant breeze brings the smells of the ocean. From where I stand, I can see the sea in the distance and the waves that die in the abandoned beaches. I'm standing there looking to the Atlantic when I feel Beatrice place her hand in mine. I try to pull her toward me, but she starts resisting and then she laughs. There's something weirdly girlish about this laugh, the laugh of a naughty girl. I reach inside the car, as far as I can go, and I take her in my arms. I carry her to the door of the house, where we're met by Beatrice's mother.

"What happened?" Graciela asks, alarmed. There's terror in her eyes when she sees Beatrice's bleeding hand. She closes the door behind me and she says, "The servants don't have to know about this. Let's go upstairs to her bedroom."

I'm exhausted, but I manage to climb the stairs carrying Beatrice. Inside the room, the curtains are drawn, and coming from the bright afternoon light my eyes have trouble adjusting. Graciela turns the lights on. I place Beatrice on the bed and sit next to her.

"I think I should call Dr. Martínez," my mother-in-law says. "He's a good friend." She walks toward the door and, before exiting, she turns around and says, "I'm so sorry about your father. We were friends for many years." Then she leaves. I hear her footsteps grow faint on the tiles and then I don't hear anything. Graciela must have gone to her bedroom or downstairs. Beatrice's hand has stopped bleeding, which means her cuts are not deep. Blood has coagulated on her palm. Her pants are stained with blood, and there's also blood on her forehead, her throat, and around her lips. I get up from bed and walk toward the windows.

"Why are you leaving?" she asks, as if waking up from a stupor.

Though it's dim in the room, our eyes make contact. "I'm not leaving," I reassure her. "I'm going to open the windows." I draw the curtains. The day continues pristine blue. The window faces a patio planted with flowers, some fruit trees, and in the distance gleams the Caribbean. I open the window. A breeze blows in strongly, as if it had been pressing against the window panes all this time. I step out on the balcony and take a deep breath. One, two, three times—each time holding the air longer in my lungs. This is a technique Beatrice and I sometimes practice before we go to sleep, so she can relax and sleep without barbiturates. She still needs sleeping pills, but these breathing exercises help me relax whenever I feel I'm about to explode. Far away, in the sea, floats a sailboat, with an immense white sail blowing in the wind. I return to the room. Beatrice's eyes are still unfocused, and when I sit next to her I see she has tears in her eyes. I lean toward her and place my face on her breasts. We stay that way for a while; I barely hear the soft beat of her heart, so soft sometimes it seems she's going to stop breathing. She touches my head with her unharmed hand and begins to stroke my hair, delicately, tenderly, trying to communicate with me without words. I start sobbing and place my ear to her heart. At first, her heartbeat reminds me of the sound of the waves unfurling at the beach, then the sound of a seashell, then the sound of the pulse of my mother's placenta, when I was still unborn. I doze off.

I wake up a short while later when the doctor arrives. My eyes are dry and Beatrice has fallen asleep. The doctor wants to know what happened.

"He knows everything," Graciela says, so I don't have to measure my words.

I tell him what happened in the car.

He pulls a syringe from his bag. "It will be better to keep her asleep for a while." He indicates that I should hold her arm, disinfects her skin, looks for a vein, and plunges the needle. Without waking up, Beatrice emits a soft moan. I hold her arm until he has finished.

"She'll sleep for a while," Dr. Martínez informs me. "It will be good for her. Now I'm going to disinfect her hand." He asks Graciela for a bowl with warm water. She leaves. The doctor dons white plastic gloves. I watch him all the while he stitches her hand.

Before he goes, he leaves some tranquilizers with instructions of when to administer them. Graciela and I undress Beatrice. Graciela makes a bundle of the bloody clothes. We put a slip on Beatrice and Graciela cleans her face with a facecloth. When I leave the room, Beatrice continues to sleep, as if she had not awakened all day. The only trace of what has happened to her is her bandaged hand. All vestiges of the accident have disappeared, forever.

I sit by the pool, under an umbrella, and ask for a drink. A uniformed boy brings me a bottle of scotch, ice, and glasses. I pour myself a double shot and gulp it down as I sit there watching the wrinkles the breeze creates on the surface of the pool. I check the time: it's four thirty. Very soon the parade will end and the last night of Carnival will begin. Tomorrow will be Ash Wednesday. My father will be buried tomorrow and everything will be over. I'm thinking about all this, enjoying the breeze, when I hear footsteps behind me. Beatrice's father, Antonio, wearing a bathing suit, sunglasses, thongs, and with a beach towel draping his slender suntanned body, approaches me. I shift position in my chair and pour him a drink. I'm about to get up when he places a hand on my shoulder.

"Please don't get up," he says. "I'm really sorry about your father." He sits down and takes the glass in his hands. "Maybe I cared about your father more than you did." He pauses and sips his drink, then puts another ice cube in it. "I knew him from before you were born. For many years your family has been like part of our family."

"Thanks," I mutter and say nothing else. I don't enjoy speaking with Antonio. Often, when we speak, we end up arguing. He stretches on his chair and lights a cigarette. He must be near fifty, I think. His hair is almost all silver, but his figure is youthful, and the tropics have not yet begun to chip away at him, at least on the outside. He keeps in great shape for someone his age; and age, instead of diminishing him, has polished him, the way certain pieces of gold and silver acquire a patina that makes their color not brighter, but more complex and subtle. I stare at him, almost hypnotized, wondering how long it will be before he starts to crumble, and whether—like my father—he will travel abroad to see doctors, trying to preserve his life, and his youth, at whatever cost. Antonio breaks the spell by saying, "For a long time I've wanted to have a good talk with you. There's lots to talk about."

"Well . . . " I try to hide my discomfort at this forced intimacy.

"I'd like to talk with you about Beatrice," he continues, "and also about your future political career. You've gone far despite your youth, but I see there are many things you don't understand. I'm going to have to give you some advice. What's more, I'm going to have to scold you whenever you don't act like a grown-up."

There's something in me that can't stand any kind of authority that tries to put constraints on me. "Yes?" I say, cutting him off. I know he understands a blunt manner, getting to the point without preambles—that's inherent in who he is.

"You're our creation," he says.

I feel uncomfortable in my chair and start twitching. I pour myself another drink before replying.

"Wait and listen to me before you say anything. Besides, I don't want to talk to a drunk. I want you sober to hear everything I have to say. Yes, we made you. You are a product of everything that I, Beatrice, and your father represent. Whether you like it or not, we shaped you. You are one of us now. That's why I talk to you in this manner: I know you understand me." He says all this calmly, without altering in the slightest the tone of his voice. "But that's not why I decided it was time to have this talk," he continues, softening his tone. "I want to remind you about your political future. You have lived most of your life abroad, and you've spent a great deal of your life in academe, and you don't understand anything about this country. When we let you marry Beatrice," and now he stares at me with his glassy blue eyes, which even under the sunglasses have an impact on me, "yes, when we allowed you to marry Beatrice, when we got you your first diplomatic job—because that was all our doing—when we had you named consul in Florida, we already knew what we wanted from you. However, you became squeamish as soon as the business got a bit complicated; you resigned from the consulate, after the investment we had made in you. Your father's interests and mine are the same, now more than ever, if you weren't aware of it. That's why I want you to understand that we are not going to continue investing in you unless you understand how the cookie crumbles. We are not going to be delighted if in the middle of campaigning for the senate you become frightened and start running. You must remember how much we've invested in you and that this is not kid's play anymore."

I get up from my chair.

"Sit down," he fumes. "I haven't finished with you. I'll tell when you may go."

I remain on my feet, shaking. I gulp down the contents of the glass and then take a deep breath. "No," I say, "I'm going. I'm as much a pawn of yours as you are a pawn of mine. I'm not stupid, and the only way you're gonna get rid of me is by killing me. I'm not a child who takes orders from you. The child is upstairs, sleeping. I developed my thinking capabilities." I say all this vehemently, but without raising my voice. Suddenly, I feel proud of being such a good pupil; I feel strong, young, and secure.

I walk out of the house fast. I'm a bit looped. I get in the car and back up at full speed, almost running into a truck full of people. Someone throws a handful of starch through the broken windshield and covers my face with it. "Fucking son of a bitch," I scream. "I shit on your mother." I roll the window up and drive toward the sea. After a few minutes, when I'm on the highway, I roll my window down. The breeze is intoxicating. I check the time: it's after five o'clock. The afternoon is dying: the sky is a blue-violet tint, and in the distance, in the direction of the sea, the horizon looks as if ten rainbows had melted over the ocean.

I take an unpaved path that branches off the main highway: it leads to a hamlet that I visited in my childhood and that now, I've been told, is a ghost town. Sometimes when we were staying in Puerto Colombia, we came here at night, by car, to a restaurant in the hills where one could dine on the terrace under the night sky, serenaded by the music made by the coconut trees undulating in the breeze, while below, in the bay, the waves crashed.

The town is encrusted on top of a hill. The sea—two or three miles below—is visible from any house. The bay is wide and two hills frame it, a castle in ruins atop one of them. I enter the town. Frenzied music greets me. I drive down a street covered with pebbles and grass. Now the sea is in front of me, agitated, full of great waves that the sun dyes a honey color. I see children in costumes, wearing just about any crazy thing they can get their hands on, women in skimpy attires and excessive makeup, drunks donning flashy hats. Forty or fifty years ago, this hamlet was a resort that many families from Barranquilla patronized. The beautiful houses of the past have now become run-down guest houses.

I drive to the beach. The sea is turbulent and there is a strong wind. The beach is semi-deserted. Here and there, I see small groups of people. I park in front of an open stand and order a bottle of rum and a Coca Cola. I pour myself a drink, as I listen to the

70

music and watch the people milling about. Little by little, people start leaving the beach. After a while I see flocks of pelicans planing above the ocean, and crabs emerging from the sand. Gusts of wind raise phantasmagoric waves of sand. I walk toward the sea. The sun is almost hidden, but the sky looks like the palette of a hallucinating painter. I walk in a northerly direction, toward the castle in ruins.

As I walk by the water's edge, I spot, in the dunes, and behind the brush, couples engaged in sex. There are a few cars parked with their lights on. I continue walking until I meet a boy who beckons at me to follow him. I have no idea what he wants. The boy continues gesturing, pointing at something, but I ignore him. I continue on my way, and after a while I run into another young man, slender, tall, tanned, built. He approaches me, and, without saying anything, he places his arms around my waist and presses me furiously against his chest. We fall on the sand, just a few feet away from the sea. He takes off his bathing suit, and while he clutches me with one hand, with his free hand he begins to undress me. Seconds later we're naked and kissing. His cock between my legs is strong, like a conviction, like a punishing weapon. I think about my father's death, while the boy's lips take my penis, and I remember how I had placed the pillow on my father's face, of how when I was a boy I looked through the interstices of the door to watch my mother making love. I look at the sky, there's a star, a full bright moon that pulls me to the Earth: it's the boy whose hands are caressing my stomach and my chest, sucking on my cock ravenously, violently, and I think about the full moon, totally satisfied, like me, after raising the pillow and suddenly I cry out and I see the boy raising his head, his mouth dripping with my semen, and then he gives me a bitter kiss and before I know it he turns me around and I feel his tongue in my ass, his saliva and my semen in my asshole, and then he kisses it, as I look ahead of me, seeing the crabs coming out of the sand in the moonlight, fast, nervous, and I think this is how I move, this is how I move, the way I had moved since that moment in the morning when I had murdered my father and I had come, the way I had come when I watched my mother make love, the way I had moved all day, and I extend my arm and try to touch something, over there, far away, the future, and I feel how the young man's hands grab me by my shoulders, his nails digging into my flesh and then I hear a wild, savage cry, like the jarring cry of a huge bird crashing against the rocks, and then I feel something filling me and hear his gasping mouth in my ear and later when I turn around he's on top of me, breathing heavily, and I feel his body vibrating on top of mine, and feel his heart beating against mine while I hear his breathing mix in with the sounds of the rough sea, the sounds of a shell in my ear, and far up in the sky I see the moon and the stars and remember that this is the last night of Carnival, that night has descended.

It's dark when I return to the city. On the way back, I run into many cars, buses and trucks crammed with people, returning to the towns nearby. The night is cool and clear. A pavonine moon shines, and the stars form geometric patterns in the sky. It has been a long and exhausting day, but night just begins. This is the last night of Carnival, and I want to enjoy it. I haven't been part of Carnival since I was a child, and my memories are not at all like the reality I've experienced the last couple of days.

I drive fast, enjoying the speed, the nooks and crannies of the highway. It's almost a sexual pleasure, letting the car gobble up the miles between the beach and the city. This is much more fun than driving on the slick American and European highways, which aren't as treacherous as this highway that has no lights. Despite having to deal with so many events from the past, today I feel firmly on my way to my future. I feel as if I were flying. I realize what a big mistake it has been for me all these years to ignore my past, everything that has caused me torment and pain.

It's hard to tell whether I'm happy or mildly drunk. I know, however, that before the night is over I have to complete my journey backwards. An old song, one of the few tunes that I remember from when I was a boy, plays. The refrain of the song says, "I forgot you, I forgot you, I forgot you." Can forgetting really be a voluntary and conscious process? The incident that just took place at the beach reminds me of other memories. The encounter has left a bittersweet taste in my mouth: I had to give the boy my watch. He threatened to hit me if I didn't. Losing my watch makes me think about the gift my mother gave me for my tenth birthday: a beautiful gold watch encrusted with emeralds. I don't know where she got the money to give me such a present; in any case, it wasn't an appropriate watch for a boy. When I put it on, my mother said, "Take good care of it. I might not be able to get you another present like this one for a long time. When you're a grown man, you'll think of me whenever you look at it." After she died, besides a few photos, that was all I had left. Sometimes I have nightmares in which I lose the watch: it's either stolen, or it falls out of my pocket, breaking in so many pieces that it cannot be repaired.

After she died, the watch took on mythic importance for me. I slept wearing it, and when I went out in the streets, I always kept it in my pants so that it would not get stolen.

When I was sent to boarding school in Bogotá, I was one of the smallest kids. It was an exclusive school for rich boys. This did not mean that horrible things didn't happen, among them thefts. I was a precocious boy who was placed in advanced classes. Thus, my classmates were generally older. I had lived mostly in isolation, reading books, without much contact with the outside world. There was strict supervision in the boarding school, but the older kids managed to get away with whatever they wanted to, especially during recess and late at night. Homosexual acts were very common. The smallest children, the weakest, were the ones who were preyed upon.

The first boy who sodomized me against my will was called Julio. One Sunday—I was one of the few boys who didn't have relatives coming to take them out on Sundays—Julio, who later, I realized, had been planning his assault, took me to the attic and asked me to perform fellatio on him. After he finished, he took my watch. Rebelling, I fought back furiously, but Julio threw a punch at me that knocked me out for a while. When I got up, my mouth was full of thickened blood. I threatened to denounce him to the authorities unless he returned my watch, but he said I would be expelled from school for being a homosexual. That's how I lost the watch my mother had given me. That year Julio graduated and I never saw him again.

Long before I was sent to the United States, I had realized that what had happened to me was not an isolated event, and that this kind of incident was common. By the time I left school I had three watches, two radios, and many other things I had stolen from younger kids. This evening, after the encounter at the beach, when the boy asked me for my watch, brought it all back.

I drive into the city, now fully illuminated, golden, resplendent. A strong breeze blows about flyers, leaves, debris, and the smell of the ocean. It's almost nine o'clock. I drive by my in-laws and see their cars parked and very few lights on. I keep on driving, without knowing where I'm heading. The streets are still crowded with revelers screaming, and drunks attacking people with handfuls of starch. After four days of partying people look tired, debauched, but ready to celebrate the last night of Carnival. I drive through the main avenue, where we had been attacked earlier in the day; there is loud music playing in the bars and restaurants, and the terraces are crammed with people in costumes drinking, or people dressed in their best finery, on their way to exclusive parties in private clubs.

The avenue is littered with confetti, crushed flowers, trash, bottles, and drunks completely coated in starch, slumped against light posts and cars. Many are dirty with mud, wet, sleeping, or passed out in fetid puddles. I continue driving. People are exuberant, but not violent. I drive by my father's house—my house—and I see it in darkness, except for the light in the terrace. I drive around the city, feeling lonely, without anyone I can really talk to. There's no one, not even Beatrice, to whom I could talk about the events of today.

I go downtown. I've always hated downtowns, especially in tropical cities, where they're always congested and full of grimy-looking people. The well-off have moved away from here with the years, moving their banks, stores, supermarkets, and hospitals nearer to their homes. The downtown area is modern, having lost the ornate and graceful architecture of old Barranquilla. Some streets, however, haven't changed. They are lined with low structures built half a century ago, painted white and yellow and a pale green, with many balconies and windows. I park the car in a garage, hand my keys to the attendant, and walk toward the old *Paseo* Bolívar, which is no longer the main commercial sector of the city. In this part of town, which is built in the ravine after which the city is named, near the river, there's no breeze, but the heat is less acute than it was at noon. In this part of town, Carnival is not winding down. There are hundreds of drunks, dancing vigorously. I keep walking down the narrow streets, where harsh music plays. There's a smell of food in the air; under the awnings there are many prostitutes offering themselves.

There's no question I'm in the poorer part of the city. As I walk, people stare at me as if I were a foreigner. These people are thinner, jaundiced looking, due no doubt to malnutrition, and their skin is much darker than mine. I have trouble believing the future belongs to these proletarians. With each passing generation their descendants grow weaker, more and more deformed by crippling poverty. It's a miracle they keep alive. How can anyone expect them to both live and think at the same time? Perhaps that's why they amuse themselves in this way, as if this were the last day of their lives, as if beyond today there was nothing.

As I continue walking, the streets are more jammed and narrower. Once in a while there's someone who looks like he's slumming: a tourist, or another bourgeois like me, looking for God knows what, feeding their sick voyeurism. On the *Paseo* Bolívar there are many stands where alcohol is sold, and every other block there is a wooden platfrom, raised above the street, where people dance to orchestras playing music from the Antilles, black African music. I have a drink and study the people. The orchestras playing along the avenue play at the same time, and the breeze blowing mixes the notes of the different pieces playing. A young woman— she looks like a hooker—asks me to dance with her. I accept. I'm quite soused, but fully in control. On the way to the platform I realize I don't know how to dance this kind of music; I never learned. But it's too late now. When I take the woman in my arms, I tell her, "I don't know how to dance."

"Don't worry," she replies, laughing, "neither do I." And then she adds, "Let me lead you."

I think about the hard life of this woman, and yet, during these four days of Carnival she forgets about all the horrible stuff she has to put up with the rest of the year. The orchestra plays a bolero, which I can do, like any other slow dance. What I cannot dance are the fast popular dances, which require special steps. I let her lead me, our bodies grinding against the bodies of the other dancers. I feel the warmth of her body against mine, the perspiration in her arms, the sweat on her breasts and her nipples pressing against my flesh. At one point, Beatrice and I danced like this together. I get sexually aroused and kiss the woman on her lips, which she offers me without resistance, and for a moment we stop dancing and we kiss, in public, our sexes grinding against each other. The song ends, and the orchestra starts playing a fast number, completely African in its rhythms. At first I have trouble getting into it, then I imitate the other dancers, who just react to the rhythms of the orchestra. Suddenly I feel that a part of me, something ancestral, something in my blood that goes very far back, farther than my mother and my grandparents, all the way back to Africa, possesses me and makes me dance. I feel intoxicated with a new knowledge of myself. At first I dance reticently, then I abandon myself totally to the music, its cadences, losing myself in the labyrinths of the sounds. My dancing partner is gyrating like a spinning top, opening her arms, as if to embrace a great love, and she skips and rotates her head, as if she were having an epileptic fit. I imitate her, and mimic her gestures and movements, gyrating, spinning, skipping, expressing in this way everything that cannot be expressed in any other way, the way one releases one's self during orgasm. It dawns on me why dancing is so important for the lower classes: this is one of their few outlets, a way of expressing all their rage and all their resentments. "Look at the white man dancing," I hear a woman shout, and then I realize that they are laughing, and the other dancers move back, making room for us, clapping, stomping their feet, emitting irrational cries, which I don't understand, although I sense why they belt them out, without fear, giving themselves in, letting themselves be pulled by the music and the night, they way I do, the way I have all day long.

The music stops, the crowd applauds and cheers. I'm so dizzy I have trouble getting off the platform. Someone in the mob says, "It's the politician. It's Villalba's son." And then I hear people muttering, "His father just died this morning! His father died today!" The music starts again, but now I've wandered away from the orchestra. The woman, sweating and panting, still follows me. "Hey," she says, "let's have a drink. Buy me a cold drink."

"I can't," I reply, "I have to go." I hand her a large bill.

She takes the note in her hand and stares at it. Then she searches my eyes. When she has my attention, she tears the bill into pieces and flings them at my face. "Asshole," she sneers. "Do you think I am a piece of merchandise?" She turns around and disappears in the crowd.

I walk away from the scene, with some difficulty, since most people are coming my way, in the direction of the dances on *Paseo Bolívar*. Music plays in every building I pass. Finally I arrive at the garage where I parked my car. There is a liquor stand. I'm hot and thirsty and ask for a cold beer. As I'm sipping it, a prostitute approaches me. "Would you like company?" she asks.

I shake my head, exasperated. The woman walks away, and then she turns around and says to the men gathered there drinking, "Do you see that faggot?" I pay for my beer and leave. As I cross the street, the woman's voice chases me. "Faggot," she screams. "Faggot." I rush into the parking lot, pay the attendant, and drive fast out of there. I turn on the air conditioning and light a cigarette. The traffic is intense, people drive without paying attention to the traffic signs. By the time I arrive home, I've stopped sweating.

Nury, Pedro, and the cook are in the living room watching TV. My entrance rattles them; they are having a bottle of rum. Nury gets up to turn off the television.

"Please don't," I say. "Just go on as if I weren't here."

She gives me a quizzical look, not sure whether I mean this without irony or sarcasm.

"Please," I say, "just keep doing what you were doing. I'm going upstairs to take a shower. Please bring me something to eat and a list of the people who have called. Thanks." Then, to Pedro, I say: "The burial is tomorrow at seven. You can all take the other car if you want to go, and you can drive them, Pedro," I finish.

Nury hands me a tray with messages and telegrams. I go up the stairs, enter my bedroom and sit on the bed. The window is open to a starry dark-blue sky. I undress and lie on the bed, staring at the ceiling. I sort the messages and the mail. There are scores of messages of condolence. I find an envelope that looks different. It's from the country club, an invitation to the ball for the last night of Carnival. In the bathroom I inspect my face in the mirror. I look haggard, dissipated. I turn on the hot-water faucet and start shaving. I still feel the smell of the boy, the salty smell of the sea, the smell of patchouli from the woman with whom I danced. Too many smells. I remain in the shower for a while, quiet, almost in a meditative state, weary. I finish showering and dry myself. In the mirror, my pale, translucent face is expressionless. My eyes look hard and red. There is a tray with food on the bed: I pick at the food, but I have no appetite. I drink down two glasses of orange juice. I put on my bathrobe, lie down on the bed, but I'm restless. Impulsively I get up from the bed and leave my room. I wander in and out of the rooms on the second floor. I don't know this house. I have no idea what I'll do with it in the future. I know that, no matter what, I won't stay in the city—I don't want a museum of memories always confronting me. I'll probably sell it and buy an apartment that will be my pied-à-terre when I need to stop in the city on business. I amble through the rooms inspecting the antiques, the objects, the paintings, the lamps, the candelabra. I enter Lucía's room. I turn on a lamp and walk around, it's a big room, with a bathroom, and a big balcony. Her room is exactly opposite my father's room—the garden separating them. It doesn't feel, though, like the room of someone who has been dead for many years: there is no dust anywhere. It's spotless, everything smells fresh, as if someone came here every day to clean and to air the room. The linen and bedspreads must be changed frequently, as if Lucía were expected back any moment.

As a boy I hated Lucía, I always saw her as "the other one," the privileged one, the one who had everything I didn't have, including my father's love. Years later I discovered how unhappy she was. Her story was not unlike Beatrice's, but her life had been briefer. I study the photographs of her: pictures of her as a girl with her mother, pictures of her in adolescence, as a debutante, dressed in her tennis whites, seated at the piano, photos of her trips abroad, of her years as a student in France and Italy, when she was at the conservatory. Pictures of her as a career pianist. And then pictures of her as a prematurely aged woman, with a sad gaze. That was how I met her, when we spent one afternoon in Manhattan. I had been told she was ill, but I didn't know how advanced her cancer was. I was fifteen years old: I wore my nicest clothes. I had no idea what to expect. I was afraid of her—because she was the favorite of my father, the professional pianist, because she represented everything I wanted to be. I also resented her. But when I saw her, in a two-piece gray tweed suit, with her sad eyes and her kind and nervous smile, I softened and I saw there was no reason to fear her. She gave me her hand: it was white, with long, strong yet feminine fingers, and her nails were short and painted a delicate pink, like the rouge on her cheeks. There was a look of intelligence in her eyes, and she was elegant, without being the least bit ostentatious; there was an aristocratic air about her, as if she were an orchid that had lived all her life in a greenhouse. Her voice was soft and she had a dry intermittent cough. There was nothing affected about her.

We walked around Manhattan. It was a golden day in October. It was comfortably cool, the sky was limpid, the trees in Central Park were ablaze, and we strolled, crushing the fallen leaves under our shoes, talking about this and that, a little shy with one another. We had lunch in the Metropolitan Museum, near the fountain, and then Lucía took me to see her favorite rooms in the museum, explaining everything to me. "You'll see, once you start traveling, you'll visit the great museums of the world," she said. The last room we visited was full of ballerinas by Degas. We sat on a bench and stayed there for a little basking in the splendid colors and shapes.

Later we visited the zoo, bought ice-cream cones and sat on the grass, in the sun. At six she asked me if I was Catholic. I said yes, although I wasn't sure.

"I don't want you to sin on my account," she said. "Let's go to Sunday Mass."

I hated the Church, but that day I lit a candle for her and prayed for the first time in many years, the way I hadn't prayed since mother's death, and I begged God to cure Lucía from her cancer, to make her happy. It was hard to say good-bye, but before we parted she gave me a picture of herself, on which she inscribed "to my dear little brother." We kissed as she put me on the train, and promised we'd write to each other often. She was leaving the next day for England. There, in London, she died some months later. In the months before her death, I received several letters in which she never mentioned her illness. When my father wrote to inform me of her death, I cried for days, weeks, months. There are moments even now, after all these years, when tears come to my eyes if I think of her. I mourn the relationship we might have had, and I mourn it because she had given me love and I had dared to hope for a future that would include the two of us.

I open the closets still full of her dresses. Among the costumes and party dresses I find a sequined dress, with frilly edges. I pull it out. In a separate box I find feathers, a sequined headband, and high-heeled shoes. I undress and begin to put on Lucía's clothes. When I finish, I'm dressed as a flapper, feathers topping my head. I pick up my clothes and run to my room, afraid that I might be discovered. I put on the shoes. They fit me perfectly. In the mirror, my resemblance to Lucía is eerie—we are both slender, pale, small-boned, and the same height. My feet are small, like hers. I start putting on Beatrice's makeup, and half an hour later the transformation has been achieved. I look like a woman, with my stockings and high heels and my headband and my emerald bag and my pink feathers and my sequined dress. I smile at myself in the mirror. I've never looked so lissome and handsome. I make a bundle with my clothes to take with me, because I don't want to return home dressed in drag. I look out the window. The house is quiet. There aren't any lights on. I pick up the bundle and bag and leave.

When I was very young, the country club was a mythic place for me. Years later, after I married Beatrice and became a member, I was disillusioned, the way we usually are when we go to visit the places where we lived in as children: they're smaller, less romantic, and not as beautiful as we remembered them.

This is the last night of Carnival, I remind myself. Tomorrow everything will be over. There will be a day of rest, and then the city will return to its usual routines. This is my first day of Carnival since I was a boy, and also my first night. As a boy, I couldn't participate in the festivities during the day, and the nights were reserved for the adults. I drive fast. The city is well lit and there is a festive mood in the air. People wander the streets looking for something to do before the night is over. Tomorrow—or rather today, since it's 1 A.M.—is Ash Wednesday and people will celebrate the burial of Joselito Carnival, the symbol of Carnival, which is buried at the end of the festivities.

A pleasant zephyr blows leaves and papers. A big, full moon, the color of orange hibiscus, shines, and when I pass the darker streets stars glitter in the sky. I arrive at the club. There are two cars in front of me. I'm a little nervous, but confident at the same time. While the guard takes my invitation, I inspect my face in the mirror. I smile. The shiny spot I've placed under the left eye glows in the dark. "Have a good time," the guard says, letting me in.

I park and stay in the car for several minutes, trying to collect myself, but my mind is racing. I see couples getting in and out of the cars and the main building. I also observe young couples wandering off into the dark golf course that lies beyond the main building. From inside pour out the sounds of the music and the cries of people. I'm doing something very risky. I know that the last night of Carnival many heterosexual men dress in black as the widows of Joselito Carnival. But what I'm doing is different: those men, are, obviously, men dressed in women's clothes, whereas I'm trying to pass as a woman. If I get caught, my political future could be on the line—there would be a scandal. I have everything to lose and nothing to gain by what I'm doing, and yet I decide I don't care what happens. I get out of the car and walk toward the main building. With my high heels, I have trouble walking on the grass, but since I don't see anyone around, I take big, unladylike strides to cross the lawn. I enter the building through the back, where the swimming pool is. The couples in love are here, kissing, chatting, slow dancing, though the music coming from inside is very fast. The swimming pool is decorated with Carnival motifs but dimly lit. The glowing moon provides most of the illumination. I reach the main door, to the left there is a ladies room. I go into the restroom before I step into the dancing hall. The bathroom is rather dirty with confetti and papers and puddles of water. I stand in front of the mirrors, take out a small brush from my bag and comb my wig. My hand shakes slightly. I smile. I retouch my lips with my lipstick. When I finish, I walk toward the door. At that moment two young women step in. Frightened, I decide to run away from there as soon as possible. In my haste, I drop my bag and its contents scatter on the floor. I start collecting the objects. The two girls laugh and start helping me. One of them hands me my brush. "Thanks," I say.

"Hi, I'm Hilda," she says. "What's your name?"

I'm afraid that my voice will give me away. But I say, "Olga."

"Olga who?" she asks, with a slight smile. She's a beautiful girl, dressed in a translucent electric blue gown; her copious chestnut hair falls to her shoulders. She talks and smiles at the same time, showing her beautiful teeth. I get up from the floor and she does too.

"I haven't seen you before," she says. "This is my friend, Helena."

Helena looks like Hilda, even in the dress she's wearing, but she's shorter and heavier and her voice is hoarse. "Hello," she says. And she adds, "Let's be friends," while Hilda goes to the door, opens it, looks out and locks it. She approaches me. I see that they're both a little drunk, and that they're planning something.

"Would you like to get high?" Hilda asks.

I don't know what to say, I'm confused. She laughs, with a high sonorous cackle. "Don't be scared," she says. "We're all friends. And it's really good stuff."

"OK," I say, but I'm shaking.

She opens a little silver box and takes out a tiny spoon from her bag. "You first," she says. "Guests first." Both girls laugh at once. She places the spoon under my nostril, with a firm hand. "OK, go ahead," she says. "Take a deep breath."

I do, and I feel the powder go up my nose, all the way to my brain. Then she fills the spoon again and places it under my other nostril. I repeat the operation. I feel the powder floating in my brain.

"You like it?" she asks.

I sneeze.

She laughs. "That's a good sign. Pure blow; the best."

"Thanks," I say and get ready to leave, but Helena takes me by the arm. She has a manly grip.

"What's the hurry?" she says. "Now it's our turn."

It's obvious they do this frequently. They move fast and with accuracy. Although it's all over in a few seconds, the time feels like an eternity to me, nervously standing there, waiting for them to finish. My head is spinning. I have so much energy I get itchy feet. I can't stand still. My head feels cooler and I can see everything more distinctly. I'm ready to run or dance or do something to get rid of the excess energy. Now I feel fully confident in my women's clothes. The two girls begin to kiss. Helena takes my hand and pulls me into a circle. We put our arms around each other and start kissing avidly, inserting our tongues deep into each other's throats. I don't get aroused; I'm too nervous. But my mouth and lips kiss them back, kiss lips and tongues expert in kissing.

Quickly, I pull away from them, dash for the door and step out. I hear the throbbing music from inside. In just the few minutes I was in the restroom, everything has changed. Now I'm ready to have a fabulous time. I enter the dancing hall, the orchestra is playing. I walk around the room, slowly, taking in everything—the lights, the sounds, the spectacle. I grab a scotch on the rocks from a waiter and gulp it down in one swallow. Then I drink another one, just as fast. I could run and scream at the same time. I'm as happy as I've ever been. Someone emerges from the crowd and asks me to dance. I give him my hand, and we step onto the dance floor, and when we're facing each other, I see it is Beatrice's father. "You're so beautiful," Antonio says, placing his hands around my waist. When he pulls me toward him, I realize he's drunk. He tightens his grip around me. I try to free myself from his embrace. "Don't worry," he says. "I'm not carnivorous."

A sensual samba is playing. My father-in-law begins to kiss my neck. I feel Antonio's sex pressing against me. I try to loosen his grip, but he's strong and he tightens his hold. I look upward, and there's a light show on the ceiling. We start turning, and twirling to the music that now plays faster. There are many men dressed as women in mourning. People dance and drink and laugh and carry on. The song ends and people leave for their tables. Beatrice's father takes my hand and leads me to a dark corner. "Let's go out," he says in my ear.

"I can't," I say. "I can't go alone."

Suddenly, children and women dressed as widows emerge from behind the orchestra.

"Let's not stay for this," he says. "It's getting late."

The men and children, and the dancers, begin to scream in unison: "Ay Jose, ay Jose, poor Jose. He's dying. He's dying. Joselito Carnival is going away. Ay Jose, don't leave me alone. Ay Jose, don't leave us like this, we poor widows need you, Jose." And men and women shout, and some of them go back to the dance floor wailing, and people rest their heads on their partners' or neighbors' shoulders and begin to sob hysterically. The orchestra starts playing funeral carnavalesque music. The echo of "Ay Jose, ay Jose," reverberates in the hall.

"Let's go," insists my father-in-law. "This is the best moment to get out of here. No one will notice."

I don't know why I follow him. We push our way through the crowd and reach the main door. When we get there, a young man steps in our path. It takes me a few seconds to realize that it is not a man, but a woman—Beatrice in a tuxedo. She looks at me, not seeming to recognize me, and then stares at her father.

"Later," he says, pushing her out of the way.

As we exit, I hear her cry, "That's what you like—whores." Then her voice is drowned by the music and the cries of "Ay Jose, ay Jose."

As we walk in the direction of the golf course I wonder whether Beatrice recognized me, though I doubt it. Her eyes looked glassy, as if she were under some potent drug. I let Beatrice's father lead me, he walks briskly. We reach the golf course and climb on a little cart and he turns it on and we drive away. The breeze is brisk now, and the sky is alive with stars and a reddish moon is heading north, in the direction of the sea. Antonio drives fast, up and down the rolling lawns. I still feel the cocaine in my head, and am very excited with the thrill of this moment. We pass couples, groups. I scream "Stop," when we pass a group of young people. Antonio stops and I get out of the cart and run toward the youths, who are smoking grass. "Who's that?" someone asks.

"She's cool," says Helena, who's there with Hilda.

Someone passes me the joint and I take it and run with it to the cart.

"Hey," a voice screams. "Give it back."

I climb into the cart, and Antonio drives away. We cross a vast expanse of lawn, and I notice couples making love, and small groups engaged in orgies. We park under a tree. I continue smoking my joint, which has burnt holes in my dress. We clamber out of the cart and lope onto the lawn. Beatrice's father takes the joint away from me. "That's enough," he says, and throws the stub into the darkness. I see where it lands and run after it. When I kneel to get it, Antonio grabs me from behind, and he lifts me. We both fall on the ground. I've fallen on the joint, which burns my back. "You beast," I scream. He tries to undress me, and then he realizes I'm a man. "You are a damned *marica*," he screams and I see him get up and lift his foot in the direction of my face. I react fast to avoid his kick. But the next kick lands in my stomach. Next he tries to kick me in the head, but I react quickly and, grabbing his foot, yank it. He falls on his buttocks. I start running toward the golf cart, but before I get there one of my high-heeled shoes gets caught in the grass. As I'm clambering into the cart, Antonio drags me out of it by my legs and throws me onto the ground. He approaches me, menacingly. I grab a handful of sand and fling it at his eyes. Taking advantage of his blindness, I push him against a tree. His head hits the trunk, making a hollow thump, and he whimpers pathetically before he collapses. Shaking, I get in the golf cart and drive into some bushes not too far away. I get out of the cart and hide behind the bushes, where I begin to sob. I don't know how long I stay there. After a while, I hear voices approaching; drunken boys emerge from behind a hill. They arrive at the tree, where Antonio lies. There are four boys. "Look, there's a man here," one of them says and they start howling. Another one says, "He's drunk. Let's take care of him." I see the boys undress my father-in-law and then they start sodomizing him. Terrified, I get in the golf cart and drive away as fast as it can go. I drive over the dunes and the hills, until the club appears in the distance. Music is still playing; it's almost dawn. The moon has disappeared and in the east the sky is now a grayish-pink color. I abandon the golf cart and run toward the parking lot, where I find my car. Nobody has seen me. I start the car and drive through the gates of the club at full speed. The city is awakening. Carnival is over. I turn on the radio, funeral music is playing. Bach, something mournful and baroque. I drive toward my house. When the piece ends, the announcer says, "It's five A.M., Ash Wednesday, nineteen-seventy-five." I park the car outside the garage doors and open the front door. There's nobody around. I run up the stairs and into my bedroom, where I undress before I get in the shower. I have to hurry. The Mass for my father begins at seven. I scrub my face with a towel. Later, I put on a black, light cotton suit and a black tie. I make a bundle of Lucía's clothes and go downstairs. There's no sign of life in the house. I change cars, and decide to drive my father's Mercedes. I drive to a secluded spot and get rid of the bundle of Lucía's clothes.

I haven't slept all night, but I'm wide awake. In the mirror, my face is haggard—it could be read as the face of someone who's been partying for days, or someone who has been suffering a great deal. I smile. The early morning light is so grayish that the city looks as if it were wrapped in white gauze. Here and there I spot drunks, people selling food, newspaper boys. I drive to the funeral parlor where the corpse of my father lies.

The funeral home is in the old part of town. It's still dawn when I get there. Years ago, this was a lovely mansion with high granite columns and luxuriant gardens. I stay in the car for a while, turn the radio to classical music—the appropriate kind of music for Ash Wednesday, a day of penance; a religious holiday that, like the lazy tropical day, is taking its time to arrive. A wind blows from the

Caribbean, and in the north the sky is red, as if there were a fire in the horizon. The entire city is tinged with that redness.

The church where the Mass will be said is near the funeral parlor, and the cemetery is in the outskirts of the city, not far from the home of Beatrice's parents. I refuse to think about Beatrice, or her father, or what might have happened to him. Stepping out of the car, I lock the door and walk toward the funeral parlor. I cross the gardens, walking on a pebbled path. I haven't seen my father's corpse since yesterday. What does he look like now, all made up? I wonder. I breathe in the as-yet-unsullied morning air. A rooster crows somewhere nearby. And then, as if it had been waiting for a signal, another one. The acacias sway in the wind, their rustling a whispering chorus.

I push the glass front door, which to my surprise is open, and I find myself in a mirrored hall, with white chairs, a dark aquamarine carpet, and a crystal chandelier dangling from the high ceiling. I wander through a few rooms until I reach the chapel, where my father's coffin is. The mahogany box is on a table covered with a purple velvet drape. The top is open. The casket is flanked by burning wax tapers, and the chapel is choked with flowers. There are so many funeral wreaths that there's hardly any space to move. The coffin lies in front of a wooden crucifix, with a rachitic Christ hanging from it. It looks almost as if the casket were there waiting for someone to come and dismount the Christ and place him in the box. I'm afraid. Never before have I experienced fear of the dead. It's the horror of confronting my dead father. But I have to do it, and forget about it, so it won't haunt me in the future.

I approach the coffin with a tentative gait, look inside, and for a moment think I'm hallucinating. The casket is empty. To make sure it's not an optical illusion, I put my hand inside—there is nothing but the silk lining of the coffin. I'm sure the corpse was sent to the funeral parlor, and for a moment I think maybe I'm in the wrong room, that this chapel is only an exhibition room. But as I go through the other rooms of the house, they're all empty. There are no coffins or corpses anywhere. I step onto the patio, and a chained dog barks at me. I make my way to the room in the back. The little room is in darkness. With my lighter I search for the light switch. On a small cot I discover a curled body. It's the guard, still wearing his uniform. Next to the bed there's a bottle of rum. I nudge him on the shoulder, but he continues snoring, with a snore that ends in a thin whistle. I shake him hard. The man stirs, mumbles something, but continues sleeping. I yell at him, ordering him to get up. The startled guard jumps off the cot and stands, staring at me, uncomprehendingly; he's still drunk.

"Wake up," I say impatiently. "I'm *señor* Villalba's son. Where is he?"

The man stares at me, absorbing what I've just said. "Excuse me," he says, and he stumbles out of the room. I follow him. The chained dog lunges at me. I grab the man by his elbow and stop him on his tracks. "What happened to my father's corpse?" I ask.

"It's over there, in the chapel," he mumbles, and he pulls away from me and continues walking. He walks into the room with the empty coffin and he looks inside, then, slowly, he turns around and avoids my eyes by looking at the carpet. "They've stolen the corpse," he says.

At first, because he's talking softly, I'm not sure I've heard him right. Then, when he says it again, I get furious. "Who the fuck would do that?" I scream.

"Somebody with a sick sense of humor," the man offers. "Today is Ash Wednesday."

I understand what that means: on Ash Wednesdays people put a large rag doll on a stretcher, dress it as Joselito Carnival, and then take him from door to door, begging for alms for his burial. Sometimes a child, or an adolescent, is carried on the stretcher. Right now my father's corpse must be going around the city from door to door.

"It's your fault," I say to the man, at the same time that I get an idea. "You'll pay for this with your job. I'll have you put in jail and I'll throw the key in the sea."

The shaken man starts crying. "Please, please," he says. "I didn't want to get drunk. Please forgive me."

"There's nothing to forgive," I say harshly. "Where's the phone. I'm going to call the police."

The guard drops on his knees and takes my hand. "Please, don't. I can't lose my job. We'll find your father. Maybe they'll return him later today."

"That will be too late," I say, pulling my hand free. "The hearse will be here soon to take the coffin to the church. I have to call the police and you'll have to take responsibility for what's happened." I wait, and then, changing my tone, I add, "Well, I have an idea. But I need your cooperation. And you have to promise me your lips will be sealed forever."

"I promise," he says, still on his knees, crying.

"Get up," I say. I start walking through the house and he follows me in silence. We go to the patio. "What are those bags?" I ask, pointing at a pile of bags in the back of the patio.

"Cement," he informs me.

"Help me," I say, picking up a bag. "You take one too."

Inside the house we place the two bags in the coffin and then lock it with the key. I go to the restroom where I wash my hands and dust off the cement from my jacket. I tell the guard to stand by the door. He's still shaking. I hand him a large bill and tell him not to worry, that everything's OK. Just keep quiet about it. I find the telephone. A clock on the wall says 6 A.M. I call Beatrice's parents. After two rings, Graciela answers. "Good morning," I say. "I wanted to know whether you're ready. I'm here in the funeral parlor."

"We're leaving for the church in a little while," my mother-in-law says.

"Okay, then I'll see you at the door." I hang up. I feel strangely elated, and I sit there, staring at the phone, until I see four uniformed men walk into the funeral parlor. I meet them, leading them into the chapel, and I help them carry the casket to the hearse. They drive away. From the sidewalk, I wave good-bye to the guard who half raises his hand. I get in my car. It's morning now, the sun still isn't out, but the mistiness of dawn is gone.

I drive fast, the morning traffic is starting already. At a red light, I see a group of children in costumes, with black ash crosses drawn on their foreheads, carrying a heavy stretcher. Could that be my father, I wonder? But the light has changed and the car behind me honks, and I have to move on. In the distance I hear the children crying, "Ay Jose, don't leave me alone. What am I going to do? I'm just a poor widow. Ay Jose."

I arrive at the church. There are cars lining both sides of the street. I park and walk up the steps of the church. It's beginning to get hot, the breeze has stopped blowing. Congregated at the church's door are Beatrice and her parents, half a dozen people, and a few photographers. Beatrice looks pale and I wonder what drug she's on that she's still standing. I join the group. I kiss Beatrice and shake hands all around. "Thanks, thanks," I say in response to their condolences, trying to look downcast. The photographers' flashes go off.

We go in. It's a modern church I've never visited before. There are few ornaments, but it is beautifully designed. The place is packed with flower arrangements and funeral wreaths and tapers burning in the altar area and around the casket. An immense, modernist Christ hangs in the place of honor. I look around and see that the church is packed, that most people look haggard, as if they hadn't slept in a couple of days. Beatrice, her parents, and I sit in the first row. I feel the eyes of the people on us, and I detect their whispers. The service begins: the priest says a brief Mass, and then he begins his eulogy. He talks about Father's contributions to society, everything he did for the community, how he was an honest and honorable man. I hold Beatrice's trembling hand. Mine trembles too. The priest makes references to the Scriptures, then the altar boy shakes the incense burner. The priest offers communion and, after he gives the holy wafer, he draws a black cross on the celebrants' foreheads. I let go of Beatrice's hand. Without thinking about what I'm doing, I leave my seat and kneel to receive communion. The priest places the wafer on my tongue and I close my eyes as he draws the cross on my forehead. I clasp my hands and pray. For something; for someone; for I don't know what.

I return to my seat. Beatrice stares at me with astonishment. I hold her gaze until she lowers her eyes. The ceremony is over. I join the pallbearers, and we lift the casket, carrying it slowly as the organ music plays. As we go down the steps, the photographers begin to shoot their flashes. We place the coffin in the hearse. Then

I shake hands with all the men and join Beatrice and her parents at the top of the steps. She places her hand on my arm, and, as we descend the steps, the flashes fire again in front of our eyes. Pedro has parked behind the hearse. He opens the door for Beatrice. Once inside, Beatrice rests her head on my shoulder. I turn around and see people hurrying to their cars. Curious bystanders observe the proceedings. Three motorcycle policemen lead the way, and the hearse follows them.

Morning has fully arrived. I see many groups of people carrying their Joselitos Carnival. The sun hangs high in the sky. I roll the window up and ask Pedro to turn on the air conditioning. As I think about everything that has taken place in the last twenty-four hours, Beatrice squeezes my hand. I turn around to see the long line of cars following us. In the distance, ahead of us, I see the open fields of the cemetery, with its colorful gardens and the gigantic marble Christ that presides over the fields. I want to be alone to cry or laugh or . . . I'm not sure what. A laugh begins inside me as I think about what has ended and what is about to begin.

When we enter the cemetery, Beatrice looks at me as if awakening from a trance and says, "I'd like to know how . . . "

I interrupt her. "Don't you worry about anything. We have our whole futures ahead of us to think about everything," I say, looking deep into her eyes. The car stops next to a newly dug grave. I caress Beatrice's hand and, before leaving the car to breathe in the air of this new day, I look toward the horizon, in the direction of the indigo ocean, and I see a boat with an immaculate white sail, wide as a circus tent, floating near the shore. In the distance, a gray ship enters the port. A monumental ship that looks like part of the sea, or something out of a dream.

"What I want to know . . . " Beatrice insists.

I cut her off again. "Let's don't be silly," I say, letting go of her hand and opening the car door. Before stepping out, I add, "We aren't children anymore."

3

The Documentary Artist

ے

I met Sebastian when he enrolled in one of my film-directing classes at the university where I teach. Soon after the semester started, he distinguished himself from the other students because he was very vocal about his love of horror movies. Our special intimacy started one afternoon when he burst into my office, took a seat before I invited him to do so, and began telling me in excruciating detail about a movie called *The Evil Mommy*, which he had seen in one of those Forty-second Street theaters he frequented. "And at the end of the movie," he said, "as the boy is praying in the chapel to the statue of this bleeding Christ on the cross, Christ turns into the evil mommy and she jumps off the cross and removes the butcher knife stuck between her breasts and goes for the boy's neck. She chases the screaming boy all over the church, until she gets him." He paused, to check my reaction. "After she cuts off his head," he went on, almost with relish, "she places his head on the altar." As he narrated these events, the whites of Sebastian's eyes distended frighteningly, his fluttering hands drew arabesques in front of his face, and guttural, gross croaks erupted from the back of his throat.

I was both amused and unsettled by his wild, manic performance. Although I'm no great fan of B horror movies, I was impressed by his love of film. Also I appreciated the fact that he wasn't colorless or lethargic as were so many of my students; I found his drollness, and the aura of weirdness he cultivated, enchanting. Even so, right that minute I decided I would do my best to keep him at a distance. It wasn't so much that I was attracted to him (which is always dangerous for a teacher), but that I found his energy a bit unnerving.

Sebastian started showing up at least once a week during my office hours. He never made an appointment, and he seldom discussed his work with me. There's a couch across from my chair, but he always sat on the bench that abuts the door, as if he were afraid to come any closer. He'd talk about the new horror movies he'd seen, and sometimes he'd drop a casual invitation to see a movie together. It soon became clear to me that, because of his dirty clothes, disheveled hair, and loudness, and because of his love of the bizarre and Gothic, he was a loner.

One day I was having a sandwich in the cafeteria when he came over and joined me.

"You've heard of Foucault?" he asked me.

"Sure. Why?"

"Well, last night I had a dream in which Foucault talked to me and told me to explore my secondary discourse. In the dream there was a door with a sign that said Leather and Pain. Foucault ordered me to open it. When I did, I heard a voice that told me to come and see you today."

I stopped munching my sandwich and sipped my coffee.

"This morning I had my nipple pierced," Sebastian continued, touching the spot on his T-shirt. "The guy who did it told me about a guy who pierced his dick, and then made two dicks out of his penis so he could double the pleasure."

My mouth fell open. I sat there speechless. Sebastian stood up. "See you in class," he said as he left the table.

I lost my appetite. I considered mentioning the conversation to the department chairman. Dealing with students' crushes was not new to me; in my time I, too, had had crushes on some of my teachers. I decided it was all harmless, and that as long as I kept at a distance and didn't encourage him, there was no reason to be alarmed. As I reviewed my own feelings, I told myself that I was not attracted to him, so I wasn't in danger of playing into his game.

Then Sebastian turned in his first movie, an absurdist zany farce shot in one room and in which he played all the roles and murdered all the characters in very gruesome ways. The boundless energy of this work excited me.

One afternoon, late that fall, he came to see me, looking upset. His father had had a heart attack, and Sebastian was going home to New Hampshire to see him in the hospital. I had already approved his proposal for his final project that semester, an adaptation of Kafka's *The Hunger Artist*. I reassured him that even if he had to be absent for a couple of weeks, it would not affect his final grade.

"Oh, that's nice," he said, lowering his head. "But, you know, I'm upset about going home because I'm gay."

"Have you come out to them?" I asked.

"Are you kidding?" His eyes filled with rage. "My parents would shit cookies if they knew."

"You never know," I said. "Parents can be very forgiving when it comes to their children."

"Not my parents," he snorted. Sebastian then told me his story. "When I was in my teens I took one of those IQ tests and it said I was a mathematical genius or something. That's how I ended up at MIT, at fifteen, with a full scholarship. You know, I was just kind of a loner. All I wanted was to make my parents happy. So I studied hard, and made straight A's, but I hated that shit and those people. My classmates and my teachers were as . . . " he paused, and there was anger and sadness in his voice. "They were as abstract and dry as those numbers and theories they pumped in my head. One day I thought, if I stay here, I'm going to be a basket case before I graduate. I had always wanted to make horror films. Movies are the only thing I care about. That's when I announced to my parents my decision to quit MIT and to come to New York to pursue my studies in film directing."

His parents, as Sebastian put it, "freaked." They were blue-collar people who had pinned all their hopes on him and his brother, an engineer. There was a terrible row. Sebastian went to a friend's house, where he got drunk. That night, driving back home, he lost control of his car and crashed it against a tree. For forty-five days he was in a coma. When he came out of it, nothing could shake his decision to study filmmaking. He received a partial scholarship at the school where I teach, and he supported himself by doing catering jobs and working as an extra in movies. He told me about how brutal his father was to the entire family; about the man's bitterness. So, going back home to see him in the hospital was hard. Sebastian wasn't sure he should go, but, he wanted to be there in case his father died.

When Sebastian didn't return to school in two weeks, I called his number in the city but got a machine. I left messages on a couple of occasions but got no reply. Next I called his parents. His mother informed me that his father was out of danger and that Sebastian had returned to New York. At the end of the semester I gave him an "incomplete."

In the summer I started a documentary of street life in New York. I spent a great deal of my time in the streets with my video camera, shooting whatever struck me as odd or representative of street life. In the fall, Sebastian did not show up and I thought about him less and less.

One gray, drizzly afternoon in November I had just finished shooting in the neighborhood of Washington Square Park. In the gathering darkness, the park was bustling with people getting out of work, students going to evening classes, and the new batch of junkies, who came out only after sunset.

I had shot footage of so many homeless people in the last few months that I wouldn't have paused to notice this man if it weren't for the fact that it was beginning to sprinkle harder and he was on his knees, with a cardboard sign that said HELP ME, I AM HUNGRY around his neck, his hands in prayer position, and his face—eyes shut—pointed toward the inhospitable sky. He was bearded, with long, ash-blond hair, and as emaciated and broken as one of Gauguin's Christs. I stopped to get my camera ready, and, as I moved closer, I saw that the man looked familiar—it was Sebastian.

I wouldn't call myself a very compassionate guy. I mean, I give money to beggars once in a while, depending on my mood, especially if they do not look like crackheads. But I'm not like some of my friends who work in soup kitchens or, in the winter, take sandwiches and blankets to the people sleeping in dark alleys or train stations.

Yet I couldn't ignore Sebastian, and not because he had been one of my students and I was fond of him, but because I was so sure of his talent.

I stood there, waiting for Sebastian to open his eyes. I was getting drenched, and it looked like he was lost in his thoughts, so I said, "Sebastian, it's me, Santiago, your film teacher."

He smiled, though now his teeth were brown and cracked. His eyes lit up, too—not with recognition but with the nirvana of dementia.

I took his grimy hand in both of mine and pressed it warmly even though I was repelled by his filth. At that moment I became aware of the cold rain, the passersby, the hubbub of the city traffic, the throng of New York City dusk on fall evenings, when New Yorkers rush around in excitement, on their way to places, to bright futures and unreasonable hopes, to their loved ones and home. I locked my hands around his, as if to save him, as if to save myself from the thunderbolt of pain that had lodged in my chest.

"Hi, prof," Sebastian said finally.

"You have to get out of this rain or you'll get sick," I said, yanking at his hand, coaxing him to get off the sidewalk.

"OK, OK," he acquiesced apologetically as he got up.

Sebastian stood with shoulders hunched, his head leaning to one side, looking downward. There was a strange, utterly disconnected smile on his lips—the insane, stifled giggle of a child who's been caught doing something naughty; a boy who feels both sorry about and amused at his antics. The smile of someone who has a sense of humor, but doesn't believe he has a right to smile. Sebastian had become passive, broken, and frightened like a battered dog. Fear darted in his eyes.

"Would you like to come to my place for a cup of coffee?" I said.

"Thanks," he said, avoiding my eyes.

Gently, so as not to scare him, I removed the cardboard sign from around his neck. I hailed a cab. On my way home we were silent. I rolled down the window because Sebastian's stench was unbearable. A part of me wished I had given him a few bucks and gone on with my business.

Inside the apartment, I said, "You'd better get out of those wet clothes before you catch pneumonia." I asked him to undress in my bedroom, gave him a bathrobe, and told him to take a shower. He left his dirty clothes on the floor, and, while he was showering, I went through the pockets of his clothes, looking for a clue to his current condition.

There were a few coins in his pockets, some keys, and a glass pipe, the kind crackheads use to smoke in doorways. The pipe felt more repugnant than a rotting rodent in my hand; it was like an evil entity that threatened to destroy everything living and healthy. I dropped it on the bed and went to the kitchen, where I washed my hands with detergent and scalding water. I was aware that I was behaving irrationally, but I couldn't control myself. I returned to my bedroom, where I piled up his filthy rags, made a bundle, put them in a trash bag, and dumped them in the garbage.

Sebastian and I were almost the same height, although he was so wasted that he'd swim in my clothes. But at least he'd look clean, I thought, as I pulled out of my closet thermal underwear, socks, a pair of jeans, a flannel shirt, and an olive army jacket I hadn't worn in years. I wanted to get rid of his torn, smelly sneakers, but his shoe size was larger than mine. I laid out all these clothes on the bed and went to the kitchen to make coffee and sandwiches. When I finished, I collapsed on the living-room couch and turned on the TV.

Sebastian remained in my bedroom for a long time. Beginning to worry, I opened the door. He was sitting on my bed, wearing the clean clothes, and staring at his image in the full-length mirror of the closet. His beard and hair were still wet and unkempt, but he looked presentable.

"Nice shirt," he whispered, patting the flannel at his shoulder.

"It looks good on you," I said. Now that he was clean and dressed in clean clothes, with his blond hair and green eyes, he was a good-looking boy.

We sat around the table. Sebastian grabbed a sandwich and started eating slowly, taking small bites and chewing with difficulty, as if his gums hurt. I wanted to confront him about the crack, but I didn't know how to do it without alienating him. Sebastian ate, holding the sandwich close to his nose, staring at his lap all the time. He ate parsimoniously and he drank his coffee in little sips, making strange slurping noises, such as I imagined a thirsty animal would make.

When he finished eating, our eyes met. He stood up. "Thanks. I'm going, OK?"

"Where are you going?" I asked, getting frantic. "It's raining. Do your parents know how to reach you?"

"My parents don't care," he said without animosity.

"Sebastian, I'm sure they care. You're their child and they love you." I saw he was becoming upset, so I decided not to press the point. "You can sleep here tonight. The couch is very comfortable."

Staring at his sneakers, he shook his head. "That's cool. Thanks, anyway. I'll see you around." He took a couple of steps toward the door.

"Wait," I said and rushed to the bedroom for the jacket. I gave it to him, and an umbrella, too.

Sebastian placed the rest of his sandwich in a side pocket and put on the jacket. He grabbed the umbrella at both ends and studied it, as if he had forgotten what it was used for.

I scribbled both my home and office numbers on a piece of paper. "You can call me anytime you need me," I said, also handing him a $10 bill, which I gave him with some apprehension because I was almost sure he'd use it to buy crack. Sebastian took the number but returned the money.

"It's yours," I said. "Please take it."

"It's too much," he said, surprising me. "Just give me enough for coffee."

I fished for a bunch of coins in my pocket and gave them to him.

Hunching his shoulders and giving me his weird smile, Sebastian accepted them. Suddenly I knew what the smile reminded me of: it was Charlie Chaplin's smile as the tramp in *City Lights*. Sebastian opened the door and took the stairs instead of waiting for the elevator.

The following day, I went back to the corner where I had found him the day before, but Sebastian wasn't around. I started filming in that neighborhood exclusively. I became obsessed with finding

Sebastian again. I had dreams in which I'd see him with dozens of other junkies tweaking in the murky alleys of New York. Sometimes I'd spot a young man begging who, from the distance, would look like Sebastian. This, I know, is what happens to people when their loved ones die.

That Christmas, I took to the streets again, ostensibly to shoot more footage, but secretly hoping to find Sebastian. It was around that time that the homeless stopped being for me anonymous human roaches of the urban squalor. Now they were people with features, with faces, with stories, with loved ones desperately looking for them, trying to save them. No longer moral lepers to be shunned, the young among them especially fascinated me. I wondered how many of them were intelligent, gifted, even geniuses who, because of crack or other drugs, or rejection, or hurt, or lack of love, had taken to the streets, choosing to drop out in the worst way.

The documentary and my search for Sebastian became one. This search took me to places I had never been before. I started to ride the subway late at night, filming the homeless who slept in the cars, seeking warmth, traveling all night long. Most of them were black, and many were young, and a great number of them seemed insane. I became adept at distinguishing the different shades of street people. The ones around Forty-second Street looked vicious, murderous, possessed by the virulent devils of the drugs. The ones who slept on the subways—or at Port Authority, Grand Central, and Penn Station—were poorer, did not deal in drugs or prostitution. Many of them were cripples, or retarded, and their eyes didn't flash the message KILLKILLKILLKILL. I began to hang out outside the city shelters where they passed the nights. I looked for Sebastian in those places, in the parks, along the waterfronts of Manhattan, under the bridges, anywhere these people congregate. Sebastian's smile—the smile he had given me as he left my apartment—hurt me like an ice pick slamming at my heart.

One Saturday afternoon late in April I was on my way to see Blake, a guy I had met recently in a soup kitchen where I had started doing volunteer work. Since I was half an hour early and the evening was pleasant, the air warm and inviting, I went into Union Square Park to admire the flowers.

I was sitting on a bench facing east when Sebastian passed by me and sat on the next bench. Although it was too warm for it, he was still wearing the jacket I had given him in the winter. He was carrying a knapsack, and in one hand he held what looked like a can of beer wrapped in a paper bag. He kept his free hand on the knapsack as if to guard it from thieves; and with the other hand, he took sips from his beer, all the while staring at his rotting sneakers.

Seeing him wearing that jacket was very strange. It was as though he were wearing a part of me, as if he had borrowed one of my limbs. I debated whether to approach him, or just to get up and walk away. For the last couple of months—actually since I had met Blake—my obsession with finding Sebastian had lifted. I got up. My heart began to beat so fast I was sure people could hear it. I breathed in deeply; I looked straight ahead at the tender new leaves dressing the trees, the beautifully arranged and colorful beds of flowers, the denuded sky, which wore a coat of enameled topaz, streaked with pink, and breathed in the air, which was unusually light, and then I walked up to where Sebastian sat.

Anxiously, I said, "Sebastian, how are you?" Without surprise, he looked up. I was relieved to see the mad grin was gone.

"Hi," he greeted me.

I sat next to him. His jacket was badly soiled, and a pungent, putrid smell emanated from him. His face was bruised, his lips chapped and inflamed, but he didn't seem withdrawn.

"Are you getting enough to eat? Do you have a place to sleep?" I asked.

"How're you doing?" he said evasively.

"I'm OK. I've been worried about you. I looked for you all winter." My voice trailed off; I was beginning to feel agitated.

"Thanks. But believe me, this is all I can handle right now," he said carefully, with frightening lucidity. "I'm not crazy. I know where to go for help if I want it. I want you to understand that I'm homeless because I chose to be homeless; I choose not to integrate," he said with vehemence. Forcefully, with seriousness, he added, "This is where I feel OK for now."

The lights of the buildings had begun to go on, like fireflies on the darkening sky. A chill ran through me. I reached in my pocket for a few bills and pressed them in his swollen, raw hands.

"I'm listed in the book. If you ever need me, call me, OK? I'll always be happy to hear from you."

"Thanks. I appreciate it."

I placed a hand on his shoulder and squeezed hard. I got up, turned around, and loped out of Union Square.

Several months went by. I won't say I forgot about Sebastian completely in the interval, but life intervened. I finished my documentary that summer. In the fall, it was shown by some public television stations to generally good reviews but low ratings.

One night, a month ago, I decided to go see a movie everybody was talking about. Because it was rather late, the theater was almost empty. A couple of young people on a date sat in the row in front of me, and there were other patrons scattered throughout the big house.

The movie, set in Brooklyn, was gloomy and arty, but the performers and the cinematography held my interest and I didn't feel like going back home yet, so I stayed. Toward the end of the movie there is a scene in which the main character barges into a bar, riding his motorcycle. Except for the bartender and a sailor sitting at the counter, the bar is empty. The camera pans slowly from left to right, and there, wearing a sailor suit, is Sebastian. He slowly turns around and stares into the camera and consequently into the audience. The moment lasts two, maybe three seconds, and I was so surprised, I gasped. Seeing Sebastian unexpectedly rattled me so much I had trouble remaining in my seat until the movie ended.

I called Sebastian's parents early the next morning. This time, his mother answered. I introduced myself, and, to my surprise, she remembered me. I told her about what had happened the night before and how it made me realize I hadn't seen or heard from their son in quite some time.

"Actually, I'm very glad you called," she said softly, in a voice that was girlish but vibrant with emotions. "Sebastian passed away six weeks ago. We have one of his movie tapes that I thought of sending you since your encouragement meant so much to him."

Then she told me the details of Sebastian's death: he had been found on a bench in Central Park and had apparently died of pneumonia and acute anemia. Fortunately, he still carried some ID with him, so the police were able to track down his parents. In his knapsack, they had found a movie tape labeled *The Hunger Artist*.

I asked her if she had seen it.

"I tried to, but it was too painful," she sighed.

"I'd be honored to receive it; I assure you I'll always treasure it," I said.

We chatted for a short while and then, after I gave her my address, we said good-bye. A few days later, on my way to school, I found the tape in my mailbox. I carried it with me all day long, and decided to wait until I got home that night to watch it.

After dinner, I sat down to watch Sebastian's last film. On a piece of cardboard, scrawled in a childish, Gothic calligraphy and in big characters, appeared THE HUNGER ARTIST, BY SEBASTIAN X. INSPIRED BY THE STORY OF MR. FRANZ KAFKA.

The film opened with an extreme closeup of Sebastian. I realized he must have started shooting when he was still in school because he looked healthy, his complexion was good, and his eyes were limpid. Millimetrically, the camera studies his features: the right eye, the left one; pursed lips, followed by a wide-open smile that flashes two rows of teeth in good condition. Next we see Sebastian's ears, and, finally, in a characteristic Sebastian touch, the camera looks into his nostrils. One of the nostrils is full of snot. I stopped the film. I was shaking. I have films and tapes of relatives and friends who are dead, and when I look at them, I experience a deep ocean of bittersweetness. After they've been dead for a while, the feelings we have are stirring but resolved; there's no torment in them. However, seeing Sebastian's face on the screen staring at me, I experienced the feeling I've always had for old actors I love, passionately, even though they died before I was born. It was, for example, like the perfection of the love I'd felt for Leslie Howard in *Pygmalion*, although I didn't see that movie until I was grown up. I could not deny anymore that I had been in love with Sebastian;

that I had stiffled my passion for him because I knew I could never fulfill it. That's why I had denied the nature of my concern for him. I pressed the play button, and the film continued. Anything was better than what I was feeling.

Now the camera pulls back, and we see him sitting in a lotus position, wearing shorts. On the wall behind him, there is a sign that reads, THE ARTIST HAS GONE TWO HOURS WITHOUT EATING. WORLD RECORD! There is a cut to the audience. A woman with long green hair, lots of mascara, and purple eye shadow, her lips painted in a grotesque way, chews gum, blows it like a baseball player, and sips a diet Coke. She nods approvingly all the time. The camera cuts to Sebastian staring at her impassively. Repeating this pattern, we see a man in a three-piece suit—an executive type watching the artist and taking notes. He's followed by a buxom blonde bedecked with huge costume jewelry; she is pecking at a large box of popcorn dripping with butter, and drinking a beer. She wears white silk gloves. We see at least half a dozen people, each one individually—Sebastian plays them all. This sequence ends with hands clapping. As the spectators exit the room, they leave money in a dirty ashtray. The gloved hand leaves a card that says, IF YOU EVER GET REALLY HUNGRY, CALL ME! This part of the film, shot in garish, neon colors, has, however, the feel of an early film; it is silent.

The camera cuts to the face of Peter Jennings, who is doing the evening news. We cannot hear what he says. Cut again to Sebastian in a lotus position. Cut to the headline: ARTIST BREAKS HUNGER RECORD: 24 HOURS WITHOUT EATING.

The next time we see the fasting artist, he's in the streets and the photography is in black and white. For soundtrack we hear sirens blaring, fire trucks screeching, buses idling, huge trucks braking, cars speeding, honking and crashing, cranes demolishing gigantic structures. This part of the film must have been shot when Sebastian was already homeless. He must have carried his camera in his knapsack, or he must have rented one, but it's clear that whatever money he collected pandering, he used to complete the film. In this portion he uses a hand-held camera to stress the documentary feeling. I can only imagine that he used street people to operate the camera for him. Sebastian's deterioration speeds up: his clothes become more soiled and tattered; his disguises at this point are less convincing—it must be nearly impossible for a starving person to impersonate someone else. His cheeks are sunken, his pupils shine like the eyes of a feral animal in the dark. The headlines read: 54 DAYS WITHOUT EATING . . . 102 DAYS . . . 111 DAYS. Instead of clapping hands, we see a single hand in motion; it makes a gesture as if it were shooing the artist away.

Sebastian disappears from the film. We have footage of people in soup lines and the homeless scavenging in garbage cans. An interview with a homeless person ends the film. We don't see the face of the person conducting the interview, but the voice is Sebastian's. He reads passages from Kafka's story to a homeless woman and asks her to comment. She replies with a soundless laughter that exposes her diseased gums.

I pressed the rewind button and sat in my chair in a stupor. I felt shattered by the realization that what I don't know about what lies in my own heart is much greater than anything else I do know about it. I was so stunned and drained that I hardly had the energy to get up and walk to the VCR to remove the tape.

Later that night, still upset, I decided to go for a walk. It was one of those cold, blustery nights of late autumn, but its gloominess suited my mood. A glacial wind howled, skittering up and down the deserted streets of Gotham. I trudged around until the tip of my nose was an icicle. As I kept walking in a southerly direction, getting closer and closer to the southernmost point of the island, I was aware of the late hour and of how the "normal" citizens of New York were, for the most part, at home, warmed by their fires, seeking escape in a book or their TV sets, or finding solace in the arms of their loved one, or in the caresses of strangers.

I kept walking on and on, passing along the way the homeless who on a night like this chose to stay outside or couldn't find room in a shelter. As I passed them in the dark streets, I did so without my usual fear or repugnance. I kept pressing forward, into the narrowing alleys, going toward the phantasmagorical lament of the artic wind sweeping over the Hudson, powerless over the mammoth steel structures of this city.

4

Twilight at the Equator

❦

Midway this way of life we're bound upon,
I woke to find myself in a dark wood,
where the right road was wholly lost and gone.

DANTE, *The Divine Comedy: Hell*

My sister Rosita was dead. She had swallowed scores of Valiums and slashed her wrists. Her body had been found by her landlady in the room Rosita rented in Jackson Heights. The news of her death came at the end of the harshest winter in memory. I felt bad for Mother, who had died four years before, not knowing what had happened to Rosita. Now that Rosita was dead, I felt as if there were no more links to my Colombian past.

The day after the police called, I went by the morgue to identify Rosita's bloodless, gypsum, frozen corpse. In the nine years I hadn't seen her, she had aged considerably—ravaged by drugs. But in death her face looked peaceful, pain free; there was even etched on her lips the slightest suggestion of a smile as if, at the moment she died, Rosita had glimpsed a world that was friendlier and less tormented than the one she had lived in.

It didn't come as a surprise when Lieutenant O'Connor of the State Police Bureau of Criminal Investigations informed me that Rosita, under the alias of Silvia, had been working for years as a prostitute in Jackson Heights.

Lieutenant O'Connor gave me the key to Rosita's room in the boardinghouse where she had died, and a note to her landlady authorizing me, as next of kin, to collect Rosita's belongings. I made my way to the house on Eightieth Street and Northern Boulevard where she had lived. I rang the bell, introduced myself to the land-lady, and showed her the police letter. The old lady gave me a sor-rowful look, and crossed herself when I mentioned Rosita's name. She showed me the way to the attic Rosita had rented. The room had that pungent smell of dried blood. As I drew the curtains to dispel the darkness, the late afternoon light poured in and the first thing I saw was a huge brown spot on the beige carpet—the stain left by Rosita's spilled blood. I told the landlady I wanted to be alone for a few minutes, and closed the door behind her. I sat down on Rosita's bed, buried my head in her pillow, and wept bitterly, opening the gates to the pain that had accumulated for so long.

Eventually, I sat up on the bed again, dried my eyes, and in-spected the small room longingly, imagining Rosita there: sitting on her chair watching television, or sitting in front of her dressing table, getting ready to go out. Overwhelmed with sadness, I de-cided to get out of there as soon as possible. I started looking for whatever possessions of Rosita I wanted to keep as mementos. I was surprised that she had copies of all my books, in English and Spanish; I also found an album of family photos, many of them going back to when we had been children in Colombia, and to the first years of our immigration to this country; photos of her wed-ding, and then no more photos, as if in the last twenty years she had found nothing worth preserving. I gathered the few posses-sions of hers I wanted, put the photo album in my backpack, and took one last look at the room where Rosita had died.

When the landlady saw me reach the ground floor, she ap-proached me.

"Can I offer you a cup of coffee?" she asked, in typical Colom-bian fashion.

I realized that this woman was the only link I had to the years when Rosita had been absent from my life, so I accepted her invita-tion. The old woman took me to her kitchen, in the back of the house.

"My name is Mercedes," she said, as she poured me a cup of cof-fee and sat down across from me. "Silvia lived here for the last year of her life. She was such a pretty girl, but she was always sad, and I know she suffered. I knew she had a drug problem, but I didn't want to kick her out because she was very quiet and, when she wasn't you know . . . twisted, she was so sweet."

"Her name was not Silvia, her name was Rosita," I corrected her.

"Ah," the woman said, tilting back her head and closing her eyes. She must have been in her late seventies, and she was short, rubicund, like a whore in a Botero painting. From her accent and her light-colored rosy skin, I could tell she was from the interior of Colombia. She kept her black hair tied in a bun atop her head, and she wore a simple black dress, as if she were in mourning. "I knew she wasn't telling me the truth about many things. I knew where she worked, but that's OK with me. All the girls who live in this house do that kind of work."

I took a sip of the strong, hot coffee. "Did you talk to Rosita sometimes?" I asked, hoping she would continue talking about her. After all, whatever this woman told me was all I had.

"I'm like a mother to all my girls," *Doña* Mercedes said. "I don't have any children myself. I came to this country alone, almost forty years ago, when Colombians didn't come here. I was a pioneer. Coming to this country was the only good thing I ever did in my life. I saved to buy this big house, as an investment, thinking one day I would sell it and move to Colombia to live with my family. They're all dead; I guess I will die here now. That's why I take good care of my girls. Silvia . . . will you excuse me if I call her Silvia?"

I nodded.

"Silvia would often come down to the kitchen for a cup of coffee. Sometimes I would offer her a meal, whatever I had made for the day. She was so skinny, you know. Once in a while I would place a plate of hot *ajiaco* outside her door. But all she wanted was to drink coffee and smoke cigarettes."

"What did she talk about?" I asked. "Did she ever mention her family?"

"No, she told me she had no family; that she was alone in the world, like me. But I knew she suffered a lot. Sometimes I would be cleaning upstairs and I could hear her crying in her room. I knew that she did . . . you know . . . drugs, but so many of the girls do. It's the only escape they have. And if it brings them a little happiness, who am I to condemn them? But Silvia was so . . . alone. All my girls get mail from their families in Colombia, and they shop for their families and send presents to their children back home. But not Silvia. Once in a while we all get together for drinks and listen to *vallenatos*, but Silvia would never join us. Sometimes I would pass her room and hear her playing Toña la Negra, or Agustín Lara—she loved melancholy boleros, you know. She was very sweet, your sister. But she didn't hang out with any of the other girls. She was a loner. We all respected her desire to be left alone because we all knew how much she cried, and how much she suffered."

We talked for a while, about the usual things Colombians who don't know each other talk about: when and why we came to the States, and whether we'd ever return.

It was dusk when I left *Doña* Mercedes's house and headed for the subway stop on Ninetieth Street. The early spring night was crisply cool, the daffodils were out, but I couldn't enjoy anything. All those years I hadn't had news of Rosita, I had thought that once I found out what had happened to her, I would feel relief. Yet tonight, my heart was heavy, and with every step I took in this neighborhood where we had been young and new immigrants to America, the profound sorrow I felt intensified.

As the pilot's voice announced our imminent landing at Barranquilla's Ernesto Cortizos airport, I peered out the window. We were flying low above a landscape partially submerged in the chestnut-colored waters of the swamps. The vegetation—grass, weeds, and scattered trees—was a swatch of dark, moody green that contrasted with the last images I'd had of a glittering New York City skyline upon my departure at 4 A.M. This was my first trip back to Colombia in five years. The last time I had been there was with Ryan, my lover, when he was still healthy. We had traveled to Colombia to celebrate our first anniversary together. Ryan, who was from Colorado, had been enamored of all things Latin.

He wanted to go to Colombia as a way of getting to know me better. We had a wonderful time together, traveling all over the country, spending time with Aunt Caty and Uncle Alejo, my favorite relatives. During that journey I realized that I was as much Colombian as I had become Americanized. Two years later, when Ryan died of AIDS, I was glad that we had made that trip. After his death, the idea of returning to a place where I had been so happy with him became unbearable.

But when Rosita was found dead, her suicide had spawned so many questions, that, at age forty, I found my life at a crossroads and it became necessary to return once more to Colombia to try to answer the baffling questions that her suicide had raised.

As the plane taxied to a full stop in front of the main terminal, the choking tension of the last few days came back. Inside the terminal I looked ahead as we passed through the glass doors, trying to locate my aunt and uncle. Many people were bunched against the doors, but I couldn't spot my relatives. Since all I carried was a knapsack and a handbag, I headed for the immigration station to get my passport stamped so I could be legally admitted to Colombia.

Once I finished with immigration, I went beyond the glass doors. Outside, I was greeted by a swarm of aggressive men offering their services as drivers. When I heard them shout in their riotous Caribbean Spanish, I felt I was truly in Colombia. The people surrounding me were that unique mulatto color of a peeled coconut—my own color. Most of the men had the copperish complexion of tropical people who subsist on poor diets.

"No, no, *gracias*," I boomed. "No, no," I repeated, firmly pulling my bags from the anxious hands that tried to yank them away from my grip. I am tall, so I tower above most Colombians. I made my way through the throng, looking over the swarm of heads for my relatives. By the time I made it to the entrance of the airport, it became apparent that my aunt and uncle were not there.

I hopped into the first taxi waiting in line, and gave the driver my family's address. Since taxis don't have meters in Barranquilla, I settled on a fare with the driver as the taxi drove down the boulevard—overgrown with tall weeds and littered with garbage—that connects the airport to the highway leading to the city. Removing my jacket, I leaned back on the seat. The highway to the city cuts through an industrial zone of ugly, impersonal-looking factories, a working-class amusement park, and shanty towns where people dwell in wooden houses painted in brilliant colors.

It was 7:30, when life in the tropics is at its most hectic and energetic, before the punishing heat of noon arrives and a slumberous torpor permeates everything until late afternoon, when the sun buries itself in the Caribbean.

I was distracted by the highway's traffic: mule-drawn carts heaped with bananas, plantains, yucca, and pineapples going to the market; miniature buses crammed with people going to work and hustle in the city; and uniformed boys and girls on their way to school, armed with their textbooks—the girls carrying red and yellow parasols to protect themselves from the sun. Ahead of us, a few yards from the road, lay a dead horse. A swarm of vultures was tearing apart its bloated stomach, ripping out ribbons of black intestines and whipping them in the air where they were attacked by tornadoes of crazed plum flies. I covered my nose, but already the stench of rotten flesh had entered the taxi. The contents of my stomach rose to my clenched teeth. I noticed the driver didn't flinch as we passed the putrid remains. I had forgotten that in the Colombian tropics horses, burros, mules, and other domestic animals (and more recently thousands of people) wasted in the open until the beasts that fed on carrion reduced them to a clump of chalk-white bones.

As we entered the city, I saw a huge billboard on the side of the road that read:

**FORBIDDEN TO DUMP
CORPSES HERE
5000 PESOS FINE**

"Oh my God," I murmured, holding the breath in my throat. Now I felt I had finally arrived, as if I had never been away. It took me a while to get my bearings, and when I had recovered we were passing through a working-class neighborhood of modest homes. Tropical style, the front doors of most of the houses were open; terraced cantinas at the corners blared salsa, merengue, reggae, and occasionally an American pop tune.

We crossed through the old downtown and entered the residential areas. I felt as if I were in a highly textured dream that contained smells, colors, sound effects, and, more disturbing, the bittersweet tugging of memory. It was uncanny how my mind was beginning to remember all kinds of things.

As Barranquilla metastasizes toward the ocean, it becomes more prosperous, its streets cleaner, the villas sprawling and graceful. Almond trees, *matarratones*, acacias, jacarandas, breadfruit and rubber trees, and purple, white, and orange bougainvillea bloom, rewarding the eyes of the traveler.

The taxi stopped in front of the gates of the apartment complex where my relatives live. I paid the driver and walked to the glass door of the security check where I introduced myself to the guard. I was let in. Six identical eight-story buildings spread out on the grounds of a well-kept park with playgrounds for children, lush gardens, and shady trees. My relatives had lived here for many years.

As I reached the front door of their building, I heard excited voices calling, "Sammy, Sammy." My family (as is customary on the Atlantic coast of Colombia), Americanized my first name. I looked up, all the way to the top floor of the building, and made out my uncle and aunt leaning over the balcony waving at me.

I walked into the small elevator, barely high enough for me to stand in upright, and so narrow that, with my two bags, there was no room for another passenger. I pressed the top-floor button.

My uncle and aunt stood at the top of the steps leading from the elevator to their apartment. I climbed the steps two at a time and, dropping my bags, embraced them.

"The car didn't start this morning as we were about to leave the house," Uncle Alejo said. "We couldn't call the airport, so we decided to wait for you here."

"Welcome to underdevelopment," Aunt Caty quipped, taking my arm as we all stepped into the apartment. "There was a storm last night and the phone lines are down. They should be repaired soon. Arritoquieta, Arritoquieta," she called out loudly.

A shy young woman appeared at the kitchen door.

"Take *Don* Sammy's bags and put them in his room," my aunt ordered her.

We went into the library, a small cool room with a low ceiling. I sat on a rocking chair by the window. In the distance, to the east, I saw the lead-colored flow of the Magdalena River and farther down *Bocas de Cenizas*, the point where the river blends into the Caribbean.

"How about a *tinto*?" my aunt asked.

A cup of coffee sounded like a good idea, so I nodded. I noted she had gained weight and looked older than the last time I'd seen her. She was now a mature woman, but her face and body retained many vestiges of her former beauty.

"Make it two," my uncle said.

When we were left alone, I studied him. He was my mother's brother, and I recognized in his face my lips, my nose, my eyes. My uncle was over sixty but still kept his boyish figure. He wore a *guayabera*, khaki cotton pants, and loafers. His hair showed no traces of white.

"I've prepared a folder for you," he said getting up and walking to his desk where he started rummaging through piles of papers. There were lots of new books on the shelves, and the library was equipped with modern technology. But the posters of Marilyn Monroe, draped in ermine and diamonds, and Jimmy Dean, sulking and leaning against a tree, still had the places of honor and looked like shrines in the sense that everything else was arranged around them. High piles of newspapers and magazines were stacked in all four corners of the room.

I heard in the kitchen the excited barking of John Wayne, my relatives' dog. My uncle rummaged through dozens of folders without finding what he was looking for.

"Caty, Caty, where's the folder I prepared for Sammy?" he began to scream. "Damn it," he cursed. "Everything is forever getting lost in this house. Caty!"

My aunt entered the room with the coffee service and was followed by John Wayne who, although no larger than my shoe, charged me, barking like a machine gun. He braked inches away from my ankle, baring his spiked, miniature fangs. His black eyes bulged as he yammered hysterically.

I found it amusing that my socialist relatives had named their beloved pet after one of the most reactionary capitalist stars; they despised John Wayne's politics, but they loved his heroic cowboy persona.

"Alejo, *mi amor*, you're going to kill me," Aunt Caty said, handing me the cup of coffee and giving me a look of complicity that said, "Your uncle will never grow up." With mock exasperation, she exclaimed, "It's right here, where I left it for you." She pointed to a folder on top of a pile of magazines next to the desk. "Remember I said I was leaving it on top so it wouldn't get lost? Alejo, Alejo."

After my long exile, I had become unfamiliar with Caribbean peoples' hyperbolic banter, and how *costeños* carry on as frantic Italian vaudeville actors who have momentarily lost the script.

Uncle Alejo dropped the bulky envelope on my lap. "I want you to read it and we'll discuss it later. I've been saving those newspaper articles for you."

I set the coffee cup on the window sill. Inside the folder I found newspaper clippings with gory headlines and gruesome photographs of bloody, mangled corpses. Like the rest of the world, I was familiar with many of these incidents. Although I no longer felt like a participant, I kept very much abreast of current events in Colombia.

My uncle said, "I don't know how much the American press prints about what's really going on here."

The phone rang in the living room.

"The phone is working again," remarked Aunt Caty. Then they both exchanged apprehensive looks. "We are convinced the line is tapped, so be careful about what you say on the phone," my aunt added for my enlightenment.

Arritoquieta appeared at the door of the library. "It's for *Don* Alejo, from the university."

"Now what," uttered my uncle getting up to answer the phone.

As soon as he was out of sight, my aunt leaned over to me and whispered, "I can't wait until December when he retires; you don't know what hell it is to be married to a politician. For thirty years, I've waited patiently until he could become my husband."

"*Carajo*, that's outrageous," my uncle said in the living room. "The gall of that man. OK, I'll be there. *Ciao*."

"Guess what, Caty?" said my uncle as he burst into the library and began explaining some incomprehensible byzantine academic imbroglio. "There is going to be another strike. I have to go there to see what I can do."

"So what's new," said my aunt. "Why don't you let somebody else take care of it for a change? Why does it always have to be you who solves all the problems? Even Superman must take a break once in a while." She made no effort to conceal her exasperation.

"Do you think I enjoy doing this? I'd rather stay here and chat with Sammy. But someone has to go there to try and keep the tempers from flaring. Otherwise, who knows what might happen? The police will be called, and then it could turn really ugly. I'll be back for lunch," he said to me. "Read the materials in the folder, will you? It's very important."

My aunt stood up and sidled up to him. She smoothed the back collar of his shirt, and checked in his front pocket to make sure he had his reading glasses and pens. "You've passed the inspection, you crazy professor," she sighed. "You can go."

"I hope the damn car won't give me any trouble starting," I heard Uncle Alejo mutter to himself as he left the apartment.

My aunt picked up John Wayne, who was lying at her feet, and placed him on her lap. Making himself comfortable, he closed his big, shiny liquid eyes.

I was twelve years old when Aunt Caty entered our family by marrying Uncle Alejo. I was drawn to her because she was an avid reader of literature and a rabid moviegoer. She shared my uncle's politics, but she loved the arts. When he received a scholarship to go to the Soviet Union to study international law, she remained behind in Barranquilla, working as a secretary in a government office and attending law school at night. Almost every Saturday, I went to have lunch with her at their apartment in Las Acacias. She introduced me to the films of Godard, Fellini, Visconti, Antonioni, but she was also crazy about the American cinema. The great stars of the 1950s were her gods. She took charge of my intellectual education, and I became a willing pupil. She tried to do the same for Rosita, but Rosita wasn't interested in books or European films. Aunt Caty gave me the early novels of García Márquez, and the works of the French existentialists, and of sensualists such as Henry Miller, Nabokov, Lawrence Durrell. With her encouragement, I started writing poems and short stories and even a play. She'd revise everything I wrote and we'd send the pieces off for publication to the Bogotá newspapers. All the years I'd lived in the States we had kept in touch.

My aunt was also the only member of my family with whom I could talk about my homosexuality. With the others, including Uncle Alejo, it was an unspoken subject. Although as long as I could remember she had been a socialist, she was also a devout Catholic. It was these contradictions in my uncle and my aunt that fascinated me. They had dedicated most of their lives to "educating" the Colombian masses. Just a few years back, they had been put on a death list by a paramilitary group, but they had refused to go into exile. I wondered how the collapse of communism in Europe had affected their lives.

John Wayne had gone to sleep on Aunt Caty's lap, occasionally bestirring himself from his dreams with a yelp. "Oh don't worry, my darling," she said, baby-talking to the dog. "I'm here to protect you." Then looking at me, she added, "He's my biggest joy, Sammy. Without him, I'd be lonely a lot of the time."

I knew how hard it was for her not to have had children, and to have a husband who belonged to a cause and was always on the go. "I see Uncle Alejo's still as involved in politics as he ever was," I said.

A look of disappointment came over my aunt's face. "The dissolution of the Soviet Union has been hard for him," she said. "And I'll be the first one to admit that the Cuban revolution has lost all prestige in Latin America. The Party" (she meant the Communist Party) "has become stagnant in Colombia. But we continue to believe in our ideals, and we'll die socialists. Do you think the people of those new countries in Eastern Europe are better off than they were before?"

"They're free," I said. "They hungered for freedom."

"Ah, freedom," Aunt Caty sallied back. "The people in Colombia are very free . . . much too free . . . free to die of malnutrition, free to live oppressed lives without hope. As you know, we went to Cuba when there was a death threat over our heads. We wanted to see if we could settle there. But your uncle and I ended up admitting to ourselves that we'd rather risk death here than live there. Yet we continue to believe in socialism. We believe that it is the only social system that cares about the oppressed. Sammy, communism isn't dead; at least not in Latin America. Look at Peru: they may destroy the Shining Path, but as long as the desperate conditions prevail, another movement like the Shining Path will emerge. There is very little Marxism-Leninism left anywhere in the world. Let's face it, it just didn't work in practice. What people forget is that it is a new philosophy, barely a century old. I pity those poor countries in Eastern Europe now entering the savagery of the capitalist system. I can't imagine that the architects of their dismantling really care for their social conditions. They certainly didn't care for the poor in England or the United States. Just as it has been proven that there can't be socialism without democracy, democracy without socialism won't survive either." Aunt Caty paused and stroked John Wayne's muzzle wistfully. She stared out the window, as if she were reading the future. "Here in Colombia conditions just continue to deteriorate," she said after a while. "The poor are poorer all the time; the narcos control the bulk of the national wealth; and new guerrilla groups—that are nothing but gangs of *bandoleros*—proliferate. We still live in an unjust society, so your uncle and I have our work cut out for the rest of our lives."

After a while, the conversation shifted to other subjects. We chatted about different relatives, and finally about the death of my grandfather, who had died a year before, and of Rosita's suicide. From the States, I had spared my aunt the details, but now I gave her a full account. I told her that Rosita had slashed her wrists, and that her body had been found in a boardinghouse for Colombian prostitutes. I told her that in the last years of her life, Rosita had been working as a prostitute on Roosevelt Avenue in Queens. I added that, according to the police, Rosita had been a heroin addict all those years.

"I'm glad that Sofia died without seeing that," Aunt Caty said, referring to my mother. "I thank God for sparing her that final blow."

"Well, she was very unhappy to die not knowing what had happened to Rosita."

"There was something very haunted about Rosita. It must have been so hard for you to discover what she became. I know how much you loved her." She paused, I could see her vacillating, debating whether to continue with this conversation or not. "I tried to befriend her when you were kids, but she wasn't interested in me. Perhaps there was a rivalry there; perhaps she resented me spending so much time with you and taking you away from her. But I see how difficult her death has been for you." A keening silence hung between us, Aunt Caty broke it by saying, "Barranquilla has changed so much, Sammy. There was always a potential for horror here, but it has mushroomed in the last decade. Did I tell you about the macabre events of this year's Carnival?" she asked, caressing John Wayne's head with the tip of a fingernail.

I shook my head.

"Well, for a while there had been stories in the press about how the men who survive collecting garbage were disappearing. But you know, nobody cares about what happens to such people in this society. Anyway, Carnival Sunday one of these men shows up at the police precinct, just a couple of blocks away from here. The man was badly cut up and bleeding. His story is that he had gone by the university where Alejo teaches and that the guards had tried to kill him. The police went to the university grounds to check his story and, in the course of their investigation, they discovered ten corpses stacked up in the kitchen. Then the story came out: the guards had been killing street people to sell their corpses to the school of medicine. For each fresh corpse, they were paid the equivalent of twenty-five dollars." Aunt Caty paused and then added, "That's what a human life is worth nowadays in this city. Twenty-five fucking dollars."

Ramón made a looping motion with his cigarette. He dragged without inhaling, and blew ringlets of smoke that the afternoon breeze wafted in the direction of the street. He was one of the most affected human beings I had ever met, and I pictured him perfectly at home in the court of Louis XIV.

I had picked up Ramón after lunch, when my relatives retired to take their siestas. He was the only friend from my adolescence with whom I still kept in touch. When I had visited Colombia with Ryan, we had spent quite a bit of time with him. Even though Ramón had his own apartment, he still went to his parents' home for lunch, and it was there that I met him. We headed for Barranquilla's shady zoo where we spent the hottest hours of the afternoon strolling under the gigantic rubber trees, meandering from exhibit to exhibit, laughing at the capuchin monkeys gnawing desperately at their tails, grooming and eating each other's ticks, pitching their still-moist turds at one another, and masturbating gleefully, shooting at the zoo visitors. We marveled at the kaleidoscopic and tuneful tropical birds and at the multiplicity of lethal vipers. All these provided us with plenty of amusement as we reminisced about the main events of our lives in the years when we hadn't seen each other.

Now we were having *frosomales* on the terrace of *El Mediterraneo*, a Greek ice-cream parlor that is a traditional focal point of Barranquilla's social life.

"Yes, Santiago, all signs of contumacy are being systematically squeezed out," Ramón shuddered, opening wide his tawny eyes. "One runs into death every time one turns a corner. For the people who are marked, it must be like living with an AIDS sentence. You made a solomonic decision to stay in gringoland; otherwise, you'd probably be pushing up daisies. Just last year, I was really afraid for Alejo's life." He paused to check out a young man in tight jeans and T-shirt crossing the street. "For myself," Ramón went on, "I gave up being a controvertist a long time ago. Yes," he seethed, frowning and wringing his hands. "I embrace the mediocrity of it all. If this place was the pits before, it's much worse now. It's rotting in a million places. This city is like an organism that didn't get vaccinated when it was born, and now it's riddled with monstrous diseases. Barranquilla is a perfect metaphor for the rest of Colombia. But I embrace the collective peristesia of the national soul. And make no apologies for it."

His pretentious choice of words, which would have sounded unbearable in an American or European, rang authentic with him—a perfect example of Caribbean rococo. I sat there, agape, grateful that his theatricality remained unchanged. What was a wonder to me was how he had managed to thrive despite the belligerent local machismo.

Like a Balanchine dancer, Ramón sprang up from his chair. "Excuse me for a sec, but I must absolutely inspect that beauty," he said, referring to the young man who stood at the opposite corner, lighting a cigarette and casting smoldering glances in our direction.

I took a spoonful of *frosomal* as Ramón and the young man made contact. For the past few years I had dreamed of this moment when Ramón and I would meet here, enjoying a *frosomal*, which is a kind of vanilla-chocolate milkshake flavored with cherry and pineapple syrup.

The sun was now in the west, descending, lifting the sluggishness of mid-afternoon. There was considerable traffic; scores of people ambled in and out of the stores, cafés, and restaurants that line Calle 72. A languorous breeze swept down the wide street, and the ungainly bushes of four-o'clocks framing the terrace metamorphosized, blooming in one breath, an explosion of scarlet petals and black eyes.

Ramón, looking in my direction, pointed at me with his pinky, as if he were trying to persuade the swarthy young stud to join us. Ramón's maneuvers brought back memories of my past as a gay youth in Barranquilla. In the ninth grade, I developed an intense crush on Pablo, one of my classmates. He was the most handsome boy I knew: gangly and muscular, with black hair and matching eyes, and the features of a young Cary Grant. All the girls were in love with him, including Rosita. Pablo was not intellectual, but he liked American movies and dancing. I liked him because when I was with him I felt enriched by his beauty—the way I would have felt, say, riding in a sports car. He was also sweet and kind. Often he stayed in my house overnight. Late at night I'd climb into bed with him and then he'd let me do with him whatever I wanted. Because I had already been sexually initiated, I sort of knew what to do. Pablo and I were inseparable. Then one day he announced that his family was moving to the United States, to Georgia. The month before he left, I tried to commit suicide by jumping from the roof of the school. I thought I was trying to kill myself because I was unhappy with school; it was many years later that it would dawn on me I had tried to kill myself because I was distraught Pablo was leaving. From Georgia, he wrote to me for a while. Then the letters stopped. Years later, I heard he had been killed in Vietnam. After Pablo left, I answered an ad for a pen pal in a magazine. The man, Adriano, was in his mid-twenties, a teacher, and he lived in Bogotá. We exchanged photos. Although the word *homosexual* was never mentioned, I was aware that we both were. I started falling in love with Adriano. I dreamt of running away to Bogotá to live with him. One day he wrote saying he was coming to Barranquilla to meet me. I panicked. How would I be able to explain this relationship to my mother? I didn't answer Adriano's letter and I never heard from him again.

I wondered if things had changed in the city since I had lived there. In my adolescence, there was only one kind of known homosexual in Barranquilla, *el marica*, the queen. The others (the vast majority) were the *cacorros*, the "straight" men who went to bed with the queens assuming exclusively the active role. What was considered homosexual was to surrender one's ass. Even then, I wanted an alternative to these clichés. Now I had returned home, afraid of sex with strangers, looking upon each new encounter as a reckless flirting with death. Although Ramón was terrified by the increasing number of AIDS deaths in the city, he still carried on with the promiscuity of the past. He felt fully protected by condoms, and refused to surrender the full expression of his sexuality.

Ramón shook his index finger at the trick, using it like a magic wand to glue the boy to the spot. Then he strutted in my direction.

"*Cariño*," he purred sitting down. "Isn't he out of Almodóvar? I have to give him a couple thousand pesos, and he'll cooperate. He's shy about meeting you. I'll give you a full report tomorrow. I feel almost guilty about leaving you here all alone, but I know that you'd do the same if you were in my heels. Anyway, I leave you in the best spot in the city for cruising. If you want company, just stay there, looking like the cosmopolitan woman you are, and before you know it someone will approach you. But wipe that Vivien Leigh look off your face. You look like she did in the last reel of *Streetcar*. We're in the tropics darling, not in New Orleans. Think Sonia Braga—that's the look that will get you boys here. Anyway, I'll come by to pick you up tomorrow night at ten o'clock American time, I promise. And I'll make it up to you then. I have a nice surprise for you." Ramón pecked me on both cheeks and sashayed down the steps, puffed up like a bird of paradise in heat.

I was too tired to cruise. I paid the check and decided to go back to the apartment. Walking north on Calle 72 I reached the corner of Avenue Olaya Herrera where I saw, on the grounds of the old soccer stadium, two trucks loaded with armed soldiers.

I went into the park across Calle 72; its grounds were as unkempt as I remembered them, but the leafy almond trees created a cool canopy. Over the years the park had become dangerous at night, so few people frequented it around dusk. In my childhood it was notorious because at night the maids who worked in the neighborhood would use it to rendezvous with their beaus. As a child, I'd come to the park to gather the ripe almonds on the ground. When I had stuffed my pockets with the yellow fruit, I'd search for a hefty stone to smash the fleshy shells and the porous wrapping underneath that hid the tender, tasty nut. Today I spotted black-coated squirrels looking for ripe fruit, digging on the thick carpet of leaves on the sand. Homeless people occupied some of the broken-down cement benches of the park, and a bunch of Boy Scouts were practicing a military drill. The children were aggressive and intent; they seemed more like ferocious midget soldiers than regular Scouts.

Arritoquieta opened the door to my relatives' apartment. She informed me that my aunt and uncle were out but that they would be home for dinner. She offered me coffee, which I declined. I went into the library. Outside, it was still light, but the room was in semi-darkness. I sat on the rocking chair by the window. I was glad to be in the apartment, where I felt safe, and not out alone in the streets. I looked out the window: the carmine sun dove in the Caribbean, creating a widespread hemorrhage in the sky. Transfixed, I watched the violent sunset bleed slowly until darkness began to set in. I became absorbed in the process of day turning into night when little squiggles began to appear over the city, darting back and forth at the speed of lightning. At first, I figured it was an optical illusion taking place in my retina, created by the hallucinating palette of the western sky. As the squiggles became more numerous, I realized that they were thousands of bats flying above the red clay roofs of the houses, the tops of the condos, the spires of the churches, the cathedral and the tallest trees. The bats were out for their nocturnal feeding. Out of nowhere, a completely forgotten incident from my childhood came back to me. I must have been five and I still couldn't read. A frenzy was created in Barranquilla by a woman who died in a doctor's office during an abortion. Momentarily losing his sanity, the doctor had hacked the woman's body into numerous pieces, stuffed them in a bag, and taken a drive all the way to the sea. Every few hundred yards or so, he dumped a chunk of the corpse in the bushes along the road. I remembered the front page photographs: one day her decomposed arm; the next, her eyeless head, maggots crawling out of all the orifices. As a child, this incident filled me with such unspeakable horror I never mentioned it to anyone. In fact, I hadn't thought about it since it happened thirty-five years ago. But as night fell from the Caribbean to the Equator, over the Amazonian jungle, above the icy peaks of the volcanoes of the Andes, all the way to Patagonia, to the bleak, glacial regions of Tierra del Fuego, this image, this memory, burst through the fortress of denial with such violence that I sat on the rocking chair in a trance, shivering, sweating a cold sweat.

I could not break the spell until some time later when the tropical sky glowed with shimmering stars the size of planets, and a moon as gigantic and luminous as the midnight sun of artic summer poised herself in the night sky, not just as a light fixture, a deity to be worshipped, but as an object of desire.

∞

The next morning, after Uncle Alejo left for the university, and Aunt Caty went out to do some errands, I decided to stay in the apartment. I wanted to be alone with the memories that had begun to surface since my arrival. I found myself mulling over Rosita's life and the years in which we had lived together.

I always referred to Rosita as "my sister," because we had grown up as brother and sister. But Rosita was *mi hermana de crianza*: she was mother's half sister, my grandfather's love child with Germania, a maid who had worked for the family. When he fathered Rosita, my grandfather was in his mid-fifties. In typical Colombian fashion, when Germania became pregnant she was fired, banned from my grandfather's household forever.

My mother, herself one of my grandfather's illegitimate children, was living in Barranquilla when she found out that Germania was working as a cook, and that Rosita lived with her. Because for my mother her family always came first, she decided to rescue Rosita from what she thought would be a life of penury, of becoming a maid like Germania, and growing up without any real choices. I was three when Rosita came to live with us. She was a baby. Father was still alive, and he adopted Rosita as his daughter. As I grew up, I understood that she was my mother's stepsister, but I could never call her "aunt," because she was younger than me. I always thought of her as my sister. Since I was an only child, we developed a strong bond as children. She was my best friend, my pal, *la reina de mi corazón*. She in turn treated me as her big brother.

Our bond deepened in our adolescence. Because I didn't get along very well with other boys my age, I ended up spending most of my time with Rosita. In school, I often got in trouble because I was more interested in reading novels than in studying. I was overweight and unathletic. One day the religion teacher had called me a marmot because I had fallen asleep during his talk. The moniker stuck, and from then on my schoolmates taunted me with it. Sometimes they'd call me at home, and ask for *marmota*. Also, because of my big ears, they called me Dumbo. Often I would get into fights, and I would come home beat-up and bleeding. Although I never discussed any of this with Rosita, I intuited that she understood and empathized with me. Rosita was already a beauty, but she too was a loner. She did not do well in school either, and she suffered from severe migraines, which sometimes kept her prostrate in bed for days at a time. Since I had asthma, I was often absent from school. Rosita was not interested in books, but we were both movie buffs. We'd spend our days cutting out the pictures of movie stars from magazines and pasting them on the walls of our rooms. We'd seize every opportunity to go see the new films that arrived in Barranquilla. We also loved the beach. On Sundays and school holidays we'd spend our days at Barranquilla's beaches, strolling, working on our tans, me reading a book, Rosita poring over magazines or daydreaming.

Rosita had a sweet disposition, but she constantly displeased Mother because she did poorly in school, because she was withdrawn, because of her chronic headaches. Mother was by then in her late forties, no longer a beauty. Her lover of many years after father died had left her for a young woman. My Uncle Carlos, who had lived with us for a few years, had married and moved away. We became poor. Every day we bought one take-out lunch from a local *fonda*—a big lunch for the three of us. As the only son, I was given most of the food; then Mother ate the rest, and whatever was left, a little soup, a piece of yucca, a bone, was for Rosita. She attended a public school, and had only one uniform to wear. When the tattered uniform was dirty, she washed it in the afternoon and dried it out with an iron overnight so she could attend school the next day. Because I was the only son, I was sent to a private school and always had good clothes.

I felt sorry for Rosita, and I especially pitied her because she never complained. It was around this time that Mother, embattled and bitter, started taking out her disappointments on Rosita.

Whenever Rosita did anything that displeased Mother, she would give her a severe beating. Rosita took these beatings without protesting. I guess she thought she'd rather get beat up than be sent back to live with Germania to become a maid. Mother would drag Rosita to the patio and beat her with the stick of the broom; often she would grab her by her hair and smash Rosita's head against the wall. The beatings would stop when I'd start screaming and throw myself between the two of them. Afterwards I'd sit with Rosita in the patio, under the mango tree, applying water compresses to her bleeding head and face.

Thinking about those years, Mother emerged as a trapped lioness trying to rip apart the cage that imprisoned her. Rosita, on the other hand, was as elusive, and shy, as an animal of the forest, seeking to blend herself into the shadows, trying to become invisible to avoid the poundings of my mother.

Mother decided to move to the United States. She still owned a house that father had left her (the only piece of property that her father or her lover hadn't taken from her), and she decided to sell it to finance our passage to New York. Mother had a friend, Isabel, who lived in Queens. Isabel offered Mother her home until we could find a place of our own. In the early 1960s, it was easy to get a visa to the States. Isabel gave Mother and me an affidavit, and Mother decided Rosita would stay with Carlos, who lived in Barranquilla with his wife. Rosita would join us later, once we settled down. Rosita begged us not to leave her behind. She cried and took to her bed with crippling headaches, but Mother said we couldn't afford the three of us to go at the same time. Seeing how unhappy Rosita was, I offered to stay behind so she could go with Mother. But Mother wouldn't change her mind.

We arrived in New York in 1966. Isabel and her husband had a two-story house in Jackson Heights, and they rented us a room on the top floor. I was enrolled in the eleventh grade. Isabel found Mother a job in a sweatshop in Manhattan where she did piecework. After school, I washed dishes in the only Colombian restaurant in Jackson Heights, where later I was made a waiter. Back then, Jackson Heights was not the Colombian enclave that it is nowadays. Already there were many Colombians living in the area, but the community was small; so small that most of the Colombian families in the area were at least acquainted with each other. Soon Mother and I moved to our own apartment, and we started the paperwork to bring Rosita to join us. I dreamed of that moment. All those months, we had written each other on a weekly basis. In her letters, Rosita did not complain about anything specifically, but she wrote that she was miserable in Barranquilla, and that she could hardly wait to join us.

When Rosita arrived, since we couldn't afford an apartment in Jackson Heights, we moved to 102nd Street and Thirty-eighth Avenue in Corona, a neighborhood that was shabbier and even more ethnic. In the year we had been apart, Rosita had become a stunning beauty, but she had also become more withdrawn. She made one Colombian friend, Ana, another girl at her school with whom she spent most of her time. Rosita continued to do badly in school, though now at least she had an excuse—she didn't speak English. She and Mother got along better. They would still fight sometimes, Mother accusing Rosita of being secretive. But the beatings stopped, maybe because Mother herself was too tired and exhausted from her own life. She would leave the house at 6 A.M. and would not return until it was night. Overnight she became an old woman, broken up by the long hours at the sewing machine and the meager salary she made. She went to church on Sundays. Occasionally, on weekends, she would get together with a friend to go hear a Colombian singer in Jackson Heights. But most of her free time was spent in bed, reading the Spanish newspapers and listening to the radio.

Rosita and I weren't as close as we had been back in Colombia. I had changed too. At eighteen I knew I was a homosexual, that what I felt for men wasn't a passing phase. Back in Colombia, I thought I'd hide my sexual preference, keeping it a secret from everyone. But in Queens High there were a few gay boys and I was attracted to them, though I was terrified to be associated with them. Sometimes I would run into one of them in the restrooms, and we'd discreetly exchange curious glances. I went to the Corona public library and read all the books and magazines that mentioned homosexuality. I began to suspect that there were more homosexuals in the world than I'd ever dreamed before.

Once I set foot in Manhattan, I was instantly seduced by its breathless rhythms, its lights, and the vastness of the hopes it seemed to offer a young person. On my excursions to the revival movie houses, I'd see many men in the streets and in the theaters who were brazenly homosexual. Sometimes I'd sit next to a man who looked homosexual to me, and once the lights were down, we'd discreetly begin to rub elbows and knees. In this state of feverish sexual excitement and fear, I saw many classic films. But when a man engaged me in conversation, either during the movie or when the lights came up, I'd flee. Thus I began to live a secret life: a model student in school, a responsible son who had a job, and a furtive homosexual during my increasingly more frequent outings to Manhattan.

Rosita found a job as a waitress in the Colombian restaurant where I worked. We wore identical uniforms: black pants, formal ruffled white shirts, black bow ties, and black shoes. After we finished working at night, we'd walk together back to our house from the relative prosperity of Jackson Heights to the sombrous blocks of Corona, where we lived on the second floor of a run-down clapboard house. During these night walks, Monday through Friday, we'd talk about school, our new life in New York, our favorite movies and movie stars, what we missed about the life we had left behind, about maybe someday going back.

When I started college in Manhattan, I spent less and less time with Rosita and with Mother. I had a tuition scholarship to City College, and I found part-time work in a bookstore. Tentatively I started coming out of the closet. One day, as I left the Thalia theater, an older guy engaged me in conversation. We started talking about movies as we walked. He invited me to his apartment for a drink. I was terrified of this encounter with a stranger, but excited that I was attracted to him and that we could talk about movies, so I accepted. That night, for the first time, I engaged in full sex with a man. His name was Peter. He fucked me. It was extremely painful, but I liked it when we kissed, when he caressed my body, when he rimmed my ass, when we lay in bed exhausted from lovemaking.

For the next six months I saw Peter once a week, on Saturday nights. We'd usually go to the movies, have dinner, and then spend the night together. Peter was a social worker who wrote poetry in his spare time. He was in his mid-thirties, which to me was old. I wasn't in love with him, but I enjoyed his company. I started enjoying sex with him more and more.

When I showed up at our home in Corona on Sunday mornings, I would tell Mother I had spent the night out with a school friend. But I knew she suspected what was happening with me. I started making American friends my own age who lived in Manhattan, and I would go with them to parties or dancing at the gay bars in Greenwich Village.

Once in a while I would go see a movie with Rosita, or accompany her to a school dance, but for the most part our lives diverged. I didn't discuss my gay life with Rosita, not for fear that she would reject me, but because I felt ashamed of myself—I felt I had betrayed her and Mother. I started spending less and less time at our home in Corona, going there only to sleep or to crash after a night out.

Rosita started dating boys. I'd see them come to the house to pick her up. In school she continued to do poorly. She was bright, but she was not interested in studying. I worried about her, since she didn't seem interested in going on to college. Sometimes she talked about going to business school to become a secretary; getting an education wasn't one of her priorities. Her relationship with Mother remained as tense as ever, and although Mother didn't beat her up anymore, there was always a great deal of bickering and continuous recriminations. I sensed that, more than anything else, Rosita wanted to get away from home as soon as possible. It was something that I also longed to do.

I was in my bedroom reading one summer morning when I heard a commotion coming from Rosita's room. Both Mother and Rosita were screaming at the top of their voices. I ran out of my bedroom and found Mother beating up Rosita, the way she used to back when we lived in Colombia. Breaking away free from Mother's grip, Rosita ran toward me and embraced me. She was crying hysterically.

"You damned ingrate," Mother shouted, shaking, her features distorted by anger. "Tell Santiago what you've done. Tell him."

Rosita offered no explanation. She clutched my chest desperately, burying her crying face in my shirt.

"She got pregnant by one of those no-good Colombians on Roosevelt Avenue. That's what she's done," Mother said.

I, too, felt betrayed. I had wanted more from Rosita; I had hoped she would have gotten an education, and a better life than Mother's.

"And she won't tell me who's the *desgraciado* who did this to her. He's got to marry her. I won't be humiliated this way. Now that's she been ruined, no decent man will marry her," Mother shrieked.

"That was back in Colombia, Mother," I said. "In this country that doesn't mean anything," I explained.

Mother's anger would not be quelled until Rosita agreed to talk to her boyfriend, Rigoberto, who agreed to marry her.

The next day, when Rigoberto came over to ask for Rosita's hand, I took just one good look at him and knew he was trouble. He sported an Afro, wore bell-bottoms and *zapatacones,* the thick-heeled shoes that were in vogue at that time. He was dressed in the equivalent of today's narco look: long hair, baggy pants, and gold lamé shoes worn without socks. Rigoberto was twenty-one years old, four years older than Rosita. He had arrived in Jackson Heights a few years prior to our arrival, and worked in a travel agency, which even back then in Jackson Heights was just a front for a money-laundering operation.

The following week, a justice of the peace married Rosita and Rigoberto in our house. Rosita had been married barely a few weeks before the problems with Rigoberto started. At first, she would come home refusing to return to him, crying inconsolably, saying that she didn't love him. Eventually, Rigoberto would come by the house, Mother would intervene, and Rosita would go back. Then, in her fifth month of pregnancy, she miscarried. Rosita had fallen down the stairs of her apartment to the first floor, and even though she never spoke about it, I suspected Rigoberto had pushed her down the stairs during a quarrel. After the miscarriage

Rosita was never the same. She became even more withdrawn and volatile, and her living situation with Rigoberto deteriorated even further: he would beat her up, she would call the police, they would come and talk to him, then leave. Their situation became such a vicious circle that, after a while, we learned to live with it, the way one learns to live with calamities like disease and war.

In my senior year in college, I found an apartment on the Lower East Side and moved in with a school friend. Corona became a distant country that I visited once a month to have dinner with Mother, usually on Sunday nights. From Mother, who was still bitter at the way Rosita had gotten pregnant and married the first man who came along, I would hear the news about Rosita's marriage: how Rosita and Rigoberto continued to fight, how she had not gotten pregnant again, the huge amounts of money that Rigoberto was making. Although it remained an unspoken subject, we both knew that he was involved in the drug trade.

A couple of times a year, Rosita would invite me to have dinner at her place. They had moved into an expensive townhouse with gardens in front and back on one of the better streets in Jackson Heights. Yet I was alarmed by what I saw: a dinner at Rosita's meant smoking joints before dinner, followed by lots of cocaine and cognac after dessert. To control her weight, she took Black Beauties. In her bathroom, there were dozens of bottles full of Valium and other pills. It was obvious to me that her life revolved around drugs.

Rosita's marriage dissolved the year I graduated from college. Because she ran away from her home—and because Rigoberto threatened to kill her if she tried to get any of his money—when the divorce came through Rosita was penniless. After her divorce, Rosita's disintegration speeded up. Hooked on drugs, she became one of those women who hang out with narco traffickers exchanging sex for easy money and drugs. She became alienated from me, too, and on one occasion accused me of being her enemy. Despite Mother's desperate efforts to get her to change her way of life, Rosita rebuffed her even more, accusing Mother of being responsible for what had happened to her. Eventually we lost touch with her. Rosita disappeared in the drug and prostitution underworld of Jackson Heights. It was as if she had fallen off the face of the earth, leaving no trace.

I had found by then what would become my life in America. To become a writer was my dream, and I took a series of menial jobs so that I could devote evenings and weekends to writing. I was no longer ashamed of being a gay man, and had a large group of gay acquaintances. However, I still felt uncomfortable coming out to my mother who, with the passage of the years, became more disappointed and unhappy. By that time Mother had stopped working in the Manhattan sweatshops; she had found a job as a cook in a Colombian restaurant in Jackson Heights. Mother went to church on Sundays, and occasionally to a spiritual retreat in upstate New York; she corresponded with her family in Colombia, and sank deeper and deeper into her santería practices, consulting the Indio Amazónico, a shaman in Jackson Heights, about Rosita's whereabouts. All those years, according to what I later learned from the police, Rosita had been working, under the alias of Silvia, as a prostitute at a whorehouse under the elevated, on Roosevelt Avenue and Eighty-seventh Street. All the Colombians in Queens knew about this whorehouse: a place for young Colombian women, who come to the States so they can send money back home to support their hungry children; a place where they serve johns off the streets for $25 for fifteen minutes; a breeding ground for AIDS.

Now I wondered whether, from the second-floor window of the hole-in-the-wall where she worked, Rosita had seen Mother going in and out of the Indio's store for years; whether she had watched Mother leaving the store, carrying bags full of herbs, roots, rocks, colored candles, incense, and the religious paraphernalia that Mother used to invoke the spirits, petitioning them to help her find Rosita. All those years that Mother had been obsessed with Rosita's disappearance, never getting a good night's rest, Rosita had been living right under her nose. All those years we had wondered whether she was still alive, or whether in the coldest winter nights Rosita had frozen to death in some filthy alley; all those years that I had stopped women in the streets, women worn down by drugs and alcohol who remotely resembled Rosita.

In her last years, Mother seemed defeated. Although we never discussed it, mother was disappointed that her only son was gay, and that her sister, whom she had raised as her daughter, had become a prostitute and a drug addict in America. For mother, the American Dream had not come true—it had turned out to be a nightmare.

For me, losing Rosita was an added loss to the loss of our country, the world we had known, the people we were back then and would never be again.

Aunt Caty and I were in the living room having coffee and chatting when I checked my watch and realized it was time to go downstairs to meet Ramón. When I got up to leave, her attitude toward me became maternal, as if I were a youngster, not a grown-up man.

"Please be very careful, Sammy. I hope Ramón is not going to take you to some dangerous place. The thing is, you don't really know Colombia anymore. I'm sure you've heard what the paramilitary groups have been doing to homosexuals," she said.

I reassured her that I wouldn't do anything reckless.

As I waited downstairs for Ramón, salsa music blasted from the neighborhood cantinas. Because it was Friday night, or Cultural Friday, as Barranquilleros call it, the street was bustling with dressed up people on their way to social gatherings.

I felt uneasy. Although I had tried to play it cool in front of Aunt Caty, I knew perfectly well what she was referring to. Since the late 1980s paramilitary groups had been killing the *desechables*, the homeless, the disabled, the blatantly gay, especially the drag queens. Most of the killings—which were in the hundreds—had taken place in Bogotá, Medellín, Cali. In Barranquilla there had been a few isolated cases, and not recently. Even so, I was aware that this was not your usual night out with the boys in New York City.

A taxi pulled up next to the curb where I was standing. Ramón was sitting in the back seat with a young man, not the same one I had seen him pick up yesterday in the afternoon. I got in and the taxi took off.

"Santiago, this is Humberto," Ramón said. "He's one of the most fabulous young men in all of Colombia, so I wanted you to meet him. He was dying to meet you, because he's also a writer. And he's read, and memorized, every single comma you've written."

We shook hands. Humberto was very attractive, in his early twenties, and he had an upper lip shaped like a swan in flight that heightened the carnality of his face.

"I admire your writing very much," he said, holding on to my hand. Right away I knew that I could have him for the night if I wanted to. The only thing that wasn't clear was whether I would have to pay him or not. But I would find that out later.

"We're going to The Godfather III, which I thought would be the most appropriate place to go since we're all such cinematographic queens," Ramón said.

Humberto, who sat in the middle, his body leaning against mine, said, "We call it The Godfather III because of the frequent shoot-outs that take place there."

I wasn't in the mood for high drama. "Couldn't we go someplace less . . . exciting?" I said.

"Darling, it's *the* place to go in Barranquilla," Ramón said with finality. "Besides, the shoot-outs are a thing of the past. Now they have bouncers who check you for weapons as you go in. If you ask me, that's the only reason to go there: to have those hunky men, with their huge orangutan hands, checking you in very very intimate places. . . . Uhmmmmm," he purred.

We all broke out laughing, yet I couldn't help but be tense about the evening ahead of us. As we chatted merrily about gay life in Barranquilla and New York, always remembering to use English and French words so that the taxi driver wouldn't understand what we were talking about, I noticed that we had entered one of the *barrios populares*, one of Barranquilla's poorer neighborhoods. The taxi stopped in front of a house at the corner of an unpaved street. I paid the driver, and we stood in front of a house with its door and windows shut. From inside the house I could hear salsa music playing. The street was dark, and next to the bar was an empty lot full of smelly garbage.

Ramón rang the bell. The door was opened a crack, and when he was recognized we were let in to an empty room, where two bouncers who looked like heavyweight boxers checked us for weapons. The one checking me put his hand inside my underwear. Ramón made orgasmic sounds as he was searched. When the men were satisfied that we didn't carry weapons, we were admitted.

We crossed a series of dim rooms, where men gathered around tables drinking or making out. Then we entered the patio, where the jukebox was playing salsa music.

High walls surrounded the patio so that the neighbors could not look in. Multicolored papier mâché lamps provided suggestive illumination. The floor was inlaid with tiles in Arabian designs, and in the center of the dance floor there was a lighted Moorish fountain. The tables for the customers were placed against the walls of the corridors, and in the back of the patio, under guava trees, tame parrots and macaws pirouetted about. A profusion of red and yellow hibiscus, the kind that opens for the night and dies at dawn, and bougainvillea in bloom, created a carnavalesque garden. We sat at a table, and a barefoot waiter in shorts and wearing a *guayabera* approached us. Ramón asked for a bottle of rum and Coca Colas. When he finished taking the order, the waiter asked, "Will there be anything else for the gentlemen?"

Ramón and Humberto exchanged looks. "Yes," said Ramón, "we'll take the Friday Night Special for three. That's all."

When the waiter left, Ramón said to me, "You're probably wondering what the Special is. We'll let it be a surprise. Suffice to say that it is one of those exquisite pleasures that only we third-worlders can enjoy."

A young man was doing salsa moves on the dance floor. He wore tight ripped jeans, sneakers, and a T-shirt draped over his muscular torso. With the exception of the people engaged in conversation, everyone was staring at him. The *salsero* was performing for all of us, so that we could admire his great body and his dancing, but he never, not once, looked up. He danced always looking at his crotch. When the record changed, the dancer joined his friends at a table, and another one replaced him. He, too, danced alone, totally absorbed in the intricacies of his steps.

"Do they always dance by themselves?" I asked.

"Mostly by themselves," said Humberto. "Though sometimes

there are two people on the floor, but far apart, with their backs to each other."

"Why is that?"

"Darling, have you forgotten?" Ramón said. "Real men don't dance together. These are working-class boys; they aren't gay."

"So why are they here?"

"For money, *cariño*. These boys are not homos. They just do it for money. They dance to advertise their talents and their baskets. If you like what you see, you go to their tables, buy them a drink, and negotiate a price for the night."

"Is this a hustlers' bar?"

"If you want to be that precise, yes. I prefer to think about it this way: they have what I want, and I am willing to pay for it. No, people don't come here looking for love, if that's what you're thinking about."

The waiter approached us with a tray. He set down on the table a bottle of rum, a bucket of ice, two large bottles of Coke, and two dishes, one with a local white cheese and another one with green wedges of mango and lime. "Whenever you're ready for the Friday Night Special, let me know."

"Thanks very much," Ramón said, batting his eyelashes. "You'll hear me meowing when we're ready."

We had a couple of Cuba Libres. Then Ramón said, "Humberto, darling, go with Santiago for the Special. I'll wait here."

I was beginning to suspect what "The Special" was. The waiter led us to a room abutting the dance floor and then closed the door. On a table there was a mirror with long lines of cocaine, cut straws, joints, a pipe, two vials with *basuco* rocks—a very poisonous kind of crack—and syringes.

We sat around the table. Humberto did a couple of lines of cocaine hungrily. Then he pushed the mirror in my direction. I considered it for a moment. Throughout most of the 1980s I had abused cocaine, designer drugs, and finally crack. At the end of my using, I was buying $5 vials in the crack houses of Ninth Avenue, behind Port Authority. But when so many of my friends had started dying of AIDS, I decided to lead a cleaner life. It was around that time I met Ryan, who, because he was HIV positive, led a life free of alcohol and drugs. After a while, I realized I no longer needed to get high to have a good time. I declined the cocaine.

"Oh, OK," Humberto said, indifferent to my abstinence. He did another couple of lines, and then lit a joint. Again I shook my head when he offered it, though at one point I had been a connoisseur of Colombian grass. When he lit the joint, because of his proximity, the smoke hit me full on my nostrils and I started getting high. That was all I needed. I didn't want to get any more stoned than that. Yet it was hard to fight the temptation. I knew that if I took a few tokes a great euphoria would come over me, and I'd instantly develop a bond with Humberto. I didn't want to spoil my chances of going to bed with him that night. But I had learned over the last years that I could have fun without doing drugs, and I wanted to keep it that way. I knew that a toke could lead to a few lines, and then to the crack pipe, and next in line was the syringe. The risk of going back to the life I led at the end of my using, to that bleak hopelessness, was too great. I got up.

"You stay here as long as you want," I said. "I just need to get some air."

I joined Ramón. "Back so soon?" he said, looking surprised.

I sat down. "I'm not in the mood," I said. "I am . . . " as I searched for the right word, it dawned on me: I'm in mourning was what I wanted to say. A wave of sadness engulfed me. Being here with Ramón reminded me of the trip Ryan and I had taken to Colombia. Ryan still did not show any symptoms at that time. Although the virus was there, a presence between us, making ours a triangular relationship, Ryan was still healthy, handsome, and we were very much in love with each other.

"I'll go join Humberto," Ramón said. "I think you want to be alone with your melancholia. You and Greta Garbo," he sighed.

I was sipping my drink, when Humberto, lit up, returned to the table—his eyes blazed from the cocaine. When a new song was played, he took to the dance floor. Although he danced like the other men, he made it clear—by giving me furtive glances—that he was dancing for me. Now that I could inspect him, I saw how beautiful he was: he had long sensual limbs, and his tight jeans revealed a nice crotch and a shapely ass. He twirled, with feline movements, an invitation to pleasures rare and exquisite. In his gestures there was the promise of total surrender. I was entranced watching him, getting aroused, when Ramón returned to the table.

"I feel like a new woman," Ramón said. "Makeup and drugs . . . and men, that's all I need to be happy." He noticed Humberto on the dance floor. "Uhm, just what I thought. He likes you. You can do with him whatever you want, darling."

"Is he a hustler?"

"No, Santiago, he's a *chico bien*, a boy from a good family, a sophisticointellectual. He's impressed with you because you're a cosmopolitan writer living in New York. Tonight he'll do anything you want. Absolutely free. Compliments of the house."

"I'm horny for him," I admitted. "But I can't take him to my relatives' house."

"Darling," Ramón snorted. "This isn't New York by any means, but here we have divine decadence, pleasures that the Emperors of China never had. As part of the Friday Night Special we have access to a room equipped with everything: condoms for all sizes and tastes, lubricants, whips, chains, torture instruments, whatever you're into. That's why I put up with everything else I hate about this country—because of the divine decadent pleasures."

It was past midnight when Ramón found someone he liked, and they disappeared into one of the cubicles off the dance floor. Left alone with Humberto, we began to talk about more intimate subjects. Humberto was a literature student at Barranquilla's private university. He had already published short stories and essays in Colombian newspapers, and he was working on his first novel. In this respect, he was no different from many of my students in New York who wanted to be writers. Then he told me about his lover, Raúl, who had died of AIDS just last year. Raúl was an older architect, and they had moved in together, which in Barranquilla amounted to a scandal. Humberto's family had cut him off. They had lived together for a short while, and suddenly Raúl developed AIDS pneumonia and died within a year. As he told me this story, he became human to me. He was more than just a handsome young man—he became a person of depth, someone whose life had been touched by suffering. Moved by his story, I reached over and grabbed his chin. Humberto closed his eyes, and grabbed my hand, squeezing it. The contact of his skin on mine gave me a hard-on. This was no different from going into a bar in Greenwich Village, chatting with a guy, asking him home. Right from the beginning you knew what the outcome would be: you'd have sex, and then you'd get up, exchange phone numbers, and you'd never call each other. I knew that in a few days I would be returning to New York, that Humberto would stay in Barranquilla where his life was, that whatever happened between us would probably have a longer life as a memory. Bluntly, I asked, "Would you like to have sex with me?"

"Yes, I'm attracted to you," he said, taking my hand and nibbling the tip of my fingers.

What happened in bed was a total surprise to me. Perhaps because we both had lost the men we loved to AIDS, perhaps because we had lost them recently, perhaps because we both came from the same culture and had experienced the isolation of a homosexual in a place that denied our existence, perhaps because the tropical night was splendorous and scented with the sweetness of honeysuckle, perhaps because the night seemed to exist just for the purpose of making love, we surrendered to each other with a passion and a totality that I had never experienced before, not even with Ryan. When we kissed, desperately, avidly, it was if we were trying to pass back and forth all the secrets in our souls. When I took his cock in my hand, I held it with wonder, for all its perfection, for all its power to give pleasure, to make me forget—for that miraculous instant—all the sadness and pain of life. We made love on the floor, standing up, on the bed, sitting up, biting, squeezing, pumping, fisting, as if this was the last chance to do with one person everything we had learned about the pleasures of the body. After climaxing, we were embracing when I noticed that he was crying with the same ardor he had made love to me. Shaken by the depth of the feelings I had experienced with this stranger, grateful to be alive, grateful to have experienced an ecstasy that had made me appreciate again what a holy instrument the flesh is, I embraced him with all my strength, and cried, too, until we both did it in unison, as if we were part of a chorus, wailing for everything we had loved and lost.

Two days later, I was a passenger on a tiny two-engine plane, on the way to El Banco, the ancestral home of my mother's family. The scenery was far more mysterious than my memories of it. We were heading toward the interior, along the Magdalena River; there were so many bodies of water created by the river and its tributaries that, from above, it looked as if we were gliding over a dense sienna-colored archipelago. The monotony of the waters was broken up here and there by patches of rainforest. A couple of times the plane soared above flocks of thousands of flamingos and white herons.

I had made this trip in my childhood and adolescence. Twice a year, in July, during the mid-year vacation; and in November, when the school year ended, I'd visit my grandparents. I both loved and hated going to El Banco. Sometimes I would stay with my grandparents; other times I would stay with my godmother, Aunt Julia, or with Aunt Carolina, both of whom were married and had families. My grandparents had twelve children, and at that time the youngest of them—two aunts and four uncles—still lived at home. My young aunts were a half dozen years older than me, and with them I'd go to the movies, to dances, or to visit their friends. Uncle Germán, the youngest of the boys, was my pal. I would spent most of the afternoons with him at Las Susanas, my grandfather's farm outside the village. We'd go hunting, or swimming, or to round up cattle lost in the vast lands of the hacienda. My grandfather had several farms, and back then was still quite wealthy. My favorite farm was Tosnován, which was a journey of two days from El Banco.

More than fifteen years had passed since my last visit. The previous year, my grandfather had died in his mid-nineties, and I wanted to see my grandmother. Actually, my grandfather's wife, *Mamá* Martha, was my mother's stepmother; my mother's mother, *Mamá* Paulina, lived in the town of El Barranco de Loba. Both women were in their late eighties.

When the plane careened onto the unpaved strip of gravel of El

Banco's airport, the first thing I noticed was the red earth of this region. As I walked toward the little airport building, the clouds were way up in the delicate, cottony, evanescent blue sky. Due to recent heavy rainfalls, the vegetation was luxuriant.

I hired one of the jeeps that serve as taxis. I told the driver, "Take me to the house of . . . " and gave him my grandfather's name. Things had not changed much in these parts, because the driver nodded. It was up to me to chit chat, but I wasn't in the mood; we remained quiet during the half-hour trip to the village. Because the soil was damp, the vehicles traveling along the main road did not raise the usual swirls of dust. The normally barren savannah was dressed in green trees and leafy bushes and grasses where Brahmin cows and other livestock grazed lazily. The openness of the landscape was contagious; and the warm dry weather was paradisial.

The town looked unchanged. The jeep stopped in front of my grandparents' house. Its windows were shut; I knocked on the door. Minutes went by and there was no answer. I knocked loudly this time, figuring that my step-grandmother was having lunch. I knew the dining room was beyond the patio, in the back of the house, and it was a separate structure. As far as I knew, my step-grandmother lived in the house with Sergio, one of my uncles. A maid opened the door. Suddenly I felt very awkward. This young woman didn't have a clue as to who I was. I introduced myself and asked her to inform my step-grandmother I had arrived. Instead of asking me to come in, she closed the door and left me waiting in the street. I felt like an intruder who had no business coming back to this house. And yet I was very fond of my step-grandmother. The door was opened again, and this time the maid asked me to come in.

"*Doña* Martha is in the dining room," she informed me. I crossed the two living rooms and the patio and then entered the dining area. *Mamá* Martha was sitting at the table, and her sister Juanita was sitting opposite her. I kissed my step-grandmother and then embraced her sister, whom I didn't know well. *Mamá* Martha asked me to sit down and join them for lunch. She reacted to my unexpected arrival almost coldly, as if my visit were nothing out of the ordinary; as if she saw me every day. I noticed that she was still in full mourning for my grandfather. She was in her eighties, but still firm: a tall woman, hefty but not fat. As in the past, when many people lived in the house, there was an ample spread of food on the table: a soup tureen, and large trays heaped with yams, potatoes, corn, green plantains, fried fish, steak, rice, and salad. There were also pitchers of fruit juices and containers with coconut, pineapple, and mango sweets. The *suero*, butter and white cheese, she informed me, they made at the house. She ate slowly, tasting all the items on the table. For a person her age, she had a ravenous appetite. Many of the staples on the table were high in sugar and fat, and yet she had lived to a healthy old age, just like my grandfather.

When coffee and dessert were served, Juanita excused herself to go take her siesta. *Mamá* Martha heaped a mound of coconut paste on a plate and passed it to me. Then she said, "I suppose you want to know what the last days of your grandfather were like." She leaned back on the chair and massaged her forehead in an upward motion with the back of her palm, as if this gesture would make her recollect better. "Julián was in perfect health until last year; he was ninety-four years old. Everyday, he'd wake up at four A.M., and then have a double whiskey and a black coffee. Every morning he'd walk the five miles to the farm, where he remained until the afternoon, when he returned home for supper. And then, one day, he had a stroke; and the next day, he was ancient." She started then to describe his painful process of deterioration, recounting the events with clarity, brevity, leaving the most dramatic anecdotes for the end of each little chapter. As I marveled at her skills as a storyteller, I remembered that in my adolescence I had shared with her my love of nineteenth-century novels. *Mamá* Martha had no intellectual pretensions whatsoever, but she loved the books of Tolstoy, Balzac, Dickens, and the Brontës. I remembered my delight in my early teens when I had discovered that *Anna Karenina* and *Wuthering Heights* were her favorite novels. Because of this bond, I'd felt close to her back then and had thought fondly of her forever after. She had never been physically affectionate, but I wondered if this was due to the fact that she had borne many children and had dozens of grandchildren, and had also had to deal with my grandfather's illegitimate children, including my mother. Her way of singling me out was very thoughtful: the day I arrived for my yearly vacations, she baked an *enyucado*, a yucca cake that I loved. Now she was describing my grandfather's last days of life, "A couple of days before he died he started saying your name, 'Santiago, Santiago,' he cried out. I have no idea why he would be calling you, since he hadn't seen you in many years." Her words hurt me. Obviously, she was unhappy that my grandfather hadn't called out the name of one of her sons or one of her own grandchildren. "Anyway, he became delirious. His ravings were frightening; he roared like a wounded lion. I was very afraid that he'd die an agnostic and go to hell. Thank God, hours before he lost consciousness, he relented to the pleadings of the family and allowed a priest to come. He converted to Catholicism and confessed before dying. Your Aunt Catalina wasn't with us when he died. But she says that she knew the exact moment he passed away because the lights went out in her bedroom." *Mamá* Martha paused, as if to gather enough strength to say something that she had been dying to say for some time. "Your grandfather was a difficult man, Santiago. He never allowed me to have a woman friend; he never allowed anyone to come visit *me* in his house. It wasn't an easy life with him, but I tried to be the best wife I could be." She made this statement flatly, without theatricality, and without any kind of bitterness that I could detect.

We finished dessert, but lingered at the table in silence. She took a sip of coffee and then asked me, "How long are you planning to visit with us, Santiago?"

"I want to leave for Barranco to see *Mamá* Paulina tomorrow, and I'll return in the afternoon because I have to be in Barranquilla two days from now. I must be in New York next week," I added, as if to imply that pressing engagements made necessary my return.

"I hope next time you come you can stay with us longer," she said in a tone that expressed disappointment at my short visit, but in which I also sensed relief that I wouldn't be staying longer.

My Uncle Sergio entered the dining room. I stood up and we shook hands, politely; we exchanged a few pleasantries. He was wearing a straw cowboy hat. He informed me he was on his way to Las Susanas, the family's ancestral farm. Since I wasn't tired, and I knew the cemetery was on his way, I said, "If it's OK with you, I'd like to visit Grandfather's grave."

"Your grandfather is buried in the Gnostics cemetery, across the road from the town's cemetery," *Mamá* Martha remarked. She got up, walked to a bureau next to the refrigerator and pulled out a long key, which she handed Sergio. A horn honked three times in the street.

"That's the driver," Sergio said. "If you're ready we can go now."

On the way to the cemetery I sat in the back of the jeep. Sergio had changed considerably since the last time I had seen him. Now in his early fifties, his hair was almost all gray. He talked village talk with the driver, ignoring me. Sergio had never married. As far as I knew, he had never even had a girlfriend. All my other uncles and aunts had moved away, and most of them had families, but he had stayed on to take care of the farm. It occurred to me that he had to be a closet homosexual, although no one in the family would have ever thought it. I wondered how conscious of it he was himself.

The jeep stopped in front of the Gnostic cemetery. Sergio gave me the key.

"Don't wait for me," I said. "I don't want to rush. I think I can find my way to the farm."

"We'll come back to pick you up in half an hour," he said. "There's a squatters' town now on the way to the farmhouse and it could be dangerous. You look like a gringo."

I thanked him and climbed the steps to the tall iron gates that were framed by an arch with an inscription in Latin. The entire cemetery was encircled by a high wall; peering through the gates I saw only five graves in it. This gave me a certain respect for my grandfather: that in such a small, and essentially Catholic and narrow-minded, community he had dared to be different. The place looked like a private wild garden, decorated with elaborate tombstones of marble and *pietra santa*. I turned the key and pushed open the creaking rusted door. Because the cemetery was contiguous to the slaughterhouse, dozens of vultures festooning the walls watched me go in. My grandfather's grave was in the back of the garden; it had a new gravestone with his name and dates. There was a cement bench in front of it, which I assumed had been built for *Mamá* Martha's visits. She had been there recently because a large bouquet of fresh pink crepe myrtle decorated the site. I sat on the sizzling bench.

My grandfather had been a tormented man. Sporadically he would go on alcoholic binges in which he would terrorize his family and the town with his guns. When I was growing up he used to claim to have supernatural powers. As a child, I heard him tell stories of being bewitched by cunning sorceresses and of how he outwitted them to break their spells and punished them by turning them into sows. He claimed he could heal sick animals by laying his hands on them. In the years when his prosperity grew, this must have been an awesome claim. The implication (this too was whispered) was that he had a pact with the devil.

My grandfather was prone to rages and to sadistic acts of violence—traits my mother inherited. I've been told how once, riding a horse, he charged against my Uncle Carlos, threw him on the ground, and lashed at him with his whip. My mother also told the story of the day she lost the tray of sweets she had been sent to sell in the streets of El Barranco: my grandfather was so angry he hanged her by the wrists from the rafters of the living room. She was lowered only when my grandfather's best friend came to visit and, horrified by the sight, pleaded with my grandfather to stop the torture.

It's true that my grandfather accepted his illegitimate daughter as part of his family, but my mother had to pay a high price: he turned her into his slave. I always felt there was something cold-hearted about the way my grandfather related to me. I don't remember him ever calling me Santiago or Sammy. Instead, he addressed me as "*sobrino.*" I felt that by calling me "nephew" he was making a kind of insinuation that made me feel tainted. He created a dark, murky bond between him, my mother, and myself. What I was made to feel was that my mother was not so much his daughter, but his sister. All his descendants called him *Papá* Julián, but the name never came out of my throat without distaste. By calling me "nephew," my grandfather made me feel not like his grand-child, but his illegitimate son—a kind of monstrous being born out of the union with his daughter.

I was shaking and sweating, and not altogether because of the scorching sun. I was suddenly full of rage against my grandfather. The jeep honking outside the cemetery snapped me out of my trance.

Riding in the jeep, I continued to be upset. A shantytown of flimsy dwellings appeared and the road cut through it. I had heard about the squatters who had settled in a portion of my grand-father's farm. Now Sergio told me the story once again: how the family had tried to intimidate the invaders into moving away, but when violence erupted and the hundred or so families refused to budge, my grandfather had to give in. With what I thought was some satisfaction, Sergio mentioned that the government had ended up buying the land for the squatters and paying my grand-father for it.

The jeep stopped in front of a wooden gate. Las Susanas was just the way I remembered it, the house surrounded by a grove of citrus and coconut trees. Sergio told the driver to return to pick us up at 5:30. We opened the gate and walked under the shade cre-ated by the fruit trees. Sergio introduced me to the caretakers—a man, his wife, and several children—as "a relative." I had expected him to say "my nephew," or my "father's grandson." We sat on rustic leather chairs under the roof of the well. Just as I used to do in my childhood, I pumped water for the hell of it: it was crys-talline and cold but, although I was thirsty, I didn't dare drink it for fear of amoebas and other parasites. I asked one of the boys to climb up one of the coconut trees and pluck a couple of fresh co-conuts for me. After I satiated my thirst, I took a walk along the edges of the grove. To the left and right of the house there were corrals carpeted with black, fresh cow dung. Swarms of exacer-bated fat flies filled the air. Facing west, I saw the pond and, in the distance, a range of milky blue mountains.

As I returned to the well, Sergio was giving the equivalent of $5 to a worker who was wearing just a pair of torn pants. "The family doesn't mind helping you out, because you're a good worker," Sergio said, making a big fuss. "But we cannot advance you money all the time."

The man, who looked like he was suffering from severe malnutrition, took the money obsequiously. "I assure you, *Don* Sergio," he said, "that my family and I are very grateful to you for helping us. If the children weren't so hungry, we wouldn't bother you."

I felt uncomfortable and wanted to walk away. Sergio began to ask the man's advice about different kinds of crops he could plant this year and the prices in the market. When the man left, Sergio said to me, "I'm going to inspect the workers in the fields. Would you like to stay here or come along with me?"

As much as I disliked him, I did want to see the farm, so I said, "I'll come with you."

"Saddle two horses," Sergio ordered one of the farmhands. And then, with a twitch of mockery in his voice, he added, "A tame one for *Don* Santiago."

While we waited for the horses to be brought to the house, Sergio turned to me and asked me about the prices of apartment rentals in New York. When that subject was rapidly exhausted he told me I was lucky to have arrived in such a mild rainy season, that usually at that time of the year it rained so much that many calves and piglets drowned in the mud. A lonely bird made a song I'd never heard before.

"It's the *carrao* bird singing," Sergio explained. "The weather has changed a lot in the past years. Last year it didn't rain and when the *carraos* arrived there was no fruit. You should have heard hundreds of them screaming in desperation because they eat only the fruit of that tree," he pointed to a fruit tree I couldn't identify. "When there's no fruit they commit suicide. They put their long necks between the branches and flip around until they break their necks."

I shuddered, and he smirked at my reaction. I was relieved to see a boy approach with two saddled horses. We left the farm and rode along the main road, until we entered a clearing; for a while we traveled through thick, tall bush. We waded a fetid *caño* whose black syrupy waters came to my waist. I remembered how these

148

waters were the breeding ground for leeches, but I wasn't about to complain, as I had when I was a child.

The horses clambered up a steep muddy ditch and we were suddenly riding on a luxuriant plain garbed in shades of emerald. The Mompox River appeared, its deep waters dark blue and inviting. African palms, with heavy clusters of nuts, lined the banks of the river. Swamp roosters and herons fed on its shores, oblivious to our presence. There were a few wild horses, but no cows. Sergio came upon two men pulling weeds. While Sergio talked to the workers, I galloped west, passing many magnificent trees whose foliage was unknown to me. In the distance, I saw a blue pond dotted with lilies.

Away from Sergio and his chores, I became aware of the chirps, croaks, and warbles of the falcons, eaglets, flocks of parakeets, *toches*, cardinals, cranes, ducks, and bands of swallows, creating an arpeggio of birds. Their songs mixed with the brassy honking of the crickets, playing an atonal yet rapturously lyrical symphony of nature.

I followed the contour of the river until, in the distance, the snow-capped peaks of the Sierra Nevada appeared, as if out of the vision of a luminist, transcendental painter. It was just simply monumental, larger than any construction that could ever be built by man. It was one of nature's skyscrapers, and the river was like an avenue in Manhattan, and the trees were like the narrow vertical canyons of New York, but in a pristine ideal state.

Hearing the voices of Rosita and my mother and Ryan calling me, I felt propelled to ride forward, following the river around its many bends, all the way to the Caribbean Sea. My American exile was obliterated in an instant and I experienced a happiness unlike any other I had ever known. It was a happiness of that particular moment; a happiness so pure because it wasn't attached to any desire. In this place, where the hand of Creation had been extremely benevolent with its gift of beauty and peace, I felt blessed, at peace with myself and the ghosts of my loved ones.

The next day, after breakfast, I walked down to El Banco's quay on the Magdalena River. The town of El Banco—the embankment—is situated on a steep incline; at its highest point rises a neo-baroque nineteenth-century Catholic church. In front of it there is a small plaza from which hundreds of narrow steps drop vertically all the way to the turbulent and turbid waters of the river. At this point, the river is so wide that its opposite shore looks as far away as the frontier of another country. Along the horizon of the setting sun loomed the robin's-egg blue mountains of the western Andes.

During my childhood and adolescence, I would often sit on one of the plaza benches at the close of day to admire the fiery sunsets, all the time frightened that if I stumbled, or took a misstep, I could fall into the river and drown. Death by drowning was very common in El Banco. So the river always held a fascination and terror for me.

I took the slanting street that leads to the market below, where the various river crafts moor. I had made the trip to El Barranco de Loba with my mother and Rosita to visit *Mamá* Paulina, or with my grandfather and uncles, for the annual migration of my grandfather's cattle to Tosnován, his farm in the jungly highlands to the north. Back then one could also travel aboard an elegant riverboat, *El David Arango,* which, in the days before commercial aviation, well-to-do people used to travel from the Atlantic coast to the interior of the nation. The cheapest mode of transportation were the river launches that looked like the boat in *The African Queen.* These launches made stops at all the villages along the river, and because they made so many stops, to pick up even solitary passengers from remote farms, the trip to El Barranco de Loba took most of the day.

Now speedboats—called *chalupas*—made the trip a lot faster. I decided to splurge and, for $20, hired a boat just for myself. I was too emotionally overcome by the sight of the river, and the memories it evoked, to be in a boat with other people. I wanted the river all to myself.

I sat near the prow, and the *chalupa* shot like a projectile upriver, skimming the dun-colored waters that carried aquatic plants and all kinds of debris downstream. Because it was the rainy season, the river was swollen, furiously fast, unfathomably deep in places. The vegetation along its banks was a riot of bright shades of green. My mother had told me stories about how in her childhood thousands of caimans could be seen sunning along the banks of the river, until alligator leather became fashionable. Nowadays caimans had become elusive. Recently, the shores of the river had been deforested, and now, instead of huge trees drooping with monkeys, parrots, herons, *collongos*, and macaws, there were flat expanses of pastures.

The people who live along its banks depend on the Magdalena to irrigate their agricultural lands; it waters the grasses where their livestock feed; it produces the fish, turtles, manatees, gators, and other animals that make up their diet. When the river overflows, whole towns are submerged, and dreadful pestilences spread, killing people and their animals, destroying plantations of banana, yucca, yam, and corn. When the river dries up, the grasses wither; the cattle live off their fat reserves and do not produce milk; the fish supply dwindles; the wild fowl look for better feeding grounds; the iguanas, deer, wild pigs, *guartinajas*, *ñeques*, and other mammals the locals depend on for their diets migrate; the cultivated lands become barren, and the people go hungry.

An hour or so later the white-sanded beach of El Barranco de Loba (the she-wolf's ravine) appeared; in the dry season, people swim and bathe at this beach. The town is what is known as a *palenque*, a settlement made in the early nineteenth century by runaway black slaves, who chose the site because of its remoteness. My mother's family had originated in this village, and my grandfather and his children had lived there until they moved to El Banco almost half a century ago.

I paid the intensely curious boat conductor. In the last decade, because of its remoteness, the region had been taken over by guerrilla groups. I knew that the insurgents had a strong hold over the entire population of the lower Magdalena, that they were the law of the land, that they kidnapped local ranchers for ransoms; that they pillaged their harvests and raided their herds. At the end of the day these animals are herded by their owners back into their corrals.

The mid-morning sun already fell with a scourging rage. I stood alone on the empty wide beach; the sand under my sneakers baked the soles of my feet. I gazed in the direction of El Barranco de Loba, a couple of miles away. Beyond the beach was a meadow where domestic animals were grazing. In the distance, where the terrain elevates in a gentle hillock, I saw the first house of the town.

I had been walking for a while on the gravel path leading to the village when a man shambled in my direction: he tottered on the trail with a drunken gait. I loped off to the right to let him pass. He was tall and dark, wore a straw hat, torn pants, and a shirt open all the way down to his belly button, but no shoes. When he was just a few feet away from me, the man removed his hat brusquely and placed it on his thigh. "Welcome," he bellowed.

"Good morning," I said, nodding and then staring at my feet, since I didn't want to be engaged by a drunken stranger.

Coming just inches away from me, he placed a hand on my shoulder. I froze and looked up. The man, who was sweating profusely, had an incipient salt-and-pepper beard, and his unfocused hazel eyes were bloodshot and coated by a filmy but gleaming membrane that was half cataract and half glassy veil. He searched my eyes.

"You're Sofía's son," he said. "I was sorry to hear she died." Then he added, "Your grandmother must be so happy about your visit."

I was astonished that this man remembered me, since the last time I had visited El Barranco I had been a young man. But so very few strangers ever visit the town that once you make an appearance you are never forgotten. The man's breath stank, as if his insides were rotting. But he didn't seem dangerous or hostile. Besides, since he had mentioned my mother by name, I reasoned he had been an old acquaintance of hers.

"*Mamá* Paulina doesn't know I'm coming," I said, and started walking toward the village.

The man followed me. "Oh she knows you're here," he said. "She's waiting for you."

I did not contradict him. I started feeling agitated as we neared the colossal *ceiba* tree that marks the entrance to the town. A part of me wanted to question this man about how he knew my mother, but I held back. Under the *ceiba* tree a cantina took umbrage; bolero music spilled out to greet me. Two men drinking beer were sitting on chairs, reclining against the wall. My companion waved at them.

"*Adiós*, Francisco," they called as we went by.

We walked on a wide street carpeted with verdant turf and decorated with huge smooth beige stones. The houses rose several feet above the ground on cement platforms. The peasant dwellings are attractive in their simplicity: walls made with whitewashed cow dung, thatched roofs, their windows and doors painted green.

"You see, the town never changes," Francisco commented as we climbed.

El Barranco did look exactly the way I remembered it. The streets were almost deserted; most of the activity concentrated in the patios, which were encircled by walls made of cacti planted close together. Through the cracks in the walls, I saw people cooking, washing, grinding corn, and children playing under the fruit trees. The town's population was primarily black. Walking by my side, Francisco often muttered to himself. We were nearing my grandmother's house when he grabbed my forearm, and forced me to stop. I was about to yank my arm free, when he pointed to a house on the left, saying, "That's the house where the murder took place."

"The murder?" I echoed, to make sure that I had understood him.

"The murder took place in that house over fifty years ago, then the family moved away." He let go of my arm and continued walking. Was he delirious? I wondered. And whose family had moved away—mine?

I was sweating and thirsty when we arrived at my grandmother's house. The front door was open. When she saw me, a pretty young girl started screaming, "Lina, Lina," (short for *Mamá Paulina*), "Sammy is here, Sammy is here."

I climbed the steps to the terrace and Francisco followed me. I entered *Mamá* Paulina's living room, which was cool and shadowy. I could hear a bunch of cackling children in the patio. "Lina, Lina, Lina," the voices cried in unison. The room contained a red clay *tinaja*, where the drinking water was kept, a small, unpainted table, and two chairs, upholstered with cowhide. A calendar on the walls was the only decoration. There was a door to my left, which opened into the only dormitory; another door opened to the open-air kitchen in the patio. I placed my shoulder bag on the table and took one of the chairs. Francisco stood at the door, grinning. When he heard voices approaching from the patio, he said, "How about a few *pesos* for a beer, *compañero*?" I was about to reach for my wallet, just to get rid of him, when *Mamá* Lina, followed by half a dozen loquacious children, entered the room. She had a wet towel wrapped around her head, and wore a dress with a black and white pattern; she was barefoot. We embraced. She had none of *Mamá* Martha's affluence of flesh. Lina smelled of coconut oil and ripe mangoes. Pulling away from me, she took my face by the chin and said, "Let me look at you, Santiago." Her eyes were moist, and her facial muscles trembled with emotion. Lina was tall, lean, like a stalk of sugar cane. Even though she was close to ninety and toothless, she seemed hale. The smaller children huddled beside her giggling, pulling her wide skirt, and the oldest—a boy and a girl—stood behind her. They were my black cousins. They looked at me with awe, as if I were from another planet. "Don't forget about me," Francisco said from the door. "Just give me a few *pesos* for a beer, Santiago."

Noticing Francisco, *Mamá* Lina grabbed the broom near the *tinaja* and marched toward him, motioning as if to sweep him away. "Shoo, shoo, drunk," Lina said, to the delight of the children who broke in riotous laughter, shrieking and skipping and repeating after her, "Shoo, shoo, drunk."

"But Lina," Francisco protested. "I brought your grandson to you. Let him give me money for a beer."

"Shoo, shoo," she repeated, fanning his legs with the broom. "Shoo, shoo. Look at him, he's heading back to the cantina. Don't go to the cantina; go to the river and get a fish for your family. Lazy drunk. Don't let my *comadre* Petra do all the work."

Defeated by her attack, and the children's chorus of hilarity and catcalls, a downcast Francisco descended the steps and stumbled away from the house in the scorching sun. Standing on the terrace, the children all chanted, "Shoo, shoo. Lina beat Francisco, Lina beat Francisco."

When Francisco withdrew, Lina addressed the oldest boy, who was in his late teens. "Juvenal, take Santiago's bag to my room, and put it in the trunk. Here is the key. Don't forget to lock it. Etilvia," she addressed the oldest of the girls, a young woman, "go to the *tienda* and get your cousin a Coca Cola."

The young people marched off to do their errands; Lina took me by the hand, and, followed by the four smaller children, we stepped into the patio. The wood kitchen was under a large straw roof, and here there was another table—where food was prepared—and chairs. We walked past the kitchen until we arrived at a *ciruela* tree from which a hammock hung. Lina ordered a chair brought for her and offered me the hammock. I did as I was told. Lina's large patio contained custard apple, mango, citrus, and sweetsop and coconut trees, red chilies, and the usual fowls, plus *pisingos*, a local duck. "I have four donkeys and ten pigs; they are feeding by the river," she informed me as if she were boasting of great riches. I knew that donkeys were prized possessions because they were used to carry water from the river and wood from the forest.

Lina introduced the smaller children to me. "This wee thing," Lina said with such affection that I could tell she was her favorite, "is Patricia. She's five years old; she's the daughter of Carmen Izquierdo." Carmen was one of my half aunts; she lived in Cartagena, where she worked in a government office. Patricia was extremely pretty. She wore her hair in two pigtails, and looked as though she, too, had taken a shower just before I arrived. The other three children were triplets. They were the offspring of Diana Marulanda, another one of Lina's daughters. Diana had lived with Lina all her life, but had died suddenly, of a heart attack, the year before. The triplets were nine years old, and they wore torn shorts, but no shirts or shoes. Like backup singers, they moved in synchronicity, but without uttering a word. They scrutinized me.

My mother was Lina's love child with *Papá* Julián. But after my grandfather married *Mamá* Martha, Lina had given birth to four children by different men. The children's fathers had left, leaving Lina with new mouths to feed. Besides Carmen and Diana, there were two sons. Lina's children had in turn married and reproduced, and, invariably, the mothers and fathers moved away, leaving the children with Lina, until they grew up and moved away. With the exception of Carmen Izquierdo, I had barely had any contact with my half uncles and aunts. Because they were black and poor and uneducated, I was brought up not to consider them as part of my family.

Etilvia returned with a cold bottle of Coca Cola, which I gulped down. When I finished, I noticed that the children were gazing at me enviously, as if I had just had a great treat which, to them, it no doubt was.

"Now children, go get cleaned up so you can take your cousin to see the improvements of the town," Lina said. The children scurried away jumping and twirling, as excited as if they were going to the circus.

"I want you to see the bridge at El Salto while we make your lunch," Lina said. "Later it will be too hot to walk." She paused, smiling at me tenderly. "I knew I wouldn't die before I saw you again," she murmured. "You've made Lina very happy because you remembered her."

Although she was my grandmother, I hardly knew her. All my life I had felt closer to my step-grandmother. Lina was illiterate, and she had lived her ninety years in El Barranco.

"You'd better go back today before it gets dark," she told me. "The guerrillas could kidnap you for a ransom. Just because you came from far away, they may think you have money."

I told her I planned to return to El Banco later that day. "Do you think the guerrillas know I am here?" I asked.

At that moment, a band of rowdy parakeets alighted in one of the mango trees. "News travels fast here," she said, pointing to the birds. "The parrots spread it. I bet you they already know."

"Do the guerrillas ever bother you, Lina?"

"Once in a while they come by and take a chicken or a pig. Once they took one of my young *burras*. But here I am, ninety years old. Nobody can bother me anymore." She smiled to herself. "Look at your grandfather; how mean he was to me when he left me to marry your *Mamá* Martha. He used to boast he had a pact with the devil, and he made all that money. Never gave me a penny. And now he's six feet under ground, and Lina is still here," she said, proud of her endurance.

Lina seemed as old and as fecund as one of the ancient trees in her yard. I was about to ask her some questions about my mother when I saw the children approaching. They had scrubbed their faces, combed their hair, and were wearing their best clothes, as if they were going to a party or to Sunday church. I got down off the hammock. Patricia approached me and grabbed my hand.

"Take Santiago to see the bridge first," Lina instructed Etilvia and Juvenal. "And make sure you're here by noon. I'm going to make a big *sancocho* for your cousin. I'm going to kill my fattest chicken for my grandson."

The children led the way. Under the punishing sun, we paraded through the green streets of El Barranco. They seemed as proud as if they were on a carnival float. We were heading for El Salto (The Fall), the lagoon in the back of the town. In my childhood, I had crossed El Salto on horse, on the way to my grandfather's farm, Tosnován. The trip by horse took an entire day because the path through the forest was narrow, rocky, precipitous. Tosnován was located in mountainous jungle, and the shrill serial chorus of the cicadas; the howls of the monkeys; the burbling of the icy creeks as they spilled from the snowy, unseen peaks of the Cordilleras; the cackle of parrots, parakeets, and macaws; the songs of tiny birds with neon colors; the roars of the jaguars, the hooting of the owls, and the rasping maraca sounds made by the vipers as they brushed the leafy ground; the small iguanas of iridescent green; the red ferocious ants carrying big chunks of vegetable matter, mowing down everything; the snake-long centipedes and weird-looking, asymetrical, poisonous spiders—the size of chicken eggs—all these things enchanted and frightened me as a child.

The first time I visited Tosnován, as we approached the farmhouse, I saw the farm children take flight in panic and climb up the mango trees, from which they observed us as we dismounted. My grandfather explained that the children were frightened because, besides their parents and a handful of farm workers, they were not used to visitors. A few days went by before the children allowed us to get near them. I was fascinated by their feral state, how they seemed just a step above the wild animals. After I had been there for almost a week, I approached one of the little farm girls. Since she was too shy to initiate conversation, I asked her how old she was. The girl, who was barefoot, her feet encased in a crust of black mud, her long hair down to her shoulders, said, "I was born the last time the parrots nested here." I was thirteen or fourteen years old at the time, and her answer astonished me. Even at that age, I sensed that there was a gap between the two of us that could not be bridged just by talking, no matter how sympathetic I was toward her. That night, I asked my grandfather about the last time the parrots had visited the farm. "The red-beaked parrots come around every seven years," he said. "They're due to nest here again next year." Although I had seen my grandfather many times tell the time of the day by looking at the position of the sun in the sky, it was during that visit to Tosnován that I began to sense how radically dissimilar this world was from the city where I lived during the school year. In my early twenties, when my grandfather's fortune declined and he had to sell the farm, I had felt a great sadness because I realized it was the end of a whole world, a whole way of being and feeling.

I started making conversation with Etilvia. She was tall, fleshy—like a young Sophia Loren painted cinnamon. I asked her if she was in school. "Oh, I finished high school last year. I was the best student in my class; I read all the books in the library," she replied eagerly. Sensing her quick intelligence, I asked, "Do you want to continue studying?"

"Yes," she said. "But how? The nearest place where I could continue my education would be Cartagena."

There was such finality in the way she said it that I felt an ache in my heart. Cartagena was just two days away by boat, but to her, because of her parents' poverty, it was as far away as another continent. Sensing how trapped she was, I wanted to rescue her from that town, from a life of penury that—at best—included marrying, having many children, her mind going dormant.

"Anyway, it's OK I'm not going to school anymore," she said. "I can see in the daylight, but I can't read at night. My eyes get very fatigued when I read."

"There is a hospital in El Banco," I said. "You should go there before your eyes are ruined."

Etilvia stared at me, with a blank expression. I understood that her parents couldn't afford the boat fare to El Banco, much less the hospital fee. Impulsively, I took out my wallet and handed her a bunch of *pesos*. Etilvia didn't count the bills, and she didn't say thank you, either. She rolled the money and gave it to little Patricia to put it in the pocket of her dress. But her eyes twinkled with gratitude.

We arrived at the bridge. It wasn't much of anything, but it did the job: its cement structure rose over the waters of El Salto. On the other shore, the narrow path had been replaced by a dirt road, which now connected El Barranco to the interior of the country. I was told that, once in a while, a vehicle would come into town from the state of Santander. We stood there admiring the cobalt blue lagoon, which was covered with lotus plants in bloom. Many swamp roosters flew airily from leaf to leaf, picking at the insects that nested in the topaz and ivory blooms. In the distance, a bloated dead dog bobbed in the still waters, and a turkey-size onyx vulture perched on it, picking at the eyes.

Etilvia said, "I like to come here with Mariela, my best friend. When the river is swollen, like now, we dive from the bridge. I wish you could meet Mariela," she added, joy creeping in her voice as she talked about her friend. "Mariela's so wild. She doesn't care about what people think. Lina gets very cross when she finds out we've jumped from the bridge."

"Is it safe?" I asked.

Etilvia smiled. "It's safe if the water is deep. Here, I'll show you."

She climbed the railing and dove into the waters below. I stood there, transfixed by her boldness. The children started screaming happily. For what seemed the longest time, Etilvia remained submerged. When she resurfaced, she called me to join her. "The water is so cool," she said. Laughing in unison, the triplets jumped in. I squeezed little Patricia's hand, to keep her from joining them.

"I don't want to mess my new dress," she said coquettishly, to set me at ease. "The water is very muddy. It will stain my dress."

Etilvia and the triplets began to play games in the water, screaming and carrying on. I had bathed in this lagoon many years ago with Rosita, with my mother, my aunts, and their friends. More than thirty years had gone by since that time, but I could almost hear their laughter now, and see their young, pretty olive-skinned bodies in 1950s bathing suits. Why had I come here, I wondered? After so many of my beliefs had crumbled in middle age, after the death of so many of my loved ones, my ideals had been replaced by a spiritual malaise that recently had made me yearn for answers I could not get. Yet part of me felt that in a world that rewarded aggression and greed, there was no room for someone searching for a center, for meaning, for a redemption that went beyond the personal, the selfish, the fulfillment of bourgeois needs and wants.

Juvenal, who had been quiet all this time, now stood next to me. He was very black, taller than me, and sturdily built, a living sculpture. He reminded me of African warriors I had seen in photographs.

A shot, followed by a volley of them, rang in the distance, and hundreds of birds, flapping their wings, imbricated the sky.

"It's the guerrillas on the other side of El Salto. Maybe they're hunting. Maybe they've executed a prisoner," Juvenal said matter-of-factly.

"Are they really that close?"

"They swim often on the other side. Sometimes they come into town to talk to the people, or to ask for things. Many of my friends have joined them out of boredom. There's nothing else to do in El Barranco." He paused. Juvenal pulled a leather pouch from his pants' pocket and, untying it, dumped the contents on his palm. Sparkling nuggets of gold filled his palm. "I know a place where I get these. After I have a bunch of them, I sell them in El Banco and give the money to Lina. When my mother was alive, she sold corn *bollos*, which she made; but now I have to help Lina feed the children."

"They're beautiful," I said, fingering the resplendent little pieces.

Juvenal smiled and, with parsimony, poured his treasure again in the pouch. "There are many dangerous vipers there," he said. "Sometimes they attack you. The other day, one of them jumped at me. It went 'ZAZZ, ZAZZ, ZAZZZZ,'" he hissed, baring his snowy teeth. "I had to pull my machete in a hurry and cut his head off."

I flinched.

"Look," Patricia said, "Etilvia and the triplets are drying out."

On the far shore, Etilvia and the boys were sitting on the sand, and shaking their heads to dry their hair.

"I think we'd better call them," I said. "We shouldn't be too late."

After we left El Salto, we went by the cemetery, but didn't go in.

"It's too bad you didn't come next month when my mother's tombstone will be laid," Juvenal said. "I've been saving money so she could have a nice tombstone." I knew that in these villages the size and the quality of work that went into a tombstone constituted one of the most important status symbols for a family. We continued walking until we came to the edge of the town, then we turned left and soon arrived at the cantina I passed with Francisco on the way to Lina's house. Since I was thirsty and sweating from the blazing sun, I offered to buy them a soda. Perhaps because it was lunch hour the cantina was empty, although the jukebox continued to blare Mexican *rancheras*. We all ordered Coca Colas. The bottles that were handed to us were like ice cubes, frosted, the liquid inside half-iced.

The children walked to the terrace facing the river in the distance, and leaned against the wall to drink their Cokes. They drank in silence, relishing every single little sip they took. There were enraptured looks on their faces as they stared at the slow-moving river. A big boat floated by, blowing its horn. The basso melancholy sound was like a magical instrument they listened to with enormous concentration. I thought how, as a child, my mother must have stood by the shores of El Barranco, waiting for the big boats to go by, waiting for their bawling horns that must have sounded to her like the song of sirens inviting her to dream about the world beyond this village. Sixty years later, I could detect this same yearning in the children's faces. I imagined little Patricia dreaming of visiting her mother in Cartagena, and wearing very pretty dresses all the time; and Juvenal, dreaming of striking ever richer mines of gold, until he could build a gold mausoleum for his mother; and the triplets, dreaming of a world in which they would each have an individuality and talk to others, not just among themselves; and Etilvia dreaming of her eyesight restored, so that she could continue to read, so that she, and her friend Mariela, could go away to a great metropolis and attend a university and fill their minds with all the knowledge and the culture their minds were capable of receiving. The intensity of the yearning in these young people's faces pierced my heart with a pain that had no name, a pain that left me wordless. I felt farther away from New York than I had felt since I had started my journey. I wondered if these children, too, would some day journey away from here. And I wondered whether their journey would lead to long lives of quiet fulfillment, or to sadness and tragedy. I wanted my arms to turn into long wings, so that I could shelter them, and fly away with them to a place where we all could live safely, in this moment forever.

Lina's delicious *sancocho* was served for me in the living room. The succulent meats, and roots and vegetables, were piled on freshly cut banana leaves. Lina and the children gathered silently around me to watch me eat. Despite my ravenous appetite, I felt uncomfortable. I would have preferred that we all ate together, but that wasn't how Lina wanted it. I ate as much as I could, and when I finished the children brought pewter plates from the kitchen and served themselves. With their plates heaped, they went to the patio to eat under the trees. The children didn't use silverware to eat, and they scooped up the thick soup with bowls made from the fruit of the *totumo* tree.

I realized what a special day this was to them. Although I don't think they ever went hungry, the concept of three meals a day was alien to them. Because of the generosity of the river and the land, there was always some kind of food available. I remembered the stories that Carmen Izquierdo used to tell me back in Barranquilla. There were times of the year when all they had to eat was whatever fruit was in season: *ciruelas,* or guavas or mangoes, plus black coffee, if they were lucky. Food was plentiful only during the months when the Magdalena produced its annual harvest of fish. Then they had *bocachicos, lebranches, lisas, coroncoros,* sardines, and *bagres,* a catfish that grows the size of a big dolphin.

The noon heat had settled on everything, creating an eerie repose. Not an animal moved, not a bird flew in the sky; even the trees became still, as if to conserve their moisture. I was full, drowsy, lethargic, the tangy taste of cumin and annatto lingering in my mouth. Lina suggested that I go lie in the hammock under the *ciruela* tree. She stayed behind to eat her meal alone.

When I woke up from my nap, I found Lina sitting on a bench next to my hammock and gazing at me. She was puffing a *calilla,* the long, thin cigar that black women, especially fortune tellers, smoke. She inhaled the way the African *palenqueras* do, by sticking the lighted end in their mouths. Lina reminded me of an ancient matriarchal sorceress, someone whose wisdom was beyond me, beyond anything I had read in books or could rationally understand.

"Lina's *sancocho* made you sleepy, eh?" she beamed, and sucked powerfully on her *calilla* before she exhaled potent aromatic clouds of smoke.

I nodded. There were so many questions I wanted to ask her, yet I found myself speechless.

"You look like a picture I have of your father," Lina said. "He was a good man to me. He bought me this house when he was living with your mother. If he hadn't done that, Lina would be living in the forest now."

"Did you ever meet my father, Lina?"

"No, he never came to visit, and Lina has never been any place farther than El Banco. But he used to send me sacks of rice and sugar and he always remembered Lina for Christmas. He wasn't like your grandfather who just took and took from me and from your mother." There was resentment in her voice when she talked about *Papá* Julián. More than sixty years after he had left her to marry *Mamá* Martha, she couldn't forgive him.

I heard myself ask, "Lina, what was the murder that took place down the road? Francisco mentioned it to me this morning."

Lina dragged on her cigar and closed her eyes; a grimace spread over her crinkled face. She pulled out the *calilla*, which was moist with saliva up to its burning tip. Then she spat on the floor. "So Francisco told you?"

"Yes, Lina," I said pressing her, now that my curiosity had been piqued. "What murder was he talking about?"

"A long time ago," she began, the way one begins a fairy tale, "long before you were born, your grandfather's oldest son, Carlos, your uncle, he killed a boy with a machete. Your grandfather's family had to leave El Barranco. They took your mother with them. That's when they settled upriver in El Banco." She paused and looked away, into the trees. "What was so bad about the murder," she said, now locking her eyes with mine, "was how your grandfather behaved. Because he had money, and the boy's family was poor, your grandfather treated the other family very badly. We didn't have the police here then. We didn't have a jail, either. No one had been murdered in the town before that time. So your uncle went unpunished because your grandfather was rich in cows and land." She paused, lost in thought, trying to remember events that had taken place long ago. "Oh, I go to Church," she said finally. "I hear the priest preach about what's in the Bible, about the sins of the fathers being passed to the sons. Your Uncle Carlos never paid for what he did, but I know what happened to that family. I heard about your Uncle Migue, the one who's a drunk and lives in the streets in the market in Barranquilla. And your other uncle, Jessie, who went to Venezuela to work in the diamond mines and was lost in the jungle. I knew all those boys when they were born. They lived down the street. And they were cursed by what Carlos did." She leaned over and grabbed my arm firmly. "It's good you found out about the murder. It's good you know now what's in your grandfather's blood. I don't want you to suffer like your poor mother and Rosita. That Sofia, she loved your *Papá* Julián more than anything, and they were never nice to her."

I thought about how odd it was that it had taken Rosita's death to make me come back here, to look for answers to the void I felt. It was just an accident that I had run into Francisco, that he had mentioned the murder, that I had been curious enough to ask Lina about it. But it was a coincidence that, in a matter of hours, shed new light on the life I had lived to that point. Now I understood my mother's blind loyalty to her family, as if she had been sworn to secrecy at the risk of her life; now I understood what it was like for Rosita to live with Carlos. I understood, too, that in the years I lost to drugs I had been following patterns that had been established long before I was born; and I understood the horror that lay at the heart of our family's history.

A few hours later, I embraced and kissed Lina as we said goodbye. I took a good look at her, trying to engrave her image on my brain, so that I would never forget it.

"I'm glad that you came before I died," she said. "Now I can die in peace."

"I'll come back again, Lina," I said, "and you'll still be here."

She smiled her toothless smile. "I'll be here under the earth, Santiago. But wherever you go, remember Lina will always be looking after you."

⦿⦿⦿

That night, back in El Banco, I had insomnia in the ghostly house. All night long scenes from the past replayed in my mind. Many of the memories were about the family gatherings at Christmas and New Year's, when most of my relatives would converge in El Banco. Those who lived in cities usually arrived on Christmas Eve. As the clan began to assemble—some reaching El Banco by plane, some by jeep, some by boat—I would be thrilled to see favorite relations I hadn't seen since mid-summer.

Leading up to Christmas Eve, the days were crammed with visits to my grandfather's farms, hunting expeditions with my Uncle Germán, fishing parties with my cousins, swimming excursions to the César River and the nearby ponds and lagoons. At night, I would go with Rosita and my cousins to the quay, where we played with firecrackers and lit Bengal lights, until we became dizzy from the smoke. There were dances, evening visits to my aunts' friends and visits to El Banco's cathedral to admire the Christmas ornaments and especially the *nacimiento,* which was a baroque recreation of the town of Bethlehem, and Jesus' family and the Wise Men and their gifts. Many nights culminated in going to the movies, but most evenings the family brought chairs out and sat on the sidewalk, and my grandfather would entertain us with stories about witchcraft, or I would hold court narrating, in great detail, my favorite movies of the year. At all times the house was suffused with the smells of the foods being prepared for the holidays: glazed hams, chicken and pork, rice *pasteles,* roast turkeys and wild ducks stuffed with raisins and sweet yams, the aroma of coconut and pineapple delicacies.

But as Christmas Eve approached, a kind of human storm usually began to brew. The house was the stage, and the family was the audience, to fights among the adults, and sometimes among the children; to hysterical scenes of crying, and insults being flung; to a young aunt's suicide attempt, by swallowing a handful of firecrackers; to an uncle getting drunk and smashing the jeep and ending up in the hospital with broken limbs; to the bitter quarrels that my aunts' husbands would start with my grandfather. One time Mother beat Rosita with her spiked heel until she bled from the head. While Rosita still bled, Mother locked her up in the room in the back of the patio where the horse saddles and other farm implements were kept. Often Rosita, my mother, and I were reminded by my aunts and uncles that we didn't really belong there, that we were not real members of the family. The only solace was found in the times Rosita and I would go by the river in the late afternoon, sit on a bench, and talk about life when we'd return to Barranquilla, to our home.

As a child, I had never understood why things always turned ugly during these family reunions. From year to year, I'd dwell on the parts I loved, trying to forget about the moments of horror that always resurfaced. On New Year's Day the entire family would go to Las Susanas for a final get-together. It was a day of great gaiety, there were no fights, everyone got along, a huge *sancocho* was cooked, goats were slaughtered and roasted, and bullfights were staged in the corrals, as well as donkey and horse races and canoe rides in the lagoon. Everything was patched up then, so that when the family dispersed again until the following year, they carried with them the memory of that day, not of the preceding ones.

But thirty years later, as I lay in the room next to where *Mamá* Martha slept, it dawned on me that all that time, all those resentments and irrational outbursts, had something to do with the fact that the family was being eaten alive trying to forget the murder that Carlos had committed. Since he was the oldest male, and therefore the successor to the patriarchy of my grandfather, Carlos was my grandfather's favorite. With the exception of Uncle Germán and Uncle Alejo, who were university students, the other four uncles were out-of-control drunks, who repeatedly got into serious trouble. One uncle in particular, Migue, had been so severely beaten in front of the family by my grandfather that afterwards he had taken to bed and slept all day long, going out only at night, when no one could see him. We called him Dracula.

It was in this house that I became terrified of sex. I must have been thirteen when Germán took me along on his outings to fuck *burras*. It was after one of these outings that I caught a terrible venereal disease. When I returned to Barranquilla, my testicles had swollen to the size of an avocado. After this time, my mother began calling me into her bedroom several times a year to inspect my testicles. During these inspections my mother checked the size of my penis to see if it was growing properly. Often she warned me about being overweight because then, she said, my penis would not grow to a normal size. Consequently, I became self-conscious about the size of my penis, and I suffered enormously when I had to undress for gym classes at school. It wasn't until I was in my late twenties that I became aware that my penis was fine the way it was.

Thinking about all that, I began to recollect the time in Barranquilla when Mother, her lover, Rosita, and I moved to the house in Barrio Boston from the four-room apartment in downtown Barranquilla where we had lived after my father died. In the downtown apartment, Mother and her lover and Rosita slept in the same room, though in separate beds. I slept in a little room off the kitchen. I was ten years old. Even then, I remember crossing the living room at night and watching Mother and her lover making love. I would get very excited watching Mother and her lover reaching paroxysms of passion. I must have wondered how it was possible for Rosita not to wake up, her bed being near the big bed where my mother and her lover lay. From that time on, I became an avid voyeur to my mother's nights of passion. Soon after that, I started to masturbate and, for the next few years, I would beat off thinking of my mother and her lover making love.

Then we moved to the house in Barrio Boston. It was a new house, modest but pretty. There were three separate bedrooms, and Rosita's bedroom was situated between my mother's and mine. We lived in that house for seven years, until we emigrated to the United States. I loved that house. I had pets: my two dogs, and chickens, pigeons, and ducks.

My mother's lover, Ricardo, was a married man. He would usually arrive at the house in the evenings, after dinner, and then my mother and he would sometimes sit on the porch to take in the air, sometimes just the two of them, though sometimes neighbors or friends came by to visit. Often they would go to the open-air movie house halfway down the block. The theater was so close to our house that I could hear the entire movies at night, although I couldn't understand what was being said because most of them were in foreign languages. The shows started at 7:30, and they were double features. My mother and her lover would return home usually after the first feature, and then they would go to their bedroom to make love.

They always left their bedroom door open. I would wait in bed pretending to sleep until they returned from the movie theater. But as soon as the lights were off, and they started engaging in sex, I would crawl across my room, and through Rosita's room, until I reached the door of Mother's bedroom.

I already knew that I was homosexual. An effeminate boy I knew would come to visit in the early afternoon, at siesta time. While he lay in bed, pretending to take his siesta, I would take my penis and press it against his lips. Sometimes he took it, sucking me delicately. I prayed that something would happen and that I would change; that one day I would wake up liking girls.

I loved Rosita above all women. She, however, was an angel to be adored from afar. We would stage beauty pageants in the neighborhood, and the girls would parade in their bathing suits. I was the only judge. I must have been fifteen, when one day, suddenly, I noticed Rosita had grown from an ugly duckling into a slender, long-legged beautiful girl. That day, I awarded her the crown as the most beautiful girl in Barrio Boston.

In this state of feverish excitement, my consciousness flooded with recollections, I had a sudden memory. Sergio and I shared the same bedroom at my grandparents' home. He slept in a hammock and I on a bed. One night, I was asleep, lying on my stomach, when Sergio climbed on top of me. He pulled down my pajama pants and tried to penetrate me. It hurt a lot. I started protesting. Sergio sealed my lips with his hand and whispered in my ears, "If you don't let me fuck you, I'll kill you, you little faggot." In terror, I closed my eyes and allowed him to sodomize me until he came. When he finished, he pulled up my pants and went back to his bed. I realized I was bleeding. I sat on my bed. The pain was excruciating, but I hobbled to one of the bathrooms in the back of the house. When I turned the light on, I saw my pajamas and legs drenched in blood. I took a long shower and stayed under the water for a long time until it ran clear. I didn't know what to do with the bloody pants. I washed them, but the stain remained. After I toweled dry, I bundled up the pants and decided to get rid of them. As I passed the garden next to the dining room, I saw a shovel in the dirt. Feeling delirious, I dug a hole next to the crepe myrtle tree and buried my pajama pants in it. I went back to bed and stayed awake all night. The next morning I came down with an asthma attack and did not have to get out of bed for the rest of the day. The following day, the wound in my ass had healed enough that I could walk without trouble.

But if all this had happened, why had I blocked it for over thirty years? Was it possible that I had imagined this incident? Just to think that I might be imagining this was enough to make me feel as though I was going crazy. I got up from my bed and opened the door to the patio. The moon and stars illuminated everything. It was well past midnight, but it was as clear as a rainy afternoon in the fall in Manhattan. I walked to the garden where I thought I had buried my pajama pants. The crepe myrtle was in full bloom, its branches heavy with flowers. I looked for a shovel but could not find one. Deracinated, I knelt on the moist black earth and started digging with my hands, in the spot where I thought I had buried the bloody pajamas. I didn't care whether anyone found me excavating like a mad rodent. Suddenly, my hands touched something. I pulled the rotting cord from the waist of the pajamas. I sat there under the branches of the crepe myrtle, and cried softly, but uncontrollably, under the clusters of tiny snowy flowers.

The following morning I flew back to Barranquilla. I squirmed in my seat throughout the flight. The memories that had resurfaced the night before, plus the discovery of the evidence, tormented me. If that had happened to me, I wondered what might have happened to Rosita. I was equally disturbed by finding out about the murder Carlos had committed. In my adolescence, when he had lived with us, Carlos had been a lover of books. His taste was different from Aunt Caty's, but he gave Knut Hamsun, Park Lagervist, Françoise Sagan, and André Gide, among others, to me to read. Twice a year he'd take me to a local bookstore so that I could buy half a dozen books I wanted to read. I was fourteen when, in one of those outings, he purchased for me *The Maker*, by

Jorge Luis Borges. After we moved to the States, I heard from mother about Carlos's wild success in business, and I was proud of him for becoming a rich man. Up until I started college in Manhattan, we had corresponded sporadically, and his letters had been full of fatherly advice. When Mother and I traveled to Colombia, we had stayed at his house, and he and Gloria had gone out of their way to make us feel welcomed. As I came out of the closet, sensing he would disaprove of me, I had drifted away from him. By that time, anyway, I had grown closer to Gloria, his wife. Like Aunt Caty, Gloria was a refined woman and she loved the arts. During her frequent visits to New York, I got to know her, and she had gone out with Ryan and me. After Carlos divorced Gloria, I fell out of touch with him. But I was proud of him for making a name for himself in business. I knew that all throughout Colombia there were branches of his company. I desperately wanted to believe that perhaps the murder had been an accident.

My relatives were having lunch when I arrived at their apartment. I had no appetite, so I asked for coffee and joined them to chat about my trip. I wanted to talk about what I had found out about Carlos, about the murder, but I realized I'd have to wait until the moment was appropriate. I was aware that because Caty was not my blood relation, she might not know anything about it. Because intimacy with her was much more developed than with Uncle Alejo, I felt she'd be able to listen and talk to me in a way that probably was alien to him.

Over lunch we chatted about my grandmother and step-grandmother, and about my visit to my grandfather's farm, and then Uncle Alejo excused himself to go take his siesta, since he had to be back at the university later that afternoon.

When we were left alone, Aunt Caty lit a cigarette as she savored her coffee. "By the way, Sammy. You're Mr. Popularity himself. You have two invitations."

"Really," I said. I knew so few people in the city anymore.

"One is from Gloria. She called this morning. When I told her you'd be back today she said she was sending her driver over at seven to pick you up. I said that I didn't know whether you had other engagements or not, but this did not seem to deter her. You don't have to go if you feel it is an imposition."

"Oh no," I said, brightening. "You know how much I like Gloria; I would love to see her."

Aunt Caty placed her cigarette on the ashtray and reached for my hand. "Sammy," she said studying my hand, as she stroked it. "I never told you in the letters, because I know you're fond of her and I didn't want to cause you pain. But after the divorce from Carlos, Gloria is almost unrecognizable. You know she was my best friend for many years; the only woman here in Barranquilla with whom I could have intellectual discussions. Perhaps I shouldn't tell you very much. She might not appreciate it. Maybe she'll tell you how it's been for her these past years. At any rate, it's safe to say that she had a severe nervous breakdown, and that she's not half the person you once knew." Aunt Caty paused and raised her head, anger set in her features. "Carlos behaved like a monster with her, Sammy. Sure, she's a rich woman now and won't have to worry about money for the rest of her life; but what a price she had to pay for that. Anyway, she invited both of us to dinner. But the two of you should be alone together. I know how much you've always enjoyed her company."

Aunt Caty let go of my hand, took a long drag from her cigarette and leaned back on her chair. "The other invitation," she said, anger rising in her voice, "is from your Uncle Carlos. He wants you to come over to his house tomorrow night for dinner. I guess he wants you to meet his Lolita. Did you know he left Gloria for a fifteen-year-old nymphet?"

I felt faint. I had decided to return to New York without seeing Carlos. It seemed to be the easiest way out. Now that I knew about the murder, I would have preferred to go back to New York without seeing him. Carrying this knowledge with me was so upsetting, and made me so obsessed, that I decided to tell Aunt Caty what I had found out.

"Caty," I began. "There's something I want to tell you."

"Yes," she said, leaning forward on the table.

As she sat there, inhaling her cigarette, her intelligent eyes focused on me with an affectionate gaze, I couldn't find the courage to tell her. I thought how unfair it was to burden her with the knowledge of Carlos's crime or even with what Sergio had done to me as a boy. So I said, "There are so many things I want to say to you. I found out many things in my trip to El Banco, but I can't tell you just now."

Caty's expression didn't change: but the light in the back of her eyes darkened. I realized that as a member of the family by marriage, she did not feel it was her place to say anything about Uncle Alejo's family that was in any way damaging. But the intensity of her burning gaze let me know that she knew plenty. "It's OK, Sammy," she uttered softly. "There's plenty of time. You still have a few days here. The trip is not over yet."

Sabanilla, a hamlet on a bay of ashen-colored waters, is half an hour away from Barranquilla by car. The houses of the villagers—most of them fishermen—are encrusted on a slope that drops precipitously, creating at its bottom a beach called Salgar. At the zenith of one of the hills that encircles the bay there's a nineteenth-century mansion in ruins that the locals refer to as El Castillo de Salgar. The elevation opposite it remained free of urban growth until the mid-1980s, when the most important drug traffickers of the area built half a dozen estates overlooking the sea.

It was on this mountain that Carlos and Gloria had constructed a compound back in the late 1980s. I had seen pictures of it, but this was my first time visiting "La Gloria," as the hacienda is called. As the gates opened, Gloria's driver took me up a gravel road that ends at the top of a hill, where the villa sits at the edge of a cliff. To my right, lush flower gardens surrounded a Thai guest house; to my left, fenced-in manicured pastures contained black and white Arabian horses grazing. Behind the pastures were the houses where the workers live.

Gloria's villa is a two-story futuristic glass structure. Flower beds and trees with festive blooms surround the villa. On one side of it is a swimming pool, inlaid with emerald-colored tiles and shaped like a gigantic turtle. On the other side is a tennis court. Gloria was waiting for me on the terrace. She wore the kind of ankle-length cotton gown worn by the Goajiro Indian women.

Balmy breezes wafted from the Caribbean. Standing there, her alabaster dress billowing in the zephyr, Gloria looked every bit as glamorous as the woman I remembered, but there was also something haunting about her aloneness at that hour, at the top of that hill.

We embraced and kissed warmly. "You look beautiful," I said, because she did look beautiful, and because I suspected it would please her. Taking me by the hand, we entered the house. Drinks in hand, Gloria took me on a tour of the place with its collection of blue-chip art they had acquired in Colombia and in the United States, the decorative pieces brought from travels around the world, the lavishly appointed rooms. I knew that Carlos had become a millionaire with his refining factories, but until that moment I had had no idea the extent of his wealth.

After the tour was over we sat downstairs, in the living room that overlooked a terrace and the Caribbean. There were many questions I wanted to ask her, but I didn't want to pry. She asked me to tell her about Rosita's death and I told her what I knew.

Dinner was served on the terrace overhanging the cliff. As the sun sank in the still waters, scarlet clouds incarnadined the halcyon sea. Rills the color of flowing lava embroidered the becalmed skin of the ocean, which was broken only by schools of balletic and silvery flying fish. Finally, Gloria started asking me more personal questions. Was I happy? Was I writing a new book? Had I begun to recover from Ryan's death? She had met him in New York, in the mid-1980s, when she visited the city often to go shopping, to take in shows, to sample the finest restaurants. I described in some detail the agony of his final months, and the depression that had gripped me after his death. Had I met anyone I was interested in, she wanted to know? I told her I had dated a few guys, but hadn't found anyone who was right for me. "And perhaps I never will," I added.

"Remember what Luis Cernuda says about love?" she asked. "That often it lasts just an instant, an instant that is an eternity." She sighed. The pause of the twilight had ceased, but solitary sea ravens and pelicans fished in the ocean, unwilling to go to their nesting places for the night. Gloria poured the coffee.

"I don't know how much Caty has told you about my life, since your uncle and I divorced," she said.

I told her what I knew.

"I'm sorry I didn't write or call you for the past five years, Sammy. Although I'm no longer married to Carlos, you're family to me and always will be. It's just that since the marriage fell apart, it's been very difficult for me, and I haven't been in touch with many people. I still see Caty because she wouldn't let me drift away from her. Even when I didn't call her or go to see her, she'd call me, and when I wouldn't answer the phone she came to see me. And I'm so glad she did, otherwise I might have died." Gloria paused, and her eyes wandered over the waters of the ocean, which had become pitch-black.

Many stars had come out, and a waning moon was emerging from behind the hill opposite Gloria's house. Gloria was in a subdued mood, she seemed as serene as the night. But there was a deep melancholia, a sadness in her voice and in her manners. She seemed broken beyond repair, as if she no longer believed happiness was possible on this earth. I sat in silence, to indicate that we would talk about her life only if she wanted to.

"Have you seen Carlos yet?" she asked.

I flinched at the mention of his name and shook my head.

"If you do see him, you'll find him much changed. He was never an easy man to live with. But for many years it was fine, it was even wonderful, because there was this charm, this sweetness about him. Of course there were terrible periods when he would lapse into behavior that to me was incomprehensible. He'd drink a lot, and get abusive and then maudlin. I'd forgive him because when he wasn't drinking he'd go back to being a good husband. I knew he was disappointed in me because I had not been able to give him a child. But I knew he loved me, and he was generous. I guess our troubles began about ten years ago, when he started making lots of money." She paused and stared at me. "Sammy, do you know how Carlos made his fortune?"

"With his oil refining factories. That's what I've been told."

Gloria clasped her hands: she no longer wore the wedding ring with a yellow diamond that Carlos had given her when he became rich. "You understand that what I'm going to tell you is not because I'm bitter toward Carlos anymore—although sometimes I am. I won't deny that I was bitter for years, and that bitterness almost killed me. One can live poisoned only for so long. You either get cured or you die. And now I want to live. I see that you don't know the truth about your uncle. Caty and Alejo have spared you. It's true that at some point his business started doing well, but the bulk of his immense fortune was made through the drug trade."

I was stunned by this revelation. Up until that moment I thought of Carlos as a successful industrialist. I said so.

"It all started when the government banned the importing of the chemicals needed to process cocaine. Carlos, however, had a license because he needed these chemicals to make his paint and lubricants. At some point he was approached by one of the cartels, and he began to sell them the chemicals they needed for an exorbitant price. That's how it all began. Later he became a partner with one of the big capos. If you don't believe me, ask Caty. Or Alejo. They'll corroborate everything I'm telling you."

Gloria fell silent. She stared into the night, which was punctured by diamante planets and stars filigreeing the firmament.

"It was around that time that he bought this land and started the work on this place. As you can see, no expense was spared. We kept so busy traveling, building, acquiring, that there was no time to really pause and think about what was happening. Carlos had always been a heavy drinker, but around this time he became a coke fiend. It was like something out of *Scarface*, but worse. It got to the point where the only way he could get high was by giving himself cocaine enemas. By that point our marriage was over. We still lived in the same house, but we were complete strangers to each other. Then, one day, he announced that he was in love with another woman. And that was it. He moved out overnight. I know it sounds weird," she said, her voice breaking, "but I still loved him. He was my husband; my hero. My Great Gatsby. For a long time after we married, he meant everything to me; I saw the world through his eyes. I lived only to please him. My greatest joy was to make him happy. When he left me for a child—she was thirteen at that time, Sammy: her parents practically sold her to Carlos, for greed and for fear—I went mad with grief. I spent my days in my bedroom, with the curtains drawn, listening to tragic operas. One day I lost my mind, I took a kitchen knife and started gashing the most valuable paintings. Then I took forty Seconals and slashed my wrists. You can still see where I cut myself." She show me her scarred wrists.

I looked away, my breath caught in my throat.

"I'm sorry, darling," Gloria said, reaching out and patting my arm. "It's just not a pretty story. I can stop if you find this too upsetting."

I knew how important this moment was to her. "Please go on," I said.

"My maid had one of the workers tear the door down in the morning, when she came to bring me breakfast and there was no answer. I had lost most of my blood. They rushed me to the hospital, and I was in a coma for weeks."

As Gloria finished speaking, in my mind's eye I saw Rosita's ravaged corpse.

"Anyway," she said, taking a sip of her coffee, her voice bringing me back to the present, "that was a long time ago. As you can see, your uncle was generous in his settlement: I guess he was buying my silence so that I would never talk to the government about his involvement with the cartels. I'm a rich woman. I can do anything I want, if I had the desire to do anything. Eventually I'd love to move away from here, and start a new life elsewhere . . . perhaps in Manhattan." Her eyes twinkled for a moment, that idea cheering her up. "We could do all the things we used to do years ago."

I reached over and clasped her hands in mine. "I would like that very much, Gloria."

"I'm a little tired," she said getting up from her chair. "Please do stay over tonight. In the morning we'll go sailing, or horseback riding. I would love to wake up and find you here."

"I'll stay over. I'd like to see more of this place in the morning." She got up.

"You can take any of the guest rooms upstairs. But stay out here on the terrace for a while. The sea at night becomes incredibly beautiful, if you look at it for a long time." She kissed me on the cheeks. "Good night, darling. See you in the morning."

Gloria glided out of the terrace, like a haunted spirit. I felt sad for her. She was like a broken-winged bird trapped in a golden cage.

The new revelations about Carlos left me confused. If killing the boy in his youth had been an accident, it would have been easy to dismiss it as perhaps an isolated incident. But if I added to that his involvement with the Colombian cartels, and the way he had treated Gloria, I had to conclude that my uncle was an evil man.

Potted hibiscus with red blooms framed the terrace; I walked to the edge of it. In the moonlight, the sea was mute, calm, its surface sleek, its even wide swells like melted lead cooling in a huge cauldron. Here and there, close to the shore, the eerie fins of sharks sliced the onyx surface of the waters. Dark birds flew overhead, flapping their sonorous wings. Despite its beauty, there was something about the place that made me uneasy, and I wanted to flee from it. Yet I couldn't tear myself away from the terrace. Gloria had been right: the still night sea—in its utter and complete darkness—had become astonishingly beautiful. But there was a monstrousness in its perfect beauty, just as there was a monstrousness in this place where Gloria lived, which had been built upon so many destroyed lives.

The blackness of the ocean extended into infinity, blending with the sky. It was easy to stand there and to feel that this blackness extended all the way to the other side of the ocean, all over the world. I tore my eyes away from the scene and, looking heavenward, saw, almost directly above my head, the effulgent stars of the Southern Cross dangling from the sky.

It was nine o'clock the following night when I arrived for drinks at Carlos's penthouse in the outskirts of Barranquilla. Part of me wished I hadn't come. After the recent revelations I no longer liked Carlos. I wished I had left Colombia without seeing him. Yet I had traveled all this way, and was so close to seeing him, that something in me pressed me to go on, for this would be perhaps the last meeting I would ever have with him. I couldn't quite trust myself about how I'd react once I was in his presence. But I was a middle-aged man, and I wanted to put my family history behind me.

Carlos's condominium was built like a fortress, high walls sheltering it. Electronic gates completed the bunker-like setting. The window nearest to the ground was at least three floors up. The building was surrounded by flower gardens and almond trees. A satellite dish looked like a huge ear pointed to the sky. As I walked on the glass bricks leading to the front door, each brick lit up as my shoes touched it. Devices that looked like the protruding tubes of snorkeling equipment were planted along the path. Each one had a monitor camera (a red eye) installed in it. As I approached the main door, a computer voice gave instructions on how to proceed. The main door opened automatically. I entered the elevator that led to Carlos's penthouse. Each corner of the elevator had a gyrating camera. As the doors of the elevator opened into a foyer of the duplex, I was met by a bodyguard. The man went to a wall, talked to a microphone announcing my arrival, and then said, "Follow me, please. Your uncle is waiting for you in the library."

The guard led me through the living room, where two silent men were playing cards. The white room with high walls was sparsely decorated, but all the objects were Art Deco. A couple of the walls had a mural depicting scenes from Carnival: people in grotesque and gaudy costumes and masks. The guard pressed some buttons on the library door and it slid inside the wall noiselessly.

Carlos was sitting behind a desk, staring at a computer. "Ah," he said without getting up, but inviting me to come in with his hand. "Here you are at last, Santiago."

The door closed behind me. I fought the agitation I felt in my heart. Since Carlos continued fussing with a mouse, and he gave no indication he was going to move away from the desk, I walked slowly toward him. When I was near him, he removed his glasses, smiled, and got up. I extended my hand, but Carlos embraced me.

"You look well," he said, placing his hands on my shoulders. Like me, he was a tall man. Standing so close to him, I was uncomfortably struck by our resemblance: it was my mother's face I saw looking back at me. Releasing my shoulders, he said, "Can I offer you a whiskey?"

"That'd be fine," I said.

Carlos limped to the bar. He was emaciated, the way some people are wasted away by cocaine. He reminded me of the way I had looked at the height of my crack addiction. But he was calm, not jitterish. While he poured the drinks, I looked around the library. The room was dimly lit, its heavy maroon drapes drawn, and the only illumination was the lamp on Carlos's desk, and the dull glow of a wall made of TV screens that showed different parts of the inside and outside of the building. There was another wall with shelves of tapes and some books, but more prominently displayed were racks of weapons: revolvers, rifles, and even machine guns.

"I take my whiskey on the rocks," Carlos called from the bar. "How about you?"

"Soda will be fine," I said, making up my mind that I would get away from this place as soon as possible. My breathing became labored; my shoulders tightened; my back began to ache. I wished I had skipped this visit.

Carlos handed me the drink and we sat on comfortable chairs facing each other. I had no idea how to begin a conversation with him.

"So what brings you back to Barranquilla, after all these years?" he asked. His eyes were watery and bloodshot. The irises seemed wrapped in a viscous black membrane, as if he had been staring into darkness for too long. His eyes gleamed like those of a nocturnal predator.

"I . . . ah," I stammered, unable to think of a response that wasn't confrontational. I began to perspire.

"You came looking for stories, didn't you?" He kicked back the whiskey in his glass.

At that moment, the door of the library opened, and a young, very pregnant, woman came in.

"Come in, Sarita," Carlos said. "I want you to meet my nephew Santiago. He's a writer, and he lives in New York."

The young woman was tall, with silky blonde hair and sculptural limbs. She looked Nordic, the child of Scandinavian immigrants. I got up as she approached us. Demurely, almost as if ashamed to be meeting a member of Carlos's family, she gave me her hand. I had no idea whether they were married or not. Or whether she was his mistress, which in Colombian society made her an outcast.

"Pleased to meet you, Santiago," she said, and dropped my hand.

Carlos invited her to join us.

"I'd like to *mi amor*, but I'm very tired. I'm not feeling well tonight."

"She's due any minute, Santiago," Carlos said. Then, boastfully, he added, "It's going to be a boy. Can you imagine? Here I am becoming a father at my age. But this is going to be only the first one," he said. "We're going to have many children, a whole army of them. Aren't we, Sarita?"

She smiled and then said, "May I pour you another drink before I go, *mi cielo*?"

"*Gracias, mi vida*," Carlos said, handing her the glass and patting her behind. "How about you, Santiago. How's your drink?"

"My drink is fine. Thanks."

When Sarita left, and Carlos and I were alone once more, he said, "So what do you think about her?"

"She seems nice," I remarked politely.

"I know you don't like women," Carlos said sarcastically. "But you have no idea what a boost it is to me to have a beautiful woman like that at my age. Also a woman who's going to make me a father."

"I may not care about women that way," I said. "But I certainly appreciate a beautiful woman when I see one."

"I'm glad you do, Santiago."

I squirmed in my seat. Perhaps I had already seen enough; perhaps just seeing how much he had changed from the way I remembered him was enough, and now I could leave.

Almost as if he sensed my train of thought, Carlos said, "Didn't mean to upset you; sorry. It's nice to see you after all these years. You are my favorite nephew. You've made a brilliant life for yourself—a writer in the United States, a college professor in New York. *Carajo*, I'm proud of you." Then, abruptly changing his tone, Carlos asked, "Did you get a chance to see Gloria?"

"Yes."

"Good. She's always been very fond of you. It's too bad what happened between us. I know it's been hard for her. But you know, I treated her well when we separated. We had to separate: I wanted to have children. And now, you saw for yourself, Sarita is going to make me a father. Finally, I'm a happy man."

"Congratulations," I said, feeling increasingly ill at ease.

Carlos gulped the rest of his drink down, got up, went to the bar and returned with a bottle of whiskey and a bucket of ice. He poured himself another drink. He offered to refresh my drink, but I declined.

"Have you become a teetotaler?"

I took a sip from my drink as if to appease him.

"What is it, Santiago?" he asked finally. "Something is bothering you. What did Gloria tell you about me?" Becoming irate, he exploded, "She's a lying bitch, that's what she is. She'd better watch what she says about me or she's going to regret it."

Knowing what I now knew about him, I realized he was capable of harming her. "Gloria didn't say anything about you that I didn't know already," I said, surprised at my boldness. After all, no matter how much I disliked him, he was my oldest uncle and I owed him respect.

"You don't fool me," he said. "I detect in your attitude a contempt toward me."

"Maybe it's your conscience," I said.

"What do you mean?" he snapped, his voice becoming threatening. "What is it about me that you despise so much? I'd think you'd be proud of me for becoming a rich man. We come from a family of *campesinos*. Peasants don't go very far in this society. I was the only one of your grandfather's children who could get away from that stinking hellhole and do it with style. Alejo, whom you admire so much, is a pathetic man. With his intellect, he could have been anything. President of Colombia. Whatever. I would have backed him. All that education abroad and when he retires from that stupid university, he won't have a pot to piss in. He's spent his whole life working for the poor, and look where that's gotten him. He's sixty years old and he'll be poor till the day he dies. I'm the only one of your grandfather's children who has become somebody. The rest of them are no-good drunks. They're my brothers, but I'm ashamed of them."

He finished his drink, and poured himself another one, this time without ice. "You're like those gringos who come here with their fucking puritan ethics and judge us because we're different from the way they are. They approve of us only when they can exploit us and we don't fight back. Well, those years are over. No matter what anybody says, the drug cartels have had a beneficial influence on Colombia. Before they came along—unless you've been away so long that you've forgotten our history—this was a medieval nation owned by a score of aristocratic families. What the cartel people have done was to break up the homogeneity of the old oligarchy. That's why somebody like me can now be a rich man, not a *campesino* without a penny to his name. What the drug lords have done is to propel Colombia into the twenty-first century. It's because of them that this country will be a major economic power in the future."

Carlos's arguments were not new to me. I had heard them spouted by many jingoistic nationalists from all over the world. Knowing what I knew about the destructiveness of nationalism carried to that degree—how it was responsible for many of the horrors of the late twentieth century—I didn't care very much for the argument he was making. What's more, I really didn't care how he had made his money. As long as I didn't profit by it, it was not my problem. I took a long sip from my drink, and then, much to my surprise, I said, "Carlos, I found out about the boy you killed in El Barranco."

Carlos leaned back on his chair, and he seemed to collapse on it. He filled up his glass with liquor. All of a sudden, I was afraid; afraid that he might get angry; afraid that he might hurt me.

"Oh, that," he murmured, closing his eyes. With his free hand, he made a gesture as if to dismiss the murder. "That," he repeated, his voice dropping to a whisper, "that was the kind of thing that happens among boys." Carlos reached for his glass and downed its contents, almost with a kind of desperation. "You know, Santiago," he said, opening his eyes. "I've never talked to anyone about it, since the day it happened. Not even to Gloria, all those years we were married. After it happened, the family never, ever mentioned it again. It must have been Lina who told you about it in El Barranco. I don't know who else would remember such a thing. I know your mother didn't tell you: Sofia's best quality was her loyalty."

"You're wrong," I said. "It wasn't Lina. It was a man from the town. A perfect stranger."

"I might as well tell you the whole story. Afterwards you can judge me if you want." He paused; the alcohol had started to take effect. He fixed his stare on me as he spoke. Except for the humming of the central air conditioning, and the almost imperceptible whirring of a fancy fax machine that intermittently received faxes, the room was chillingly hushed. He began speaking. "Juan Jacinto was my best friend. His house was around the corner from ours. He was a year older than me and from the time we started school we were always in the same grade.

"His family was very poor—they didn't have land or animals. His father made a living catching fish, turtles, alligators, and animals from the forest; and his mother made sweets that Jacinto's sister sold going from house to house. That's something that your mother did, too.

"My father had a farm and cows so there was plenty of food in our house. We bought fish from Jacinto's father, and *bollos* from his mother's kitchen.

"The townspeople used to say that we looked like brothers. We enjoyed doing the same things: we'd go into the forest to trap birds—*mochuelos*, troupials, canaries. We loved going swimming in the river and the lagoons. We used to look for gold in the streams that flowed from the Sierra Nevada.

"When we reached puberty, we started having crushes on the girls of El Barranco. Jacinto and Leila, a neighbor, started making out in the woods. After school, instead of spending time with me, they would go off by themselves. I was hurt. I had lost my best friend. We continued to see each other but not so often. One day, we were seventeen, we went swimming in the lagoon behind the town. We were both naked. We didn't own bathing suits back then. After a long swim, we lay on the sandy beach talking about this and that. Juan Jacinto began to tell me about Leila and the things they did together and I noticed that his penis got hard. He asked me if I'd like to masturbate together. I had already begun to masturbate a year before, but it had always been a solitary practice. When he started doing it, and I saw his penis get hard, I got an erection. At some point, as I was nearing my climax and he was heaving, I . . . touched him . . . I don't know why I did. I . . . couldn't help myself. I had never touched a man . . . intimately. We both ejaculated, and as we were lying there, trying to catch our breath, he said to me, 'I didn't know you were a *marica*.' 'You son of a bitch,' I screamed angrily. 'You went along with it; you liked it as much as I did.' He threw a punch at me; we exchanged furious blows. I broke his nose. When I saw him bleeding, I grabbed my clothes and ran away, still naked. The rest of that day I thought that the fight would blow over. After all, we had been best friends all our lives. I didn't want to let what had happened affect our friendship. It had just been a moment of temporary insanity. Many boys will do that sort of thing, and it doesn't mean that they're *maricas*.

"The next day, I was walking to the house carrying water from the well, when I saw Juan Jacinto and two other boys standing on the corner. As I passed by them, they called out, 'Where are you going, you little fag? Wannna suck our cocks *mariquita, mariquita.*'

"I was hurt but didn't react; I was stung by Jacinto's betrayal. I was closer to Juan Jacinto than to any of my brothers. I couldn't forgive him for telling about what had been a private moment between us. When I got to the house, after I poured the water in the earthen jar, I kept hearing their words ringing in my ears. Then a blind rage exploded in me. My mother was in the kitchen making *sancocho*. I went to the kitchen, feeling possessed. I saw the long knife mother used to remove the fish scales with, and I grabbed it and bolted out of the house, as I heard my mother calling, 'Where are you going with my knife, you crazy boy?' I ran out into the street. It was near noon and the sun almost blinded my eyes. Juan Jacinto was still on the corner with his friends, they were just loitering there, waiting for the girls to go by so they could say sweet things to them. Everything happened so quickly that I've never been able to understand it. I know I approached them running. I know I was surprised when I saw the knife dripping with blood in my hand. Then I heard the other boys screaming, calling for help. I found myself on top of Juan Jacinto. He was on his stomach, and I sat on his buttocks—and once, twice, many times, I stabbed him on the back of his neck, until we were separated by the men of the village.

"I got up, the knife sprinkling blood. The men let me go. I ran all the way home and locked myself in my bedroom, where I lay in my hammock, rocking from side to side, clutching the wet, sticky knife." Carlos finished his story, and stared at me pitifully, as if asking for my forgiveness.

Somehow this wasn't what I had expected. At least in his own retelling, Carlos appeared as a sympathetic figure. In those circumstances, I could imagine myself committing a murder too. Yet I did not want to feel pity for him, or to understand his point of view. I knew that even if he had committed the murder under the circumstances he had described—and he looked so crumpled, so vacant, so devastated when he finished speaking one almost had to believe his version of the events—I wasn't about to feel sorry for him. But if I couldn't judge him for what he had done in a moment of passion, what about what he had become? Just to think about the bodyguards outside gave me the creeps. Only criminals lived that way.

"That's when the family moved away," he went on. "It wasn't

so much the murder, after all. Your grandfather could live with that, and there was no jail in El Barranco and no police and so I couldn't be brought to trial. What my father couldn't live with," he said pouring himself another glass of whiskey, "was the stigma of having the townspeople calling his eldest son a *loca*. You don't know what that was like in a hellhole like El Barranco in those years. . . . How dare you," he screamed, shaking, "judge me? It's all very well for you to be a faggot because you live in New York where everyone is one. If you really had balls, you would have stayed here. Try and be a faggot in Barranquilla, and see how far that's going to get you."

"I'm not here to discuss my homosexuality," I said.

Carlos got up. I was afraid he was going to hit me. "You fucking faggot. You have the nerve to imply that I am a fag like you."

I got up too. "Actually, I don't give a damn what you are. And I've seen as much as I can take of you."

Carlos took the bottle of whiskey and guzzled the liquor from the neck of the bottle. His face had turned red, and now his bloated features became very pronounced. He finished drinking the entire bottle, and then threw it over my head. It smashed against one of the racks where he kept his weapons.

I was angry, my heart beating furiously. I started to turn around, ready to leave that room, never to see him again.

"Where do you think you are going?" he screamed, lurching in my direction. "You can't come here and accuse me of being a *marica*, and a criminal, and just leave like that." His words were slurred, and he staggered, as he took another step in my direction.

"I'm leaving, Carlos," I said. "You can't stop me. And all I hope is that you pay for your sins some day."

"You fucking faggot," Carlos screamed as he turned around and lunged in the direction of the rack with the weapons. "I'll kill you, you fucking cocksucker. I'll put a bullet in your ass."

Before I could move, Carlos grabbed a gun and pointed it at me. "Sit down," he hollered. "You leave when I tell you to leave. If I decide to spare your life . . . I don't want any faggots in my family."

I didn't want to die. After everything I had gone through in the past years, life was precious to me. Yet I did not want to die groveling at the feet of this man I despised. I stood still. Carlos took a step forward.

"You can shoot if you want," I said, afraid yet reckless. "I'd rather die than stay with you in this room another minute. You make me sick, Carlos. You're a vile, revolting creature, and now that I've told you that I don't care what happens next. I'm going to turn around, because I don't want to die seeing you. You can shoot me in the back, like the coward you are." I did a 180-degree turn and began walking toward the door. I fully expected him to shoot, but I kept walking all the same. I opened the door and walked out of that room and the next, while the bodyguards stared at me. I kept walking until I was out of his apartment, out of his building, and didn't once looked back until I was in the street. I was elated, scared, my heart hammering in my chest. Tomorrow, I would be leaving for New York. I would be going back to the safety of the world I knew, to the place that for the first time looked like home to me. By journeying back to my origins, I had found out every-thing—more than—I had wanted to know. I knew that had I stayed in Colombia, I might have become like Carlos or like Sergio. After confronting him, I felt free. As I loped down the road, under the starry equatorial sky, I knew that coming back home had freed me from the tyranny of dreaming of returning to the sullied paradise I had left as a boy, for which now I could cease to yearn.

5

The Day Carmen Maura Kissed Me

I was on my way to the Algonquin Hotel to have a drink with my friend Luis whom I hadn't seen in several years. It was 4 P.M. in mid-June, and looking up the vertical canyons of midtown Manhattan, I saw a lead-colored, spooky mist engulfing the tops of the skyscrapers, threatening rain. As I passed Sardi's, my eyes snapped a group composition made of three men, TV cameras, and a woman. Living as I do in Times Square, I've become used to TV crews filming in the neighborhood around the clock. But the reason I slowed down my pace was that there were no curious people hanging around this particular TV crew. The four people were not students, either—they were people my age. I noticed, too, they spoke in Castilian Spanish. Then, to my utter astonishment, I saw her: *la divina* Carmen Maura, as my friends and I called her. Almodóvar's superstar diva was taping a program with these men outside Sardi's. It's not like I'm not used to seeing movie stars in the flesh. O'Donnell's Bar, downstairs from where I live, rents frequently as a movie set. Just last week, coming home, I ran into Al Pacino filming in the cavernous watering hole. You could say I'm star-struck, though; and I'm the first to admit it was my love of the movies that lured me to America. But after ten years on Eighth Avenue and Forty-third Street, I'm a jaded dude.

Carmen Maura, however, was something else. She was my favorite contemporary actress. I looked forward to her roles with the avidity of someone whose unadventurous life needs the vicarious thrills of the movies in order to feel fully alive. I adored her as Tina, the transsexual stage actress in *Law of Desire*. But what immortalized her in my pantheon of the divine was that moment in *Women on the Verge of a Nervous Breakdown* when, putting on a perfectly straight Buster Keaton face, she orders the girl with the cubist profile to serve spiked gazpacho to everyone in her living room. After I saw the movie, I fantasized carrying with me a thermos of gazpacho to offer a cup to (and put out of circulation) all the boring and obnoxious people I encountered in my humdrum routines.

Carmen stood on the sidewalk, under the restaurant's awning, speaking into a microphone, while the cameraman framed her face and Sardi's sign above her head.

Riveted, I stood to the side of the men and diagonally from the star, forming a triangle. For a moment, I fantasized that I was directing the shoot. What's more, I felt jealous and resentful of the technicians working with Carmen. To me they seemed common, unglamorous, undeserving of existing within range of the star's aura. I stayed there, soaking in her presence, thinking of my friends' reactions when I shared the news with them. Momentarily there was a break in the shooting and, getting brazen, I felt compelled to talk to her. The fact that I was dressed up to meet Luis at the Algonquin helped my confidence. I was wearing what I call my golf shoes, a white jacket, a green Hawaiian shirt, and a white baseball cap that says Florida and shows two macaws kissing. Therefore, Carmen was unlikely to mistake me for a street bum.

As I took two tentative steps in her direction, I removed my sunglasses so that she could read all the emotions painted on my face. I smiled. Carmen's eyes were so huge, liquid and fiery, that the rest of the world ceased to exist. For an instant I felt I existed alone in her tunnel vision. I saw her tense up, and an expression of bewilderment, unlike any I had seen her affect in the movies, showed in her face. Carmen exchanged looks with her men, who became very alert, ready to defend their star from any danger or awkwardness.

"Carmen," I popped, in Spanish. "I love your movies. You've given me so much happiness and I want to thank you for it."

The star's full-toothed smile took me aback. Her men smiled, too, and went back to loading their camera or whatever they were doing.

"We're taping a show for Spanish television," Carmen said. She was wearing a short white skirt, and a turquoise silk blouse and red pumps, and her Lulu hair was just like it was in *Women on the Verge of a Nervous Breakdown* except a bit longer. Her lips and fingernails were painted an intense red, and her face was very powdered. Extremely fine blonde fuzz added a feline touch to her long, sleek cheeks. "This is where *Women on the Verge* received an award," she was saying as I landed back on earth.

A momentary silence ensued, and we stood face to face, inches away from each other. Her poise and her ease and her friendliness were totally disarming, but suddenly I couldn't help feeling anxious. I decided to finish the encounter before I did something silly or made her yawn. It seemed ridiculous to ask her for an autograph so, as a good-bye, I babbled, "You're the greatest actress in the contemporary cinema." That, somehow, wasn't enough, did not convey the depth of my emotions. So I added, "You're the most sublime creature that ever walked the face of the earth."

Any reserve she may have left, melted. Diamond beams flashed in her coal-black eyes, which were huge pearls into which I could read volumes.

"*Ala!*" she exclaimed, an expression that means everything and nothing. Before I realized what was happening, Carmen glided toward me, grabbed my chin, and kissed me on the cheek, to the left of my lips.

I bowed, Japanese style (Heaven knows why!), and sprinted down the street. At the corner of Broadway and Forty-fourth, I turned around and saw that Carmen and her men had resumed their taping. My heart wanted to burst through my chest. I was out of breath, almost hyperventilating. I felt strangely elated. Aware of the imbecilic smile I must have plastered on my face, I put on my sunglasses. Although the Don't Walk sign was on, I crossed the street. A speeding taxi missed me by half an inch, but I didn't care—at that moment I would have sat smiling on the electric chair. Standing on the island in the middle of Broadway and Seventh Avenue, I had to stop for a moment to recollect where I was going and why.

"Wait till Luis hears about this," I thought.

My friend Luis is a filmmaker and a movie nut; it was our love of the movies that had brought us together. He had been educated in the States, where he graduated in filmmaking at UCLA. We had met in Bogotá, in the early 1970s. I made my living at that time reviewing movies and lecturing about the history of the cinema at the Colombian Cinémathèque. Luis, who was wealthy and didn't have to work, published a film magazine and made documentaries. We were leftists (although we both despised the Moscow-oriented Stalinist Colombian left), smoked heaps of Santa Marta Gold, ate pounds of mushrooms, and it wasn't unusual for us to see three or four movies a day. We were the angry young men of the Colombian cinema; we had declared war on the older generation of Colombian filmmakers whom we considered utterly mediocre and bourgeois. I'm speaking, in other words, of my youth. Later I moved to Europe and even later to New York where I now made a living as a college professor. Nowadays I'm haunted by the Argentinean refrain "In their youth they throw bombs; in their forties, they become firefighters." Luis, on the other hand, had remained in Colombia where he continued making documentaries and feature films that were distributed in Latin America but had never been released in the States. Slowly we had drifted apart. He never called me anymore when he was in New York. But this morning, when I heard his voice, the years in between had been obliterated in one blow and I had joyously accepted his invitation to meet for drinks at the Algonquin the way we used to do in the old times when we dressed in jackets and ties so we could sit in the lounge and watch film critics, movie directors, and stars whom we idolized and who frequented the place at that time.

It began to sprinkle heavily when I was about a couple of hundred yards from the hotel's awning. I broke into a fast sprint in order not to mess up my jacket and shoes.

The last time I had been in the Algonquin had been to meet Luis. I felt as though I was walking into a scene from the past. Maybe the crimson carpet was new, but the rest of the place was just as dark, and quaintly plush, as I remembered it. I told the waiter I was meeting a friend for drinks. There were a few people in the vast room. I scanned the faces, looking for Luis. The times had changed, indeed: a couple of kids in shorts and T-shirts sat drinking beer and munching peanuts. But I couldn't find Luis. I was about to ask for a table when a woman waved at me. I waved back as a polite reflex. When she smiled, I recognized her: it was Luis, I mean Luisa, as he was called in drag. I forgot to mention that even though Luis is heterosexual, and has lived with a girlfriend for a long time, he is a militant drag artist.

Blushing, I said to the waiter, "That's my party."

Luisa offered me her hand, which I judged would be inappropriate to shake, so I bowed, kissing the long fingers that reminded me of porcelain pencils.

"You look like a Florida tourist in Disneyland," Luisa said in English, the language in which we communicated in the States.

In this regard we were like the nineteenth-century Russians who spoke French among themselves.

"Guess who I just met," I said, taking the other chair.

"Let me guess. You have stars in your eyes—the ghost of D. W. Griffith."

"You're as close as from here to the moon," I said noticing the waiter standing between us. We both ordered Classic Cokes and this, too, was a sign of how much we and the times had changed. I told him.

"Was Almodóvar with her?" Luisa asked, reaching for a peanut.

"Who cares about Almodóvar!" I snapped. Of course neither Luis nor Luisa would have been thrilled by my encounter. I remembered they both worshipped film directors; for me, the star was everything. I was disappointed. In my short memory, I had thought running into Carmen Maura was the most fortuitous coincidence that could have happened before meeting my old friend.

I shook my head fully exasperated. "She was taping a program with some guys for Spanish television." I desperately wanted to change the subject. Luisa chewed the peanut interminably. There was nothing effeminate about Luis when he was in drag. I can easily spot transvestites because of their theatricality and ultrafeminine gestures. But Luisa behaved like Luis: reserved, parsimonious in gesture, and with exquisite aristocratic elegance. She wore brown alligator boots, a long banana-colored skirt, a wide black snake belt around the small waist, and a long-sleeved blouse that closed at the neck with an eighteenth-century school of Quito silver brooch. The chestnut mane of hair was long and flowed all the way to her fake bust. It helped that Luis was extremely skinny and that his features were delicate and that he had a marvelously rosy complexion. His jade-colored eyes, framed by profuse pale lashes, were utterly beguiling. Luisa could have been mistaken for a structuralist pre-Columbian expert, or an Amazonian anthropologist, or a lady photojournalist who photographed ancient cities in Yemen, or some place like that. It took me a few seconds to remember the dynamics of the friendship: Luis and Luisa were the passive ones, the listeners who laughed at my jokes. I was their court jester.

Obviously I had gotten out of the Carmen Maura incident all the mileage I was going to get. I was rescued from my predicament by the waiter who set the Cokes down, asked us whether we wanted anything else, and left mortified by our drinking habits.

Instead of asking about our friends in common back in Colombia, I began with the most generalized question I could think of, "So what's the gossip?"

"I can't go back to Colombia," Luisa said with a twinge of sadness in her voice. She sipped her Coke to give me time to digest the news. "I had to get out of there in a hurry. I was in the middle of shooting a movie. Can you imagine the timing of these people!" Luisa reached for her big straw pocketbook and pulled out a small wooden box. It looked like one of those boxes in which guava wedges wrapped in banana leaves are packed for export, except that it was painted black. She set the box between our glasses.

"It's a box for *bocadillos*. Is it for me?" I asked.

"Not, it's for me. But open it," she prodded me.

Suddenly the box looked creepy, weirding me out. "What is it? A bomb?"

Luisa teased my curiosity cruelly, with her characteristic Gothic humor. "You're not even warm. Just open it."

"No, you open it," I said, thinking she was about to play one of her nasty jokes on me.

"Okay," Luisa acquiesced, removing the top of the box.

Inside the box there was a crudely made replica of Luisa. Now I got it: it was supposed to be a small coffin, and something like dried ketchup was generously splashed over the little doll.

"That's real blood," Luisa said pointing at the red stuff.

"What the fuck is that supposed to mean?" I asked, horrified.

"Have you become such a gringo that you don't know what's going on in Colombia?" Luisa wanted to know.

"I read the papers," I said, shrugging. "I know paramilitary groups are killing prominent members of the opposition. Furthermore," I continued with my recitation to show Luisa I was still a Colombian through and through, "I know they're killing left-wing sympathizers and outspoken liberals. I keep in touch," I said, as if to absolve myself of all guilt. Yet it just blew my mind to even think that Luisa might have become a leftist. If we had resisted the temptation back in the early 1970s, when the pressure had been intense, I refused to accept that twenty years later Luisa had finally succumbed to Marxism-Leninism. On the other hand, I had heard of people in Colombia who had become socialists just out of exasperation with the telephone company.

"First they call you. And they say something like, 'We saw your wife yesterday in the supermarket.' Or, 'We know at what time your little son comes home from school.' That's the first warning. Then they send you a blank telegram. And finally, you receive this little coffin, which means you have forty-eight hours to get the hell out before they pop you," she explained.

I felt nauseous. "Do you mind?" I asked, taking the top of the box and covering it. Next I gulped down half of my Coke. I looked around: Kathleen Turner was now seated at the table nearest to us. She was accompanied by an equally famous journalist. In the past, we would have been dizzy at the proximity of these luminaries; we would have sat there eyeing them, imagining their conversation, reviewing what we knew about them.

"But why did they send this . . . thing to you? Have you become a member of the Party?"

"I hope never to sink that low," Luisa smirked.

"Then why?"

"Those creeps are our moral majority. They hate communists, liberals, non-conformists, and homosexuals."

"But you're not gay."

"Of course not. But you tell them that. You try to explain to them that I dress in drag because of . . . artistic necessity. Just like Duchamp did. And Chaplin."

"I hear Muammar Qaddafi loves to dress in drag," I said, realizing immediately how inappropriate my remark was.

Luisa smiled. "He must do it for religious reasons, or something like that."

"So what are you going to do?"

"I'm going to Spain for a while. I'll look up Carmen Maura and say hello for you when I'm in Madrid," she teased me. "Sylvia will meet me there in a few weeks," he added, referring to his longtime girlfriend. "She had to stay behind to wrap up my affairs. Then we'll wait a year or two until the situation blows over. I don't think I could live permanently abroad. Colombia is home for me."

Becoming defensive, I said, "But you can't blame me for not living there. It sounds like I would have been one of their first targets, don't you think? I'd rather be a homeless artist than a dead queen."

Luisa sighed before she took a long sip. "Tell me about you. Are you happy? What have you been up to all these years?"

"You'll have to wait until I write my autobiography," I joked. Becoming serious, I thought: how could I make her understand my present life? A life so different, so far removed from all that stuff? She probably could see for herself that New York had become a third-world capital, like Bogotá; and America a class society, like Colombia. But how could I explain my new interests nowadays: bodybuilding; a vegetarian diet; abstinence from sex, nicotine, and most mood-altering substances? How could I explain that my current friends were not into revolution, not into changing the world, but into bioenergetics, rebirthing, Zen, Buddhism, healing circles, Quaker meetings, *santería*, witchcraft studies, neo-paganism, and other New Age phenomena?

We did go on to lighter subjects as we consumed a few Classic Cokes. We gossiped about old acquaintances and friends in common, the Colombian film industry, the despised enemies of the past, and our favorite movies. We agreed to meet for a farewell movie before Luisa left for Spain.

It was past six o'clock when we left the Algonquin, which by then was abuzz with all kinds of artistic and quasi-artistic people talking deals.

It had stopped raining, and the rain had washed away the layers of dust and papers that had accumulated since the last summer shower. The oppressive mist had lifted, too, and the worst of the dreaded rush hour was over so that, although Manhattan was alive with the promise of night's splendors, the atmosphere felt almost relaxed. Or maybe it was just my mood.

At the corner of the Avenue of the Americas, we hailed a cab. I kissed Luisa on both cheeks, closed her door, and waved good-bye as her taxi disappeared in the uptown direction. I felt rejuvenated. It cheered me to realize that my affection for my friend was intact and that we'd probably go on meeting for many more years. I meandered across town, enjoying the nippy air and the pinkish glow of the bald sky over the metropolis. The sun must have hovered someplace over the Hudson, but night seemed to be pushing not far behind it. The lighted buildings and billboards blazed like a high-tech aurora borealis. As I passed Sardi's, I noticed its emerald-green sign, and the mailbox next to which I had stood watching Carmen, and the lamppost next to it, which now projected a circular beam of red-gold light under which I bathed, basting. I was about to continue on my way when, looking across the street, I spotted Carmen and her men still shooting their program. I stood still, becoming aware of the street separating us and the cars streaming by, and the slick Manhattanites, and the pristine tourists hanging in front of the theatres that lined Forty-fourth Street. None of these people were interested in *my* Carmen. It was as if on the screen she had been created for all people, all over the world, but in the streets of Manhattan she was visible only to my eyes. I knew also that the magic of the moment when we first met was past; that it would have been inappropriate to interrupt her now, or to say hello, or to remind her that just a couple of hours ago she had kissed me. As if to snap the picture forever, I closed my eyes upon the scene and then started walking toward home, without once looking back.

I crossed Eighth Avenue. As I passed in front of Paradise Alley, the porno palace next door to O'Donnell's Bar, the score or so of crack addicts hanging out in front of my place of residence were no longer hideous to me. This evening I accepted them as the evil spirits necessary in all fairy tales. Pity arose in my heart for them. In their dead angry eyes, I heard their hopelessness and suddenly they seemed as doomed and tragic as the people who were being wiped out back home. The man and the woman smoking crack in front of my door moved reluctantly as I opened it and leaped over the puddle of piss that the rain had not washed away. Taking the steps two at a time, I felt happy and sad in the same breath. It was a new sensation, this happy/sad feeling I experienced. It was sadness for all that was sad in this wide, mysterious world we tread upon; and it was the unreasonable happiness produced by the tinsel gleam of the glamorous dreams that had brought me to America and for which I had had to wait for many years before briefly, heartbreaking in their fleetingness, they became real.

JAIME MANRIQUE was born in Colombia where his first volume of poems received the Eduardo Cote Lamus National Poetry Award. He has taught creative writing and literature at Mount Holyoke College, New York University, Hampshire College, Goddard College, the Graduate Faculty, and Eugene Lang College of the New School for Social Research. Mr. Manrique lives in New York City.